She lifted her hands and pushed down the remaining petticoat, then turned slowly, within his embrace, to stand naked in front of him.

There was colour on her cheeks and her eyes were lowered. It came to him that for all her directness and bravado Laura was shy. *'It has been a long time,'* she had said. Six years for a sensual, beautiful woman who had known physical passion was indeed a long time. Time to ache—and time to grow reticent.

'Would you like me to put out the light?' he asked.

She looked up at that, eyes wide. 'Oh, no! I want…I want to see you.' A smile trembled on her lips. 'I want to be very bold and I fear to shock you.'

'Shock me?' Avery tugged his neckcloth free and stripped off his coat and waistcoat. 'I would love you to shock me, Laura.'

He finished undressing, his arousal stoked by her unwavering gaze. When she ran her tongue along her lower lip he almost lost control like a callow youth.

He dragged a ragged breath down into his lu

AUTHOR NOTE

I always enjoy a 'secret baby' plot, and I began to wonder what would happen if it was the hero with the baby and the heroine with the secret. What would drive a respected diplomat to take on the scandal of raising someone else's love-child, and what lengths would a woman go to in order to take back her daughter from him? Gradually I got to know Lady Laura Campion, whose unhappiness leaves her uncaring that society calls her *Scandal's Virgin*. It took me longer to discover the motives of Avery, the gorgeous, intelligent, haunted Earl of Wykeham—other than that the cause of all the deception and heartbreak, six-year-old Alice, has him firmly twisted round her little finger!

I hope you enjoy getting to know them all too, and discovering how Laura and Avery manage to untangle years of deceit, passion and distrust without bringing scandal down on Alice's innocent head.

SCANDAL'S VIRGIN

Louise Allen

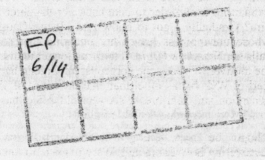

FP
6/14

MILLS
BOON

Published in Great Britain 2014
by Mills & Boon, an imprint of Harlequin (UK) Limited,
Eton House, 18-24 Paradise Road, Richmond, Surrey, TW9 1SR

© 2014 Melanie Hilton

ISBN: 978 0 263 90962 3

Harlequin (UK) Limited's policy is to use papers that are natural,
renewable and recyclable products and made from wood grown in
sustainable forests. The logging and manufacturing processes conform
to the legal environmental regulations of the country of origin.

Printed and bound in Spain
by Blackprint CPI, Barcelona

Louise Allen has been immersing herself in history, real and fictional, for as long as she can remember. She finds landscapes and places evoke powerful images of the past—Venice, Burgundy and the Greek islands are favourite atmospheric destinations. Louise lives on the North Norfolk coast, where she shares with her husband the cottage they have renovated. She spends her spare time gardening, researching family history or travelling in the UK and abroad in search of inspiration. Please visit Louise's website—www.louiseallenregency.co.uk—for the latest news, or find her on Twitter @LouiseRegency and on Facebook.

Previous novels by the same author:

THE DANGEROUS MR RYDER*
THE OUTRAGEOUS LADY FELSHAM*
THE SHOCKING LORD STANDON*
THE DISGRACEFUL MR RAVENHURST*
THE NOTORIOUS MR HURST*
THE PIRATICAL MISS RAVENHURST*
PRACTICAL WIDOW TO PASSIONATE MISTRESS**
VICAR'S DAUGHTER TO VISCOUNT'S LADY**
INNOCENT COURTESAN TO ADVENTURER'S BRIDE**
RAVISHED BY THE RAKE†
SEDUCED BY THE SCOUNDREL†
MARRIED TO A STRANGER†
FORBIDDEN JEWEL OF INDIA††
TARNISHED AMONGST THE TON††
FROM RUIN TO RICHES
UNLACING LADY THEA

*Those Scandalous Ravenhursts
**The Transformation of the Shelley Sisters
†Danger & Desire
††Linked by character

and as a Mills & Boon® special release:

REGENCY RUMOURS

and in the Silk & Scandal mini-series:

THE LORD AND THE WAYWARD LADY
THE OFFICER AND THE PROPER LADY

and in Mills & Boon® Historical Undone! eBooks:

DISROBED AND DISHONOURED
AUCTIONED VIRGIN TO SEDUCED BRIDE**

Did you know that some of these novels are also available as eBooks? Visit www.millsandboon.co.uk

To all my friends in the Romantic Novelists' Association.

Chapter One

April 1816—the park of Westerwood Manor, Hertfordshire

Keep still! The circular image shook, swooped over immaculately scythed grass, across flower beds fresh with young growth, over a flash of bright blue cotton... *There.*

The watcher's hand jammed so hard against the branch that the rough bark scored the skin from the knuckles. *Yes.* Glossy ringlets the colour of autumn leaves, determined little chin, flyaway brows over eyes that must surely be clear green. *Beautiful. She is so beautiful.*

And then the girl smiled and turned, laughing as she ran. The telescope jerked up and a man's face filled the circle. Hair the colour of autumn leaves, stubborn chin, angled brows, sensual mouth turned up into a smile of delight.

'Papa! Papa!' The child's voice floated back through the still, warm air. The man stooped to scoop her up and turned towards the house as she buried her face in the angle between neck and broad shoulder and clung like a happy monkey. Her laughter drifted on the breeze towards the woodland edge.

The telescope fell with a dull thud onto the golden drift of fallen beech leaves and the woman who had held it slid down the tree trunk until she huddled at its base, racked with the sobs that she had stifled for six long years.

'You saw her then.'

'How did you guess?' Laura Campion let the door slam shut behind her.

'Look at the state of you. All blubbered up. You never could get away with tears, my la— ma'am.'

Trust Mab to exhibit the delicate sensibility of a brick. The scratch of wicker on wood as the maid pushed aside the mending basket, the sharp tap of her heels on the brick floor, the creak of the chain as she swung the kettle over the fire, all scraped like nails on a slate. But the words steadied her as gushing sympathy never would have done. Mab knew her all too well.

'Yes, I saw her. She is perfect.' Laura pulled out a chair and sat down at the table. Her boots were tracking leaf mould across the floor and she tugged them off and tossed them onto the kitchen doormat without a glance. 'She looks like Piers. She looks like *him*.'

'You just said.' Mab slopped hot water into the teapot and swirled it round.

'No, I mean she looks like the Earl of Wykeham. Piers's cousin Avery.' Laura tightened her lips, stared round the kitchen of the little house that had been home for just two days and fought for enough control to continue. 'She calls him *Papa*.'

'Aye, well, that's what he says he is.' Mab Douglas dug a spoon into the tea canister. 'I only had to ask at the shop who lives in the big house and they were all of a clack about it. How his lordship came here just a month ago from foreign parts with a love child and no wife and doesn't even have the grace to be shamefaced about it.'

'Foreign parts!' Laura tugged at her bonnet strings. They'd do nicely to strangle *his lordship* with. 'He stole her from Derbyshire, though I expect that's foreign enough for them around here.'

'They won't know nothing about that, it was six years ago and he must have taken her abroad with him right away. He's been at that Congress in Vienna, and then he stayed on to help sort out some political nonsense in the Low Countries, so they say.

'Besides, Mr Piers is dead and Lord Wykeham is head of the family, after all. In the village they say he's spending money on the estate.' The boiling water splashed onto the tea leaves. 'Perhaps he thinks he should be responsible for Mr Piers's child as well as his old home.' Mab, at her most infuriatingly reasonable, being devil's advocate.

'That might be the case, if the child did not have a mother.' The bonnet ribbon tore between Laura's twisting fingers. 'But she does.' *Me*.

'Aye, and there's the rub.' Mab poured two cups of tea and brought them to the table. 'You drink that up, now.' She sat down, five foot nothing of plump, middle-aged, bossy femininity, and shook her head at Laura with the licence of a woman who had looked after her since she was ten years old. 'He knows you're the child's mother, but he thinks *you* don't want her. He doesn't know you thought she was dead. The

question is, where do you go from here now
you've found her?'

'He has never met me.' It was time for calm
thinking now the first shock of emotion was
past. Laura smoothed her palms over the dull
fabric of her skirts. She was so tired of the black
she had worn since her parents died of influenza fifteen months ago. She had been about
to put her mourning aside and return to society,
but that had been before the bombshell that had
rocked her world. Now the solemn garments
made the perfect disguise.

'There is no reason he would suspect I am
not who I say I am—the widowed Mrs Caroline Jordan, retired to the country to regain my
strength and spirits before I re-enter society.'

'And how are you going to meet an aristo-
cratic bachelor who lives in the big house in the
middle of a park?' Mab was still being logical.
Laura didn't want logic. She wanted a miracle or, failing that, to sob and rant and… 'And
what are you going to do if you do get in there?
Snatch the child?'

'I do not know!' Laura closed her eyes and
dragged in a steadying breath. 'I am sorry, Mab,
I didn't mean to bite your head off. All I knew,
right from when I discovered those letters, was

that I had to find my daughter. I did not dare plan beyond that. Now I have found her and I have no idea what happens next.'

'He called her Alice,' Mab said and laid her hand over Laura's. 'They told me in the village. Miss Alice Falconer. That would have been her proper name if you'd married Mr Piers, wouldn't it?'

It was hard to speak around the thickness in her throat, to find the words in the confusion of her mind. When they did spill out they seemed unstoppable. 'She is six years old. I heard her cry, just once, before they took her away and then they told me she was dead. I heard her say one word today and you tell me her name, the name strangers told you. I should be so happy because she is alive and healthy and yet I feel as though I have lost her all over again. How could they do that?'

How could her parents—the respected Lord and Lady Hartland—have told her the baby had died? How could they have secretly given the child—their granddaughter—away? Admittedly, their chosen recipients, the Brownes, were respectable tenant farmers on one of the earl's distant estates, but even so…

'They thought they were doing the right thing

for you,' Mab soothed. 'You were only just eighteen. What they did meant you could have your come-out two months later and no one any the wiser.'

'Really? What, I wonder, was I supposed to say to the nice young men they expected to propose to me? *So sorry, my lord, but I'm not a virgin. In fact, I've given birth.* I could hide the one—I gather there are shabby tricks, straight out of the brothel—but did they hope I'd find a complete innocent who wouldn't notice something amiss?' She knew she sounded angry and bitter and those weren't nice things, either of them. But she did not care. Being angry and bitter had got her through five London Seasons as the most notorious débutante of them all.

Scandal's Virgin, they called her, which was an irony if ever she heard one. But Lady Laura Campion, daughter of the Earl of Hartland, had the reputation of being frivolous, flirtatious and outrageous. And, to the intense frustration of the men who pursued her and the chagrin of the matrons who decried her behaviour, no one was ever able to say she had taken that one fatal step to ruin.

Yes, she would drink champagne on the terrace at a ball. Yes, she would slip away into the shrubbery and allow kisses and caresses no innocent should allow. And, yes, she would wear gowns more suitable to a fast young matron, ride with careless abandon and dance four times in an evening with the same man, if the fancy took her.

Any other young woman after five Seasons would be considered to be on the shelf, unmarriageable, the subject of pity. *But*... No gentleman could ever claim she had given herself to him, despite the wagers in the betting books of every club in St James's. No one had ever managed to catch her doing more than kissing a rake behind the rosebushes. And no one could deny that she was beautiful, amusing, loyal to her friends and the daughter of one of the richest and most influential of peers. Despite the nickname and the shocked glances from the chaperons' corner, Scandal's Virgin continued her apparently heedless way though the social whirl and no one guessed that her heart had shattered at the death of a lover and the loss of his child.

'If the man loved you, he might not care,' Mab ventured.

Laura snorted. She had hoped that, once. But observation soon taught her that men were hypocrites. That theoretical lovelorn suitor would care, for certain.

In January of 1815, just as she was preparing for yet another Season full of distractions to stop her thinking of the hollowness inside, her parents succumbed to the influenza. It was sudden, shocking and completely unexpected, but within ten days of the first fever they were gone. Laura, draped in black veils, retreated to Hartland Castle and the virtual solitude of mourning, interrupted by the occasional descent of Mr Bigelow, the lawyer, and letters from Cousin James, the new earl, apprising her of his efforts to sell out of the army and return home.

He was grateful, he wrote, that Cousin Laura continued to oversee things at the Castle and urged her to call upon whatever resources from the estate she saw fit to transform the Dower House into her new home.

Eventually she made herself order the work, advertised for a lady companion, failed to find one she liked, shrugged and decided to do without for the present. Mab was all the company she needed. Finally, a year after their deaths, she gritted her teeth and started to go through her parents' personal possessions, the things that were not entailed with the estate.

Mab had fallen silent while she sat lost in memories. Now Laura was vaguely aware of her gathering together the tea things and stoking up the fire. 'Why do you think Mama kept them?' she asked abruptly.

'The letters?' Mab stirred a pot and shrugged. 'No one thinks they are going to die suddenly and that someone else will go through their possessions, do they? And they had to do with her granddaughter, after all.'

The box had been inside a locked trunk under a stack of old accounts, dog-eared notebooks of recipes, bundles of bills for gowns going back years. Laura had almost ordered the whole thing taken down and burned unsorted and then she had seen a few sheets of music, so she dragged those out and put them aside.

Once her father had allowed an antiquarian to excavate an ancient mound on the estate and Laura thought of him as she dug her way down through paper layers of history, rescuing the music, smiling over a recipe for *restoring greyed hair to a perfect state of natural glory* and finally breaking a nail on the hard, iron-bound surface of a smaller chest.

It was locked, but she found the key on the chatelaine her mother had always kept about her. When the lid creaked open it revealed a neat bundle of letters. She began to set them aside for the fire unread, thinking they must be old love letters and recoiling from the ghosts of someone else's old romance. She had enough spectres of her own. Then something about the handwriting caught her eye.

Muddy brown ink, a hand that was not so much untutored as unpractised, and poor quality paper. These could not be *billets-doux* or family letters. Puzzled, Laura drew them out and began to read. Even now, knowing the truth, it was hard to withstand the emotional impact of what was revealed. Laura stood, left the kitchen for the back parlour of the little rented house and paced over the old Turkey carpet until her stomach stopped its roiling.

First, the joyful shock of discovering that her baby had not died. Then the monthly letters, three of them, from the farm in the Derbyshire Dales. The child was thriving, the money was arriving, the Brownes, who had just lost a newborn, were very grateful for a healthy babe to raise as their own and for his lordship's generosity. And then, May the fifteenth 1810, the news that she had caught some fever, they knew not how, and had sickened rapidly. *The little mite passed on peacefully in the early hours this morning,* Mrs Browne wrote in her spiky hand. *We will see her decently buried in the churchyard.*

It had taken a day and a sleepless night to recover from the shock of hope snatched away just minutes after it had been given. The next morning, still stunned into a strange calm, Laura had ordered her bags packed and a carriage prepared. At least there would be a grave to visit, not the vague assurance that her child had been discreetly secreted amongst the coffins in the family vault, unnamed, unacknowledged.

When she and Mab had arrived at the solid little greystone farmhouse she simply walked straight in, her carefully rehearsed words all lost in the urgency of what she had to say.

'I am Lady Laura Campion and I know the truth. Where is she?' she had demanded of the thin, nervous woman who had backed away from her until she simply collapsed onto a chair and buried her face in her apron.

Her husband moved to stand between Laura and his sobbing wife. 'He said no one would ever know. He said he was her cousin so it was only right she was with him.'

'What?' This made no sense. They had written that the child was dead...

'He said no one would ever find out if we said she had died and we just kept our mouths shut.' Browne shook his head, shocked and shamefaced. 'I knew we never ought to have done it, but he offered so much money...'

'She is not dead.' It was a statement, not a question. Laura had stared at him, trying to make sense of it all. *He? Cousin?* 'Tell me everything.'

A gentleman calling himself Lord Wykeham had come to the farm unannounced. He had known everything—who the baby's mother was, who was paying them to look after her. He had shown them his card, they saw his carriage with the coat of arms on the door, they were convinced he was the earl he said he was. He had a respectable-looking woman and a wet nurse in the carriage and he had offered them money, more money than they could imagine ever having in their lives. All they had to do was to write to Lord Hartland and tell him the child was dead.

'Babes die all the time,' Mrs Browne had murmured, emerging from the shelter of her apron. 'All ours did. Broke my heart...' She mopped at her eyes. 'I still had milk, you see. Her ladyship, your mother, made sure I could feed the little mite.'

They lived remotely in their distant dale. No one knew that they had a different child in the house, it had all been so simple and Wykeham had been so authoritative, so overwhelming. 'You'll want the money,' Browne said, his weather-beaten face blank with stoical misery. 'It was wrong, I know it, but the milk cow had died and the harvest was that bad and even with what your father was paying us...'

Laura had looked at the clean, scrubbed kitchen, the empty cradle by the fire, the grey hairs on Mrs Browne's head. *All her babies had died.* 'No, keep the money, forget there ever was a child or an earl in a carriage or me. Just give me his card.'

Now Laura took the dog-eared rectangle from her reticule and looked at it as she had done every day of the eight weeks it had taken her to track Wykeham down, organise her disguise, create a convincing story for her staff and neighbours.

She had wanted evidence she could hold in her hand of the man who had stolen her baby, stolen every day of her growing, her first tooth, her first steps, her first word. Piers's cousin, the rich diplomat, Avery Falconer, Earl of Wykeham. Now she no longer needed a piece of pasteboard: she had seen him, that handsome, laughing, ruthless man her daughter called *Papa*. The calling card crumpled in her hand as Laura tried to think of a way to outwit him, the lying, arrogant thief.

'Papa?'

'Mmm?' Saying *yes* was dangerous, he might have missed the whispered trick question. That was how the house had become infested with kittens.

'Papa, when may I go riding?'

Avery finished reading the letter through and scrawled his signature across the bottom. Sanders, his secretary, took it, dusted over the wet ink and passed the next document.

'When I am satisfied that your new pony is steady enough.' He looked back to the first sentence and tapped it with the end of the quill. 'Sanders, that needs to be stronger. I want no doubt of my opposition to the proposal.'

'I will redraft it, my lord. That is the last one.' John Sanders gathered the documents up and took himself and his portfolio out. The third son of a rural dean, he was efficient, loyal, discreet and intelligent, the qualities that Avery insisted on with all his staff.

'But, Papa…'

'Miss Alice.' The soft voice belonged to another member of his staff, one possessed of all those qualities and more. 'His lordship is working. Come along, it is time for a glass of milk.'

'I will see you before bedtime, sweetheart.' Avery put down his pen and waited until Alice's blue skirts had whisked out of the door. 'Miss Blackstock, a word if you have a moment.'

'My lord.' The nurse waited, hands clasped at her waist, every hair in place, her head tipped slightly to one side while she waited to hear his pleasure. She was the daughter of his own childhood nurse and the only one of his staff who knew the full truth about Alice. Blackie, as Alice called her, had been with him when he had finally tracked the baby down to the remote Dales farm.

'Please sit down. I think it may be time for Alice to have a governess, don't you think? Not to usurp your position, but to start her on her first lessons. She is very bright.' *And impetuous. As her father had been*.

'Indeed, yes, my lord.' Miss Blackstock sat

placidly, but her eyes were bright and full of questions. 'You'll be advertising for someone soon, then? I'll speak to Mrs Spence about doing out the schoolroom and finding a bed-chamber and sitting room for the governess.'

'If you would.' Avery looked out over the rolling lawn to where the parkland began at the ha-ha. It was small but beautiful, this estate he had inherited from his cousin Piers and which he had signed over to Alice along with its incomes. He would do his utmost to give her all the standing in society that he could, and this place restored to prosperity as part of her dowry and an education with an excellent governess would be the start.

'There is no hurry to arrange the accommo-dation here. However, will you ask her to ar-range the same thing at the Berkeley Square house immediately?'

Miss Blackstock stared at him. 'You are tak-ing Miss Alice to London, my lord?'

'I am. I intend staying there for the remain-der of the Season.' There was no reason why he should explain himself, even to an old re-tainer, but it would help if she understood. 'I plan to marry.'

'But, my lord…' Miss Blackstock hesitated,

then opted for frankness. 'Might Miss Alice perhaps…discourage some of the ladies?'

'Her existence, you mean?' Avery shrugged. 'I would not wish to marry a woman who thought less of me because of one, much-loved, child. Anyone who will not accept Alice is simply unacceptable themselves.'

'It will certainly winnow the wheat from the chaff,' the nurse murmured. 'When will you go up to town, my lord?'

'In two weeks. Late April.' *Wheat from the chaff, indeed.* Avery's lips twitched as the nurse shut the door behind her. It was a long time since he had been in London for the Season, it would be interesting to see what the quality of this year's crop of young ladies was like.

Chapter Two

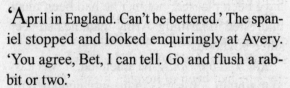

'April in England. Can't be bettered.' The spaniel stopped and looked enquiringly at Avery. 'You agree, Bet, I can tell. Go and flush a rabbit or two.'

The shotgun, broken open for safety, was snug in the crook of his arm, just in case he did spot one of the furry menaces heading for the kitchen garden, but it was really only an excuse for a walk while the sun was shining and the breeze was soft.

I'm getting middle-aged, he thought with a self-mocking grin. *Thirty this year and enjoying the peace and quiet of the country. If I'm not careful I'll turn into a country squire with a placid wife, a quiverful of children and the prospect of the annual sheep shearing for excitement.*

After an adulthood spent in the capitals of Europe, in the midst of the cut and thrust of international diplomacy, he had thought he would be bored here, or that country life would bring back unpleasant memories of his childhood, but so far all he felt was relaxed. The parkland was in good order, the Home Farm and the tenant farms thrived, as his regular rides around the surrounding acres showed him. Piers would have been pleased, not that he had been much interested in farming. Army-mad, he had been since boyhood.

Relaxed but randy, he amended. It was easy to maintain a mistress in the city and keep his home life separate, but a remote country manor and a small child were a combination guaranteed to impose chastity. And decency told him that setting up a London mistress at the same time as hunting for a wife was cynical.

Still thinking vaguely about sex, Avery rounded a group of four beeches and stopped dead. A dry branch cracked under his booted foot.

'Oh!' The woman in black sitting on the fallen trunk of the fifth tree jumped to her feet, turned and recoiled at the sight of him, her eyes wide in her pale face. He had an impression of fragility, as much of spirit as of form, although she was slender, perhaps too slender. Her eyes flickered down to the gun and then back to his face and her hands, ungloved and white against the dull sheen of her walking dress, clenched together at her waist.

'I beg your pardon, madam. I had no intention of frightening you.'

'I suspect I am trespassing.' Her voice was attractive, despite her alarm, but there was a huskiness in it that made him think of tears. She was in mourning, he realised, not simply soberly clad, and there was a wedding ring on her finger. A widow. 'I was told in the village that there was a public path across the estate, but I saw a deer and went closer and then I lost sight of the path... If you will direct me, I will take myself back and cease my illegality, my lord.' Now she had recovered from the shock her tone was cool and steady.

'You know who I am?'

The spaniel ran up, ears flapping, and sat at her feet. She bent to run her hand over its head with the confidence of a woman used to dogs, but her dark eyes were still on Avery. 'They described you in the village, Lord Wykeham.' There was nothing bold or flirtatious in

her study of him, she might as well have been
assessing the tree behind him, but heat jolted
though him like a sudden lightning flash and
was gone, leaving him oddly wary. His thoughts
had been sensual, but this was as if a fellow du-
ellist had lifted a sword in warning.

'You have the advantage of me, madam,' he
said, and knew his diplomatic mask was firmly
in place.

'Caroline Jordan. Mrs Jordan. I have taken
Croft Cottage for a few months.' She seemed
quite composed, but then she was not a young
girl to be flustered by a chance meeting with a
stranger. She was a young matron, twenty-four
perhaps, he hazarded. And a lady of breeding,
to judge by her accent, her poise and the expensive sheen and cut of the black cloth. Standing
there under the trees in her elegant blacks, she
looked as much out of place as a polished jet
necklace on a coal heap.

'Then welcome to Westerwood, Mrs Jordan.
You are indeed off the path, but I believe I can
trust you not to kill my game or break down my
fences. You are welcome to roam.' Now what
had possessed him to offer that?

'Thank you, Lord Wykeham. Perhaps you
would be so kind as to point me in the direc-

tion of the path back towards my cottage.' She moved and again he was conscious of a stab of awareness, and this time it was most certainly sensual, even though she had done nothing flirtatious. A disturbing woman, one who was aware of her feminine allure and confident in it to the point where she felt no need to exert it, he surmised. Yet her eyes held a chill that was more than aloofness. Perhaps she was completely unaware of the impact that she made.

'It falls along my own route, if you care to walk with me.' He kept his voice as polite and reserved as her own as he skirted the fallen trunk, whistled to the dog and walked towards the path, trodden down by his own horse. He did not offer his arm.

'Is it you who jumps this?' she asked, with a gesture to the hoofprints dug deep in the turf in front of the trunk she had been sitting on. 'Not an easy obstacle, I would judge.'

'I have a hunter that takes it easily. You ride, ma'am?' She kept pace with him, her stride long and free with something about it that suggested she would be athletic on horseback. *And in other places,* his inconvenient imagination whispered.

'Before I was in mourning, yes.' She did not

glance at him as she spoke and Avery found himself wishing he could see the expression in her eyes, the movement of her mouth as she spoke, and not merely the profile presented to him, framed by the edge of her bonnet. Her nose, he decided, was slightly over-long, but her chin and cheekbones were delicately sculpted. Her cheek, pink with exercise, showed the only colour in her face beside the dark arch of her brow and the fringe of her lashes.

'Was it long ago, your bereavement?' he ventured.

'Some time, yes,' she said in a tone of finality that defied him to question further.

Well, madam, if that is how you wish to play it, I will not trouble you further! He was not used to being snubbed by ladies, but perhaps it was shyness or grief. He was more used to diplomatic circles than London society and the ladies who inhabited those foreign outposts were no shrinking violets.

'This is where our ways part.' The path had converged with the ha-ha where the stone slabs set into its side provided a crude set of steps up to the lawn. Bet, the spaniel, was already scrambling up them. 'If you take that path there…' he pointed away towards the edge of the woods '…it will take you back to the lane that leads to the church.'

'Thank you, my lord. Good day to you.' She turned away as Bet gave a sharp yap of welcome. It made her start and stumble and Avery put out a hand to steady her.

'Papa! There you are! You will be late for tea and we are having it on the lawn.'

Mrs Jordan turned to look at Alice as she stood on the brink of the drop and the movement brought her into the curve of Avery's arm. He loosened his grip and for a moment she stood quite still where she was, so close that he could swear he heard her catch her breath. So close that a waft of lemon verbena teased his nostrils.

'Ma'am? Are you all right? I apologise for my daughter's abrupt manners.'

It seemed the widow had been holding her breath, for it came out now in a little gasp. 'It is…nothing. I turned my ankle a trifle when I twisted around just now.'

'Is the lady coming for tea, Papa?'

'No…I…'

Damn it, she's a stranger here, she's in mourning, she knows no one, what's the harm? 'Would you care to join us, Mrs Jordan? Perhaps you should rest that ankle a little.' When

she still stood there, unspeaking, he added,
'And we are eating outside.' Just in case she
thought he was a dangerous rake who employed
children as a cover for his nefarious seductions.
He was even more out of touch with country
manners than he was with London ones.

'Thank you, Lord Wykeham, I would enjoy
that.' She tipped up her head so she could look
directly at the child above them. 'Good afternoon,' she said, as serious as if she was address-
ing a duchess.

'Good afternoon, ma'am.' The girl—*my
daughter,* Laura thought—bobbed a neat little
curtsy. 'I am Alice.' She was bare-headed and
dressed in a green cotton frock with a white
apron that showed evidence of a busy day's play.

'Allow me,' Lord Wykeham said before
Laura could respond. 'These steps are more
secure than they look. If you take my hand as
you climb, you will be quite safe.'

'Thank you.' She put her ungloved hand in
his, her fingers closing around the slight rough-
ness of the leather shooting gloves he wore. Her
fictitious twisted ankle and the awkwardness
a lady might be expected to show in climbing such an obstacle would account for her un-
steadiness, she supposed, as she set foot on the
first step.

* * *

As she reached the top Alice held out her hand, her warm little fingers gripping Laura's. 'Let me help.'

The shock went through her like a lightning strike. Laura tripped, fell to her knees and found her fingers were laced with Alice's. *'Oh!'* Tears welled in her eyes and she blinked them back as she fought the instinct to drag her daughter into her arms and run.

'Your ankle must be more than just turned.' That man was bending over her. She hunched her shoulder to exclude him from the moment. 'Let go, Alice, and run and tell Peters to bring out a chair and a footstool for Mrs Jordan.'

Laura could have snarled at him as Alice loosed her grip and ran up the slope of the lawn. Somehow she turned the sound into a sob of pain.

'Allow me.' Before she could protest he swept her up into his arms and began to follow the child. 'I will send for Dr Pearce.'

'There is no need.' The words emerged sounding quite normal. Laura tried to make herself relax as much as any lady held in the arms of a complete stranger might. She could not follow her instinct and hit out at him, slap his face, call him all the words that buzzed like furious hornets in her brain. 'I am certain it will be better for a short rest.'

'Even so, I will send for him.'

Not a man who accepted disagreement with his opinions, but then she already knew he was arrogant and ruthless.

'Thank you, but, *no.*'

'As you wish.'

I do. Does no one ever say no *to you?*

Laura dredged up some composure from somewhere and tried a tiny barb. 'Lady Alice is a delightful child.'

There was a pause, so slight that if she had not been attuned to his every reaction she would never have noticed, then, without breaking stride, Lord Wykeham said, 'She is not Lady Alice, simply Miss Falconer.'

'Oh, I beg your pardon. I thought in the village they said you were an earl. I must have misunderstood.'

'I am an earl. However, I have never been married and certainly not to Alice's mother.' He must have interpreted her small gasp of surprise at his easy admission as one of either shock or embarrassment. 'I see no reason why the child should suffer for the sins of her father. I will not have her pushed into the background as though she is something I am ashamed of.'

'Indeed not.' Laura fixed her eyes on the sharp edges of waistcoat and coat lapels and added, with malice, 'And she looks so very like her father.'

That went home. She felt the muscles in his arms contract for a moment, but his breathing did not change. 'Very like,' Lord Wykeham agreed, not appearing to notice the strange way she phrased the comment.

It was so strange, fighting this polite battle while in the arms of her opponent. With a less-controlled man, and probably with a less-fit one, she might have expected his body to betray his feelings even though he commanded his expression and his voice. He could have no suspicions of her, so this composure must be habitual. And she need not fear betraying anything by being so close against his body, for he would expect any lady to be flustered by such an intimacy.

He was warm and smelled not unpleasantly of clean linen, leather and man. She had missed that, the intimate scent of male skin, the feel of muscle against her softness, the strength that was so deceptive, so seductive. It turned a woman's head, made her believe the man would keep faith with as much steadfastness.

They had reached the top of the slope. Laura risked a glance forward and found any danger of tears had gone, banished by anticipation of the secret, one-sided duel she had just begun to fight.

The lawn levelled off beneath the spreading boughs of a great cedar. Windows stretching to the ground had been opened to the spring breeze and a table and chairs brought out to stand beneath the tree. A maid set out dishes on the table and Alice was speaking to a footman who stooped to listen, his face turned to see where she was pointing.

'What a charming house.' It should have been her home. Her home, Alice's home. She had never been there, but Piers had described it to her in those brief, breathless days of their courtship. It would be their love nest, away from the smoke and noise and social bustle of London, just the two of them. She had spun fantasies of making a home in this place so that when her hero returned from war he would find love and peace here. She could almost see him now, long legs stretched out as he sat beneath the cedar, so handsome in his scarlet regimentals.

'Yes, it is pleasant and well laid out. A little on the small side compared to Wykeham Hall and the estate is not large, but it is good land.'

'This is not your principal seat, then?' Laura asked as they reached the table.

'No. I inherited it from a cousin. Here is the chair for you.' He waited while the footman put down a sturdy one with arms and Alice, staggering a little under the weight, dragged a footstool in front of it. 'There.'

Lord Wykeham settled her into place with a brisk efficiency that, unflatteringly, showed no reluctance to yield up possession of her. Laura watched him from beneath her lashes as he went to take his own seat. And why should he wish to keep hold of her? She had exerted none of her powers to attract him, all she had done was to suppress her instincts to storm at him with accusations and reproaches.

And if I find it necessary to charm him? Can I do that, feeling about him as I do? Why not? I am a good enough actress to attract many men when all I want to do is play with their hearts a little. It would be no hardship to look at him, that was certain. He was as handsome as Piers had been and more. This was not a young man, still growing into his body and his powers. The earl was mature and powerful…and dangerous.

Laura smiled at Alice and felt the frost that grew around her thoughts when she spoke to Wykeham thaw into warmth. She had every excuse to look at her daughter now and to talk to her. *If only I could hold her.*

'Thank you very much for fetching me the footstool.' She lifted her foot onto it and caught a flickering glance from the earl before she twitched her skirts to cover her ankle and the high arch of her foot in the tight ankle boot. *Hmm, not so indifferent after all. Useful…* Was that shiver at the thought of flirting with such a man or disgust at herself for even contemplating such a thing?

'Does your foot hurt very badly?' Alice stood right by the chair, her hands on its arm, and regarded Laura's face intently. Her eyes were clear and green. On her, as with her true father, the winging eyebrows made her seem always to be smiling slightly. On the earl they added a cynical air that only vanished when he smiled.

'No, it is much better now I am resting it, thank you. I am sure it is only a slight strain.' Was there anything of her in the child? Laura studied the piquant little face and could see nothing that would betray their relationship except, perhaps, something in the fine line of her nose and the curves of her upper lip. Alice had none of her own colouring—dark blonde hair, brown eyes, pale skin. Perhaps, as she grew towards womanhood Alice would develop some similarities. It was dangerous to wish it.

'Why are you wearing a black dress? Has someone died?' Alice asked.

'Alice, that is an intrusive question.' The earl turned from the table, displeasure very clear on his face.

'It is all right.' It was easier to establish her story in response to the child's innocent questions than to attempt to drip-feed it into conversation with the earl. 'Yes, Alice. I lost my husband.' It was true in her heart: Piers had been her husband in everything except the exchange of vows in church. 'And then my parents died.'

Alice's hand curled round her forearm, small and warm and confiding; the touch so precious that it hurt. 'That is why you have sad eyes,' she said, her own lip quivering. 'I lost my mama. Really lost her, because she isn't dead. Papa says she had to go away and won't come back.'

I can't bear this. I must. 'I am sure your

mama would if she could,' Laura said and touched her fingertips to the child's cheek. 'I am certain she will be thinking about you every day. But we cannot always do what we wish, even if it is our heart's deepest desire.'

'Alice, run inside and ask Miss Blackstock to join us for tea.'

Laura glanced at Alice, but the child did not appear frightened by Wykeham's abrupt order or the edge to his voice. It did not seem that she felt anything but trust and love for the man she believed was her father. She waited until the small figure whisked through the window and then said what she was thinking without pausing to consider. 'Why did you not tell her that her mother was dead?'

Chapter Three

Lord Wykeham did not snub her as he had every right to do. 'I will not lie to her,' he said abruptly. 'Do you take cream or lemon with your tea, Mrs Jordan?'

'Lemon, thank you.' Laura was hardly aware of the automatic exchange. 'But you—' She caught the rest of the sentence, her teeth painful on her tongue. *But you let her think you are her father.* 'You do not think that is more difficult for her to accept?' His expression became even more sardonic. 'I beg your pardon, my lord, it is not my place to speak of it.'

'Alice likes you,' he said without answer or comment on her question. 'Have you children of your own, Mrs Jordan?'

'I lost one child. I have no others.' It was quite safe to mention that she had given birth

to a child, he would never associate her with
Alice's mother, of that she was confident. His
natural supposition, should he trouble to think
about it, would be that she had married perhaps
three or four years ago, some time after her first
come-out to allow for the normal processes of
upper-class courtship and marriage. She was almost twenty-five now, and her mirror told her
that she did not look older.

'She is a naturally loving and friendly child,
I imagine.' He nodded and passed her a plate
of small savouries. 'Has she many playmates
in the neighbourhood?'

'No, none. Alice has lived virtually her entire life abroad. We have only been back from
the Continent for just over a month. There has
been a great deal to do, but you are right to
make the point, Mrs Jordan, I should make the
effort to socialise locally in order to find her
some friends of her own age.'

'My lord, I had no intention of criticising.'
Which was an untruth. How fast he caught her
up. As a diplomat the man was used to watching faces, listening to voices and hearing the
reality behind the facade. She would have to
be wary. She glanced towards the house, then

quickly away. He must not see the hunger she was certain was clear in her eyes.

'Hinting, then,' he said with the first real smile he had directed at her. Laura felt her mouth curve in response before she could stop it. When the man smiled he had an indecent amount of charm. And that was confusing because there should not be one good thing about him. *Not one, the child-stealing reptile.* She dropped her gaze before he could read the conflict.

'Papa! Here is Blackie.' Alice, who never seemed to walk anywhere, bounded to a halt in front of Laura. *That energy is so like me as a child.* The pang of recognition was bittersweet. 'Mrs Jordan, this is Blackie.'

The nurse bobbed a neat curtsy. 'Miss Blackstock, ma'am.'

'Miss Blackstock. Miss Falconer is a credit to you.' *And you are a credit to Lord Wykeham's care for Alice,* she thought, reluctantly awarding him a point for the care of the child. Not such a reptile after all, if Alice could love him and if he could choose her attendants with such care. Being fair was unpalatable, she wanted to hate him simply and cleanly.

'Thank you, ma'am.' There was a stir as the

nurse took a seat beside Alice, then a small tussle over the need to eat bread and butter before cake. All very normal for an informal family meal and not at all what she had expected and feared she would find. And that, Laura realised as she nibbled on a cress sandwich, was disconcerting.

She had been braced to rescue her child from some sort of domineering, manipulative, bullying tyrant and found instead a happy girl and, she was coming to suspect, a doting father behind the facade of firmness.

Tea was finished at last, a final sliver of cake wheedled out of the earl despite Miss Blackstock's despairing shake of the head, and Alice wriggled off her chair. 'May I get down, Papa?'

'You *are* down,' he said.

Alice dimpled a smile at him and came to gaze earnestly at Laura. 'Will you come and visit again, Mrs Jordan? We are very cheerful and there is always nice cake and perhaps you won't feel so sad then. You could play with my kittens.'

'Miss Alice!' Miss Blackstock got to her feet with an apologetic look at Laura.

'It was indeed very nice cake and I feel very

cheerful now after such good company,' Laura said. Could she come again? Dare she? She must not promise the child something she might not be able to fulfil.

'Jackson!' A footman came striding across the grass in response to the earl's summons. 'Send to the stables and have Ferris harness up the gig to take Mrs Jordan back to the village.'

'Please, I do not wish to be a trouble, I can walk,' she said as the man hurried away across the grass to the side of the house. 'My ankle feels quite strong now.'

'I cannot countenance you attempting it without an escort and it is probably best if we do not emerge from the woods together.' The smile was back, this time with a hint of something that was not exactly flirtation, more a masculine awareness of her as a woman.

'As you say, Lord Wykeham.' To drop her gaze, to hide behind her lashes, would be to acknowledge that look. She sent him a carefully calculated social smile that held not one iota of flirtation. 'Thank you.'

'I do not know what to do.' Laura paced across the parlour and back, her black skirts flicking the bookcase at one side and the sofa on the other as she turned. 'I thought she would be unhappy and lonely, but I think she loves him and he loves her.'

'What were you planning to do if she'd not been happy?' Mab demanded. 'Kidnap the poor mite?'

'Go to law, I suppose,' Laura said. 'And, yes, I know it would ruin my reputation, but it is the only remedy I can think of. This isn't a Gothic novel where I could snatch Alice and hide in some turreted castle until my prince came along and rescued us both.' *Not that I have a prince. Or want one.*

'But she is happy and well cared for and loved, so why not leave things be?' her henchwoman demanded, fists on hips. 'I can't be doing with all this handwringing, I've my dusting to get on with.'

'Because he doesn't deserve her! He lied, he deceived and he bought a child as if she was a slave. He has no right to her.'

'She's base-born,' Mab stated, attacking the bookshelves with a rag. 'No getting round that. He's family and she's better off with him, provided he's kind to her. He can protect her better than you can.'

'He is rich, he is privileged, he is—'

'And so are you,' Mab pointed out with infuriating logic. 'But he is a man so he can protect her in ways that you cannot. His reputation isn't going to be dented by having an acknowledged love child, but yours would be ruined and all the influence you can muster goes with it.'

'I do not like him.' Laura flung herself onto the sofa and slumped back against the cushions, exhausted by tension.

'What's that to do with the price of tea?' Mab demanded. '*You* haven't got to live with him. Alice has.'

'*I am her mother.*' The words were wrenched out of her. 'All those years when I thought she was gone. And then to find that she hadn't died, and to have hope and to have that wrenched away and then to discover she was alive after all. And now... Now I have got to do what is best for Alice. But it hurts so, Mab. It hurts.'

'Oh, lovie—' Mab tossed the rag aside '—don't you be crying now. You've done too much of that these past months.'

'I'm not crying.' Her eyes were dry. It was inside that the tears flowed. Or perhaps she was bleeding where some organ she could not put a name to had been wrenched out. It could not be her heart, she could feel that beating, hard and fast.

Mab stomped across the room and sat down on the sofa. 'She loves him and he'll do the best he can for her by the sounds of it. He'll be one of those gentlemen who'll stick by family come hell or high water—it's part of their pride. You've just got to be glad for her and get on with your own life. He'll be off abroad again soon, those diplomatic gentlemen are all over the place. Think of all the sights she'll see, the things she'll do. And when she's all grown up he'll give her a big dowry and find her a nice man to marry and she'll be happy, just you see.'

'I know.' *I know. It is the right thing. I am happy that she is alive and so clever and bright and kind and lovely. But she will never know that Piers was her real father, she will never know that her mother loved her and wanted her.* 'I am going to stay for a week. Just a week. I will see her again, I will make certain she is truly safe and happy and then I will go back to London and take off my blacks and rejoin society.'

'A good thing, too. But who's going to chaperon you, then?' Mab asked. 'You turned down all those fubsy creatures that came in answer to the advertisement.' She stood up and administered a brisk pat on the shoulder before going to hunt for her duster.

'I have written to my mother's cousin Florence. She is a widow and she isn't in very comfortable circumstances. She says she'd be delighted to be my companion.'

'What? Lady Carstairs? The one your mama always said had feathers for brains? She'll be no use as a chaperon.'

'I am too old to need one of those. I just need a lady companion to give me countenance.'

'Huh.' Mab snorted.

'Yes, I know, I am shockingly fast and have no countenance to preserve, some would say, but I am not seeking a husband. So long as I am received, I really don't mind.'

'There'll be many a man who'd overlook a slip-up in your past.'

'For the sake of my bloodlines and dowry, you mean?' Just as there would be gentlemen who would overlook Alice's birth when the time came, all for the sake of her powerful father and the money he would dower her with. 'I don't believe there is and I don't want a man who would *overlook* something for anything but love.' And none of them would get close enough to her heart to arouse such emotion. She did not have the courage to risk it, one more wound would kill her.

Coward, a small voice jeered. Once she had been prepared to do anything for love. Not now. Now the only battle she was prepared to fight and be hurt in was the one for Alice's welfare

Mab suddenly slapped her own forehand with the palm of her hand. 'I'll disremember my own name one of these days. You had some callers while you were out. It went right out of my mind when you came back just now in that smart carriage, white as a sheet. They left their cards. I'll go and get them.'

'Three.' Laura picked up the cards and found all were from married ladies and all had the corners turned to indicate that they had called in person. 'Your visit to the village shop has obviously caused some interest.'

'A right gossipy body she is behind the counter, so she'll have told everyone who came in. I was careful to say who you were so they'd know we were respectable and there'd be no problem with credit. Who you are pretending to be,' Mab corrected herself with a sniff.

'Mrs Gordon, The Honourable Mrs Philpott and Mrs Trimmett. She is the rector's wife, I assume, as the address is the rectory. I will call on them tomorrow, they all have At Homes on Tuesdays according to their cards.'

'What, and risk them finding something out?'

'Why should they suspect I am not who I say? I am not pretending to be someone whose status might excite their curiosity and it will look strange if I do not.' Laura fanned out the cards in her hand and realised she had reached a decision. 'I will stay for a week and I will find out all I can about Lord Wykeham. These ladies and their friends will be agog about his arrival and full of information.'

'You always say you despise gossip,' Mab muttered.

'And so I do, but I will use it if I have to. I'd wager a fair number of guineas that all these ladies know just about everything there is to know about what goes on at the Manor. All I have to do is give them the opportunity to tell me.'

One of the disadvantages of her disguise was not having a footman in attendance, or a carriage to arrive in, Laura reflected as she rapped the knocker on the rectory door the following afternoon.

'Madam?' The footman who opened the door to her was certainly not a top-lofty London butler, which was a relief. She could hardly assume the airs of an earl's daughter if he snubbed her.

Laura handed him her card. 'Is Mrs Trimmett at home?'

He scarcely glanced at the name. It was certainly more casual in the country. 'Certainly, Mrs Jordan. Please enter, ma'am.' He relieved her of her parasol and flung open a door. 'Mrs Jordan, ma'am.'

There were two ladies seated either side of a tea tray. One, grey-haired and plump, surged to her feet. 'Mrs Jordan! Good day, ma'am. How good of you to call, please, allow me to introduce Mrs Gordon.' She had all the rather forceful assurance of a lady who knew her position in the community was established and who spent her life organising committees, social gatherings, charity events and the lives of anyone who allowed her to.

Laura and Mrs Gordon—a faded blonde of indeterminate years—exchanged bows and Laura sat down. *Two birds with one stone,* she thought with an inward smile. 'I am so sorry

I was out yesterday when you were both kind
enough to leave your cards. As a stranger to
the village it is most welcome to make new acquaintances.'

Over cups of tea Laura endured a polite in-
quisition and obligingly shared details of her
fictitious bereavement, her depressed state of
health and her need to have a change of air and
scene before facing the world again. The two
ladies tutted with sympathy, assured her earnestly that Westerwood Magna was a delightful,
healthful spot where she would soon recover
both health and spirits, and delicately probed
her background and family.

Laura shared some of her invented history
and nibbled a somewhat dry biscuit.

'You will find everyone most amiable and
welcoming here,' Mrs Gordon said. She was,
Mab had reported, the wife of a city lawyer
who had retired to a small country estate and
spent his time fishing and breeding gun dogs.

'I do hope so,' Laura murmured, seizing her
opportunity. 'I fear I may have inadvertently in-
convenienced the lord of the manor yesterday.'

'Lord Wykeham?' Both ladies were instantly
on the alert.

'Yes, I became lost crossing his park and

strayed off the footpath. The earl came across me and I was startled and turned my ankle. In the event he was kind enough to offer me refreshment and send me home in a carriage.' It was impossible to keep that sort of thing secret in a small village and she saw from the avid look in their eyes that they had already heard that she had been seen in a vehicle from the Manor.

'Well! How embarrassing for you,' Mrs Trimmett remarked with ill-concealed relish as she leaned forward in an encouraging manner.

'It was a trifle awkward, but he acquitted me of trespass. Oh, you mean the refreshments? Just a cup of tea on the lawn with one of the female staff in attendance. I would not have gone inside, naturally.'

'Naturally,' they chorused, obviously dying to do just that themselves.

'Do tell us,' Mrs Gordon urged, 'what is the earl like? My husband has left his card, of course, and they have met, but he has not yet called.'

'He was perfectly punctilious and civil, but I found him arrogant, you know. Perhaps it is just those devilish flyaway eyebrows—'

The two ladies opposite her went very still,

their eager expressions frozen into identical stilted smiles. Too late Laura felt the draught from the opening door on the nape of her neck.

'The Earl of Wykeham,' the footman announced.

Chapter Four

It seemed impossible the earl had not heard, which left two alternatives, once Laura had stifled the immediate instinct to flee the room. She could apologise and probably dig herself even deeper into the hole or pretend the words had never been uttered.

'My…my lord.' Even Mrs Trimmett's self-assurance seemed shaken. 'How good of you to call. May I make Mrs Gordon known to you?' The matron managed to utter a conventional greeting. 'And Mrs Jordan I believe you know,' she added as the earl moved into the room.

'Mrs Gordon. And, Mrs Jordan, we meet again. Are you quite recovered from your fall yesterday?' His voice was silk-smooth, so bland that Laura was suddenly doubtful whether he had heard her *faux pas* after all. Willing away what she was certain must be hectic colour in her cheeks, she sipped the cooling tea. *Thank Heavens he has been seated to one side of me!*

'I have no pain at all now, thank you, Lord Wykeham.' Laura shot a glance at the clock, mercifully in the opposite direction to the earl. She had been there twenty minutes which meant, by the rules governing morning calls, Mrs Gordon should be departing soon, her own half-hour having passed. 'I was just telling the ladies that I trespassed in your delightful park yesterday.' She smiled and shook her head at Mrs Trimmett's gesture towards the tea pot. She would finish this cup and then could most properly make her escape. Mrs Gordon was obviously determined to hang on now this intriguing visitor had arrived, never mind the etiquette of the situation.

'No trespass at all and my daughter, Alice, was delighted to meet you.'

Both the older women stiffened and the polite smiles became thin-lipped. *He has done that on purpose,* Laura thought. *It wasn't thoughtless—he wants to see how they react.* Then the realisation hit her. *That is my daughter they are pokering up with disapproval over.*

'Miss Alice is a delightful child,' she said.

'Such charming manners and so pretty and bright. A credit to you, my lord. I do hope she soon makes some little friends in the area. Do you have grandchildren, Mrs Trimmett?'

The vicar's wife looked as though she had been poked with a pin. 'Er...no, they are all in Dorset. Such a pity.'

'Mine will be coming to stay next week,' Mrs Gordon said. 'My two dear granddaughters, aged six and eight. Perhaps Miss Alice would like to come to tea?' Her expression was such a mixture of smugness and alarm that Laura almost laughed. She could read the older woman's mind—an earl's daughter...but illegitimate. The chance of an entrée to the Big House...but the risk that her neighbours might disapprove.

Laura told herself that she had defended Alice and perhaps made some amends for her tactless remark about Lord Wykeham, which, whatever she thought about him, had been inexcusable.

'I am happy to accept on Alice's behalf,' he said.

Laura risked a sideways glance and encountered a pleasant, totally bland smile with just the faintest hint of mischief about it. Or was she imagining that? 'Well, this has been delightful, thank you, Mrs Trimmett. I am hoping to find Mrs Philpott at home,' she added as she got to her feet. Lord Wykeham stood, looming far too close for comfort in the feminine little parlour.

'I called on her about an hour ago,' Mrs Gordon said. 'So you will certainly find her at Laurel Lodge. Such a pleasure to meet you, Mrs Jordan.'

With a further exchange of civilities, and a slight bow to the earl who was holding the door for her, Laura left, hoping it did not appear such a flight as it felt.

A smart curricle with a groom in the seat stood outside the vicarage. The earl's, she assumed, sparing the pair of matched bays an envious glance as she passed. The groom touched his hat to her as she set off around the green that led past a group of cottages and towards the turning that Mab had told her led to Laurel Lodge.

Laura dawdled, hoping that fresh air and time would do something to restore her inner composure. She touched the inside of her wrist above the cuff of her glove to her cheek and was relieved to find it cool and not, as she had feared, flaming with embarrassment. What had possessed her? Probably, she concluded, a desire to hear Wykeham abused by the other women, to hear some scandalous gossip about him to confirm her in her dislike of him. And now all she had done was to ensure he would not dream of inviting her to the Manor again. She had quite effectively cut herself off from her daughter.

'Very rustic this, my lord,' Gregg observed, his arms folded firmly across his chest; his face, Avery knew without having to glance sideways, set in a slight sneer.

'That is one of the characteristics of the countryside, yes,' he agreed.

'Hardly what we're used to, my lord.'

'No, indeed.' And singularly lacking in theatres, taverns, pleasure gardens and other sources of entertainment for a good-looking, middle-aged groom with an eye for a pretty girl and a liking for a lively time, he supposed. 'We'll be off to London in a week or two,' he offered his brooding henchman. Tom Gregg had been with him for over ten years and enjoyed a freedom not permitted to any of his other staff.

Gregg gave a grunt of satisfaction and Avery went back to pondering the mystery that was Mrs Jordan. Just what did she find so objectionable about him? Other than his eyebrows, which could hardly be provocation enough to make a well-bred lady express a dislike to two near strangers. Her manner to him had been impeccable, if cool, and yet he was constantly aware of a watchfulness about her and, ridiculous as it might sound, a hostility. Perhaps she was like that with all men. It could be, he supposed, that her marriage had been an unhappy one, but his instincts told him it was more personal than that.

Which was a pity, as well as a mystery. Mrs Jordan was an attractive woman and Alice liked her. And, he supposed, with a wry smile at his own vanity, he was not used to ladies taking against him.

'You turn right here, my lord.' Gregg gestured towards a lane leading off the green.

So now he had a choice. He could allow himself to be routed by a sharp-tongued widow in drab weeds or he could endure her dislike for half an hour at Mrs Philpott's house. No, damn it, he thought, guiding the pair into the lane, Mrs Philpott had young relatives, so he had been told, and he was not going to deprive Alice of some possible playmates because of Mrs Jordan's prejudices.

And there she was, strolling along the lane in front of him as though she did not have a care in the world. No maid with her again, he noticed, and certainly no footman. But this was broad daylight in a placid little village, so perhaps there was no conclusion to be drawn from that about her resources, her respectability or her background.

His horses were walking, the ground was soft and it seemed she had not heard him. Avery allowed the pair to draw alongside her without speaking and noticed the start she gave when one of them snorted. She was so composed in voice and expression and yet her body seemed to betray her feelings as though she had no command over her nerves. He recalled the flush of pink at the nape of her neck when she realised he was in the room and must have heard her cutting words. He had wanted to touch that warm skin, he had wondered how far the blush had spread...

'Mrs Jordan. Good afternoon once more. May I take you up as far as Mrs Philpott's house?'

Her eyes flickered to Gregg's sturdy figure. 'Thank you, Lord Wykeham, but I am enjoying the exercise.' She turned and walked on.

So, she did not want to talk in front of his groom. Fair enough. 'Gregg, take the reins,' he said. 'Be outside Laurel Lodge in half an hour.' This needed settling.

She did not glance at it as the curricle passed her, but he made no attempt to keep his long stride silent, so her lack of surprise when he reached her side was only to be expected. This time she was completely in control of her reactions. 'My lord? I hardly feel I require an escort for a few hundred yards up a country lane.'

'But I require a conversation.'

'And an apology, no doubt. Please accept my regrets for my discourteous words at the vicarage, my lord.'

'I wish you would stop calling me *my lord*.' It was not what he had meant to say and her startled glance showed he had surprised her as much as himself.

'And what should I call you?'

'My name is Avery, Caroline.'

'And are we on such terms that we call each other by our Christian names? I believe I would recall it if we were childhood friends or cousins.'

'I would be friends. I am unclear what I have

done to make you dislike me. If I have offended you in some way, I would like to repair that.'

'How could you have offended me?' she asked without looking at him. 'We have only just met. And why should you wish me as a friend?'

'Alice likes you. More feminine influence in her life is desirable, I think.'

She caught her breath and something in the whisper of sound seemed to touch him at the base of the spine. *So that's what this is... I desire this prickly, difficult, wan-faced widow.* Avery stopped and, as though he had put out a hand to restrain her, she did, too. 'Look at me.'

Caroline half-turned to face him and studied his face, her own expression grave. As she had in the park, she seemed to look with an intensity that probed not just his appearance, but his thoughts and his character. Every muscle under the fine skin of her face seemed taut, there was wariness, almost fear in the dark eyes, and now something else. Something he would wager she did not want to feel at all.

'Whatever else there is between us,' Avery murmured, thinking out loud, 'there is physical attraction.'

'You flatter yourself!' She looked as outraged as he might have expected and also utterly taken aback.

'No, there is nothing to be vain about in an instinctive reaction. But I am right, am I not?' He had dragged off his right glove as they spoke and now he touched his fingers to her cheek. Warm, soft skin. The muscles flinched a little beneath his touch, but she did not step back, or brush his hand away or slap him. 'Has someone hurt you, Caroline?'

He read the answer in her eyes, an almost bottomless lack of trust, but her reply showed no weakness. 'Again, you flatter yourself to believe that my unwillingness to flirt with you is due to some flaw in my own experience.'

'I do not seek to flirt.' And he did not, he realised. Such superficiality would only make the itch to touch her far, far worse. 'I only want your company for my daughter and to understand what it is that sparks between us and yet seems to cause you so much pain.'

Her lids fell, covering the darkness of her eyes. When she opened them she seemed to have come to a decision. 'I have no reason to trust men, least of all strong, authoritative men who seek to order the lives of others. But it is a long time since… I cannot help it if there is some awareness in me of a virile man. I do not wish to discuss this.'

Or act upon it, that was very clear. *What manner of man had her husband been? A tyrant? A domineering bully? And yet a man who had awakened her sensually.* The two things were not mutually exclusive, he told himself.

'I do not seek to take advantage of you, merely, as I said, to understand.'

'And understanding people is your stock in trade, is it not?' Caroline Jordan began to walk slowly towards their destination. His uncharacteristically impulsive words had not, it seemed, deepened her distrust of him.

'It is. I study their motives, their strengths and weaknesses. The points on which they will yield and the points upon which they will stand fast until death.'

'I will visit Alice, if you wish,' she said, almost as though her words followed on from what he had just said. The charged intimacy still surrounded them like a mist and yet she seemed capable of ignoring it. 'Does she have a governess?'

'No, but I intend to employ one for her very soon. She is naturally very bright, I think. However, I do not want to stifle her enthusiasm and energy through rigorous teaching.'

'You must choose carefully.' She seemed calmer now, more at ease with him. Avery pulled on his glove and fell into step beside her. 'A young woman, one with a natural manner and energy herself would be best. Alice is just like I—'

'Yes?'

'Like I recall my best friend Imogen was at about that age. An older, more formal woman would stifle her character.'

It was not what she had meant to say, he suspected. 'Caroline,' Avery said and she did not react. 'Caroline?'

'Oh! I beg your pardon, I was woolgathering. You should not call me by my given name, you know.'

Woolgathering? In the middle of a conversation that started with a discussion of sexual attraction and moved on to a subject she professes an interest in? It was almost as though she did not recognise her own name...

'I was considering the question of governesses,' Caroline said. 'I know women are supposed to be able to think of seven different things at once, but I fear I cannot.'

It was the closest she had come to making a joke in his presence. Avery reproved himself for his suspicions. That was what came of spending too much time in the company of professional dissemblers, outright spies and manipulative women.

He heard Caroline take a deep breath as though either shedding a burden or taking one up. 'That must be Laurel Lodge, Avery. Do you think it would be discreet to arrive separately?' Then she answered her own question even as he was masking his surprise at her use of his name. 'Foolish to pretend, for they will all get together and gossip about us anyway.' As he opened the gate for her she slanted a look at him. 'And foolish to allow them to think there is anything to hide.'

'You are quite correct.' Avery knocked, wondering at the composure Caroline layered over the vulnerability that lay like a brittle layer of ice beneath the poise. *Yes, there is nothing to hide except an awareness of each other at a very basic level that is, perhaps, nothing to be surprised about.*

Laura caught Avery's eye across the tea table and suppressed a smile. Their arrival together could not have provided Mrs Philpott, her daughters, two female callers and a youth making a cake of himself over Miss Maria Philpott, with more delicious grounds for speculation if they had planned it. The village was small, the pool of genteel company a mere puddle, a mysterious widow and an internationally well-known diplomat and earl would create a gossip broth that might last for months.

Avery. It had been a struggle to smile and to make herself relax and allow the familiarity he asked for, but it was necessary if she was to spend time with Alice. Letting go had been like falling from the certainty of one position—dislike and distrust—to the uneasy foothold of distrust and…what exactly? Physical attraction, he had said. And he was right, she could not delude herself. He was a very attractive man to look at, he had intelligence, power, an unabashed masculinity. And he reminded her of Piers in some ways, but a Piers matured, and this man had never been the impetuous romantic his cousin had been.

One of the two female visitors asked her something and Laura made herself focus and smile. Yes, indeed, it was a delightful village and just what she wanted to recover her health. Yes, it was most kind of Lord Wykeham to escort her, although she was sure such a pleasant place was quite safe for a lady to walk alone.

His lordship was flattering Mrs Philpott on the subject of her nieces, who were playing in the garden under the eye of their governess. Perhaps she could advise him on the best way to find a governess for his daughter?

Mrs Philpott, Laura decided, was somewhat more sophisticated and worldly-wise than the vicar's wife. She did not bat an eyelash at mention of Miss Falconer and it was she who made the suggestion that Alice might like to come and play with the girls.

That was satisfactory, Laura decided. Alice would have the opportunity to make friends and she could leave now, the civilities achieved. After all, she would not be here more than another week, although she had no intention of saying so just yet, so she had no need to cultivate acquaintances now she had established her respectability.

Avery accepted another cup of tea and seemed to be handling the languishing looks of Miss Philpott, a fresh-faced brunette, with skill. Now would be a good time to make her escape, for he could hardly abandon both tea and young lady without giving offence.

* * *

Laura made her way home along the lane, repeating mentally, *Caroline Jordan, Caroline. Caroline.* She had almost been caught out by Avery when he addressed her by her assumed name. If she were to survive a week of close encounters, she must learn to respond to that quite naturally.

What was he hoping for with his remarks about physical attraction and his desire for first-name intimacy? Was this some unusual attempt at seduction? Laura shivered. It had not been easy to deal with that startling statement and the self-recognition that went with it. A man like him would treat a widow very differently than he would an unmarried lady. Perhaps he thought her sophisticated enough for a fleeting liaison.

And she had not lied when she had admitted that it had been a long time. There had been no need to spell it out, he knew they were talking about the last time she lay with a man. The awful thing was, the remembered image of Pier's face as he kissed her, as he lay over her, within her...that face was changing, shifting, becoming the face of Avery Falconer, Earl of Wykeham. Her adversary.

Chapter Five

'Astride! In *breeches?*' Avery sounded as scandalised as any prudish matron.

'Certainly astride,' Laura countered. 'Then she can learn balance and control and gain confidence before she has to deal with a side-saddle.'

Alice, clad in clothes borrowed from Cook's grandson, stood watching them, her head moving back and forth like a spectator at a shuttlecock game. The argument had been going on for ten minutes now and the groom holding the little grey pony's head was staring blankly across the paddock, obviously wishing himself elsewhere.

'Is that how you learned to ride?' Avery demanded.

'Certainly.' And she still did when she could

get away with it. 'I am only concerned with Alice's safety.'

'Very well.' As she had guessed, that clinched the argument. Avery lifted the child and swung her into the saddle. 'Now you—'

Alice promptly slid her feet into the stirrups, heel down, toes out, and gathered up the reins. 'Aunt Caroline showed me on the rocking horse in the nursery yesterday while you were out.'

'Aunt?'

Laura shrugged, her nonchalance hiding the warm glow of pride at Alice's quick learning, her trust. 'I appear to have been adopted.'

'So long as you do not mind the familiarity.' Avery took the leading rein from the groom. 'I will take her this first time, Ferris.'

'I am coming, too.' As if she would not watch her daughter's first riding lesson!

Avery cast a dubious look from the paddock's rough grass and muddy patches to her neat leather half-boots, but did not argue. *Sensible man,* she thought. *I wonder where he has learned to humour women.* But he would not be so casual about anything that actually mattered to him.

'Gather up the reins so you can feel the contact with his mouth, press in with your knees and just give him a touch with your heels to tell him to walk on,' Avery ordered.

Alice gave a little squeak of excitement as the pony moved, then sat silent, her face a frown of concentration.

'Let your hands and wrists relax.' Laura reached across to lay her hand over the child's clenched fingers just as Avery did the same thing. Their gloved fingers met, tangled, held. Alice giggled. 'Poor Snowdrop, now we're all riding him.'

'Relax,' Avery murmured and Laura shot him a stern glance. It had not been the child he was speaking to. 'Shoulders back,' he added as he released her hand to correct Alice's posture.

'And seat in.' Laura patted the target area. 'That's perfect. When you ride side-saddle your back and posterior will be in exactly the same position as now.'

They walked around the paddock twice, speaking only to the child, hands bumping and touching as they reached to adjust her position or steady her. Laura was in heaven. Despite the looming masculine presence on the other side of the pony, and despite the crackle of awareness at every touch, she was with her daughter, able to help her, see her delight. She praised, she reassured, she smiled back as Alice beamed at her, and fought down the emotion that lurked so close to the surface. *Five days left.*

'I want to trot now.'

'No,' Avery said flatly.

'Why not?' Laura countered. 'It is hard work, Alice. You must push down with your heels, tighten your knees and rise up and down with the stride or you'll be jolted until your teeth rattle.'

'She'll not be able to post when she's riding side-saddle,' Avery pointed out.

'Which is why you see ladies trotting so infrequently, but it will strengthen her legs. Pay attention to your balance and don't jab his mouth, Alice. Use your heels, that's it.'

Off they went, the tall man jogging beside the pony, the excited child bouncing in the saddle, *bump, bump* and then, 'Aunt Caroline, look! I'm going up and down!'

She stood by the gate and watched them until the circuit was completed and Avery came to a halt beside her, not in the least out of breath. For a diplomat he was remarkably fit. She had supposed he would spend all his day at a desk or a conference table, but it seemed she was mistaken.

'Enough, Alice. You'll be stiff in the morning as it is.' He lifted her down. 'Now run inside to Blackie and get changed into something respectable before luncheon.'

He took Laura's arm as the child gave her pony one last pat and then ran off towards the house. 'Thank you.'

'For what?' *For indulging myself with my daughter's presence for an hour? For reassuring myself that you really do care for her and will look after her?*

'For finding her those clothes and persuading me of the benefits of allowing her to learn to ride astride. She is very confident now and that's half the battle. In a week or two we can try her with a side-saddle.'

Laura was not aware of making a sound, but he glanced at her. 'We won't have to have one made. Ferris found a small one in the stable loft. You will stay for luncheon?'

'I—' *I would move in if I could, absorb every impression, every memory. In a week or two we could teach her to ride side-saddle...* Oh, the temptation to stay, to dig herself deeper and deeper into Alice's life, into her affections.

'You hesitate to come inside a bachelor household when I am at home? Alice and her nurse will be adequate chaperons, don't you think?'

'Of course they will. I would be happy to accept.' Not that she now had any worries about what the ladies of the parish might say if they found out. She would be gone in a few days and her purpose in meeting them, to help find Alice some little playmates, had been fulfilled. It was her own equilibrium she was concerned about. That and the man by her side.

Without Alice's presence to distract her Avery seemed to loom over her, tall, solid, an immovable object as much in her mind as in reality. Alice loved him; he, Laura was forced to accept, loved her. He was intelligent, good company, handsome and part of her wanted to like him, wanted...*him*. And yet he had stolen her child with every intention of keeping her from her mother. He had bribed another man's tenants into lying and he would ruthlessly do whatever it took to get what he wanted. She should hate him, but she could not. Instead she envied him, she was jealous of him and she feared him.

And none of those emotions were attractive ones. Hatred was condemned from the pulpit as a sin, of course, but somehow it seemed a more straightforward feeling. If one could express it, of course, Laura pondered as she walked beside Avery Falconer to the house. *Piers's house.* That was another pain, the way Avery had slipped so easily into the role of master here. And it was something else she should not resent, for the tenants were being treated well, the land was in good heart, the servants had employment. It was not this man's fault that his cousin had died, that Piers had broken his word to her, left her before they could marry, abandoned her for some romantic notion of duty and valour.

She was not wearing a bonnet and the breeze blew strands of her hair across her face. Laura pushed them back, wishing she could hold her head in her hands and think, clearly, rationally and not be filled with so many conflicting feelings.

She was conscious that Avery was looking at her, but she kept her eyes down, reluctant to meet his now she was the sole focus of his attention. Ever since he had made that remark about physical attraction he had said or done nothing the slightest bit improper or provocative. As a result Laura found she was constantly braced for words and actions that never came. And she was thinking about him as a man, an attractive man, a desirable man.

Was it a strategy? Was Avery playing with her, hoping she would be intrigued by that statement? Perhaps this was an opening gambit in a game of seduction.

'That was a heavy sigh. Are you tired?'

'Yes. Yes, I am,' she said before she could think better of it. 'I am tired of playing games. Two days ago you spoke of physical attraction between us and then nothing. You do not explain yourself, you do not flirt, you do not try to make love to me. I do not want any of those things, you understand. It is just very unsettling to have them…hovering.'

Under her arm his guiding hand tensed. 'I did explain. I said I felt that attraction and tried to understand it.'

'You had no need to mention it at all.' It had kept her awake at night. 'It makes me uneasy. And I suspect you intended that.'

'Do you want me to flirt with you?' he asked. Then, when she did not answer, 'Do you want me to make love to you?'

'No!' Laura wrenched her arm away. Avery caught her hand in his, the impetus of her movement swinging her around so they were face-to-face. His face was serious, his eyes dark and intent and assessing. He desired her, she could read it in his face, could see it in his parted lips and the stillness of him. 'I do not flirt.' It was a lie. Her entire life away from this place was a game, a flirtation, an empty farce.

It was very quiet. The stable block was behind them and they had just entered the shrubbery that swept around the east side of the house, thick with laurels and box, the smell of the evergreens aromatic and astringent. A robin was singing high up in an ash tree and the gravel of the path crunched beneath Avery's booted feet. Her pulse was thudding.

'No, you have not done anything that might be construed as flirtation. I wonder then that I sensed what I did. Wishful thinking, perhaps,' Avery said and she saw from the faint smile that he had seen her colour rise. 'You said you did not trust men. Have you come to trust me a little, Caroline?'

'Yes,' she agreed, wary now, only half-believing what she said. Or what she felt. He was going to kiss her. And then what would she do?

'Why?' He was so close now that their toes bumped. She was aware of the smell of saddle soap and horse from his gloves and the warmth of his breath and the cock robin overhead flinging his challenge at every other bird in the vicinity. *Another arrogant male.*

'Because Alice loves you,' she replied with simple truth and watched his mouth, only his mouth, as the smile deepened, slightly askew so a faint dimple appeared on the right, but not on the left. And even then, even though she expected it, the kiss surprised her when it came.

Avery bent his head and brushed his lips across hers, an electric, tickling touch that made every hair on her nape stand up. He did not touch her or try to deepen the caress, but simply tucked her hand under his arm again and walked on.

'You are a wise woman to trust the innocent judgement of a child over your own fears.'

'I did not say I was afraid of you.' Her mouth trembled and she pressed her lips together. A proper kiss she could have dealt with. She would have returned it as an equal and then, as she always did, have made it very clear that nothing would follow. A crude attempt to do more she could have dealt with, too. She had no scruple about kneeing a man in the groin or biting an ear or whatever unladylike manoeuvre was necessary to leave him gasping on the ground in fear for his manhood. She had done that also, more than once.

But that brush of the lips—what was that? Was she being teased as she had so often teased? Best to ignore it, pretend it never happened, pretend that there was no heat in her belly and that she did not ache for his hands on her breasts and his mouth, open over hers. *Oh, Piers, how could I feel like this for another man?* Was it because of the resemblance between the cousins? She pushed away the thought that she could be so foolish.

'I have drafted an advertisement for a governess,' Avery remarked as they came out of the shrubbery onto the lawn.

'Which newspapers will you put it in?' *So, he can ignore it, too, infuriating man. It should make me like him less, but somehow it does not. Yet I suspect he knows that. Games. We are both playing games.*

'All the London ones and the local press, as well. Will you check it over for me?' She nodded. 'In that case, if you would like to join Alice in the dining room, I will fetch it. Just through here.'

The long windows that faced the garden front were all raised to let in the balmy spring air and

Avery helped her over the low sill into a blue-painted room with a table set for luncheon. As she stepped down onto the polished floor he continued outside, presumably to his study.

There was no sign of Alice yet. No doubt Miss Blackstock was scrubbing off every trace of pony and stables and dressing her in a suitable dress for a proper little girl. She should wash, too.

'Can you show me where I can wash my hands?' she asked the maid setting a bowl of fruit on the table.

'Yes, ma'am, this way if you please.'

It was an unexceptional way of exploring, although, disappointingly, all the inner doors off the hall were closed. The girl led her through to a small room with a water closet on one side and a washstand on the other and left her. Laura lingered over cleaning her hands, working up a froth of lavender-scented soap, trickling the cool water through her fingers.

A fantasy was forming in her mind. She would write to her solicitor, her steward, everyone, and explain she was going abroad for an indefinite period. Then she would tell Avery that she would become Alice's governess. He could not deny that the child liked her, responded well to her. He trusted her enough to ask her opinion, he knew from conversation that she was educated, cultured. A lady.

Laura blotted the wetness on a linen towel, watched the fabric grow darker, limp with the water from her hands. It seemed very important to focus on getting every inch of skin quite dry while her mind scrabbled at that fantasy like an overexcited child tearing the wrappings from a present.

And then, as though she had opened the gift and found not the expected doll or sweetmeats, but a book of sermons, acrid as dust, her hands were dry and her mind clear. She could not do it. How long could she live so close to Alice and not betray herself? She would be a servant in her own daughter's home, someone with no real power, no control. Sooner or later Avery would find her out and then she would have to leave and Alice would lose someone she might have grown very fond of. It was too painful to think the word *love*.

Avery was crossing the hall when she emerged, her hair smooth, her expression calm, even the trace of a blush from that kiss subdued by cool water and willpower.

'What do you think?' He handed her a sheet

of paper. 'Will you look at it now in the study, before Alice comes down?'

He watched Laura as she stood, head bent over the draft. Her hair was rigorously tidy, each strand disciplined back into a severe chignon. It did not look like hair that relished control, it looked as though it wanted to be loose, waving, its colours catching the sun in shades from blonde to soft brown. Her cheeks were smooth, pale with less than the natural colour of health in them and none of the blush that had stained them when she had thrown that challenge at him in the shrubbery.

Her lips moved slightly, parted, and her tongue emerged just to touch the centre of her upper lip. He guessed it was a habitual sign of concentration, but it sent the blood straight to his groin. Those lips under his, smooth and warm. They had clung for a moment against his while he had wrestled with the urge to possess, feel her open under him, to taste her. He was confusing her and he wished he understood why.

'You state that the person appointed must be willing to travel.'

'Yes, that is essential. I expect to be sent

abroad again before the year is out and I will take Alice with me.'

'You had best say it means to the Continent, then, and not simply on a tour of the Lakes.' Her lips quivered into a slight smile and were serious again.

Avery fought with temptation and yielded to it. 'I was wondering… I know you said Alice would benefit from a younger governess, but I wondered about a widow.'

A shiver went through Caroline, so faint he saw it merely in the movement of her pearl ear-bobs. He held his breath. Was he being too obvious? And what, in blazes, was he thinking of in any case?

Chapter Six

What could he tell from Caroline's stillness? The downcast lids did not lift, nor the dark lashes move. Perhaps he had imagined that shiver, perhaps she had no notion he was talking about her. 'Not all widows are middle-aged,' she pointed out after a moment.

'No, indeed. Such as yourself.' Avery wondered just how old she was. The ageing effect of her black clothes, and the paleness of her skin, made it difficult to tell, but he doubted she could be much over twenty-five. 'I was just wondering if someone with more experience of children would be better.'

'And not all widows have had children,' Caroline said, her voice so lacking in expression it might as well have been a scream.

Hell and damnation. She told you she had

lost a child. Get your great boot out of your mouth, Falconer, and stop daydreaming. It had been a nice little fantasy about Caroline Jordan as Alice's governess, but what did that make him, lusting after his daughter's teacher, a woman who would be under his protection in his house? *A lecher, that's what,* Avery told himself. He despised men who took advantage of their female dependants.

'You see how much I need you to stop me wandering off at tangents,' he said.

'It seems strange that a man who can steer the fate of nations at the conference table finds it hard to advertise for a governess.' Caroline sounded faintly amused, thank heavens.

'The devil's in the details,' he said, snatching at a cliché in desperation. He had told the Duke of Wellington to stop interfering before now. He had faced down the most powerful of the Emperor Alexander's ministers and he could negotiate in five languages, but this one woman, with her emotional buttons done up so tightly over whatever was going on in her bosom, had him in knots.

And that's because when you are dealing with Wellington you aren't thinking with the parts of your anatomy that are giving you hell now. Although it isn't simply desire.

'Papa! Aunt Caroline! Luncheon is ready and I am *starving.*'

'Coming, Alice.' Avery lowered his voice as he took the paper from Caroline. 'Do you suppose a governess will be able to stop her stampeding about like a herd of goats and shouting at the top of her voice?'

'Oh, I hope not.' Mrs Jordan's smile was curiously tender. 'Not all the time.'

Avery watched Caroline during the meal and Caroline watched Alice. Not him. Which meant he had either so comprehensively embarrassed her that she did not dare risk catching his eye or that she was completely indifferent to him. And yet his reckless remark about desire had discomforted her to the extent that she had challenged him about it this morning. She had neither screamed, nor slapped his face when he had kissed her, but she had given him no encouragement either.

So…not a merry window or even one sophisticated enough to contemplate an irregular liaison. He suspected she was not mourning her husband in anything but the outward show of black clothing and quiet living. There was a mystery there.

'Was your husband a landowner, Mrs Jordan?'

'In a small way. He was a military man.' She prepared an apple for Alice, scarcely glancing at him as she controlled the peel that curled from her knife.

'From this part of the world?'

'We lived in London when we were together.' Her hand was quite steady with the sharp blade. 'There, Alice. Now, I was careful to get it all off in one piece, which is very important for this magic to work. If you hold up the peel, very high, and drop it, it will make the initial of your husband-to-be.'

Alice giggled. 'That can't be right, Aunt Caroline. You peeled it, so you will have to drop it.'

'I have no intention of marrying again.'

'Please?'

Avery watched, amused that the wide-eyed green stare, combined with the faint tremble of the lower lip, worked just as well on Mrs Jordan as it did on him. He shuddered to think of the impact on young men when Alice was old enough to make her come-out. He would have to carry a shotgun at all times.

'Oh, very well. It will come out with a Z or an X or something improbable.' Caroline held up the peel and dropped it. She and Alice studied it with all the care of scientists with a lens. 'I cannot make anything of it,' she said at last. 'The magic obviously works and it knows I will not marry again.'

Avery leaned across the table. 'It is a lower-case *a,*' he said. 'It is facing me, that is why you cannot read it. See, the round shape and the little tail.'

'A is for Avery,' Alice exclaimed.

There was a deadly little silence, then Caroline said, 'Your papa will be marrying a titled lady, Alice. She is probably dropping her apple peel at just this moment and it is coming out as a capital A, the right way up.'

'You have the makings of a diplomat,' Avery remarked softly as Alice became engrossed in making letters with pieces of peel while she nibbled on her apple segments. 'I am sorry if we have embarrassed you between us this morning.'

'I am not embarrassed,' Caroline said and

returned her attention to the piece of fruit on her own plate.

And she was not, he realised. But she was distressed. He was learning to read her emotions behind the calm facade and her eyes were sparkling as if with unshed tears and her hand shook, just a little, as she wielded the sharp little knife. What the devil had her husband done to her to make her so fragile on the subject of marriage?

He is going to marry some day and Alice will have a stepmother. She will call her Mama and she will love her. They will be a family in some glamorous European capital while Avery is a diplomat and then they will host great house parties at Wykeham Hall when they return to England. Alice will grow up and another woman will help her choose her gowns and will share her secrets and those first tears over a flirtation. Another woman will... Stop it!

It was self-indulgent and as foolish as prodding a bruise to see if it hurt. Of course it hurt, but her heartbreak was not important. Alice was what mattered. Only Alice. Laura glanced up and saw Avery was watching her. He knew she was upset and his face was grave. Strange how she was beginning to be able to read his face, the thoughts behind the skilful diplomatic mask. Would there have been as much subtlety and intelligence in Piers's face as he matured to the age this man was now?

He smiled at her, a little rueful, the expression of a friend who wants to help, but is not quite sure how. He would not look like that if he knew she was deceiving him or who she was, she thought with a kick of conscience.

'May I get down, Papa?'

'Ask Mrs Jordan's permission.'

'Certainly. Go and play, Alice.' Inevitably the door banged behind her. Then they were alone and she could say the thing her conscience was prodding her to say. 'I apologise.'

'Whatever for?' Avery was leaning back in his chair, but he sat up at that.

'I thought you arrogant and I made judgements about how well a single man could raise a child. It was wrong of me. Prejudiced.'

'And I apologise for making assumptions about how a widow might wish to flirt.'

'That is what it was? You must forgive me if I am a trifle innocent about these things.' She was not, of course, but she wanted to maintain the fiction that her world was not that of the *haut ton.* But while he was being so frank, she could seize the opportunity to remove a small worry about Alice's welfare. 'Do you not keep a mistress?'

The look he gave her was forbidding, but he answered without hesitation. 'I have done. Not very recently and not in this country. And I would never allow a future mistress anywhere near Alice, if that is what is worrying you.'

'So, when you were hinting just now that I might take the position of governess, that negated any chance you might offer me a very different position?'

'That is frankness if ever I heard it!' That question jolted him out of his composure, which was interesting. When he recovered his countenance, with a speed that spoke volumes for his self-control, she thought he might be faintly amused under the surprise. 'Allow me to be equally frank in return. I thought about that for a moment. And I am ashamed of myself, I own it, so you have no cause to look at me like that from those wide brown eyes.'

'Like what?' She had thought her emotions were well hidden.

'As though you are disappointed in me. Although perhaps I should welcome some heat in your regard after your usual Arctic chill.'

'You talk nonsense, my lord. I must leave now.' *Before this becomes any more complicated.*

'You will come tomorrow?' he asked as she retrieved her bonnet, reticule and shawl from the hall stand.

The servants had made themselves scarce. *Perhaps they know better than to intrude when their master is with a woman. No, that is unfair, I trust him when he says he would never expose Alice to one of his* chères amies.

'No,' Laura said crisply. 'It is not convenient tomorrow. Please say goodbye to Alice for me.'

Avery opened the door for her without speaking and she walked briskly down the drive, feeling his eyes on her back for every step. *That had been remarkably like a tantrum,* she told herself as she turned left into the lane in the direction of the village. *Or a lovers' quarrel. Only we are not lovers and he did no quarrelling.*

It was not difficult to work out what was upsetting her, only to know how to cope with it. The situation with Alice was clear enough, if painful. At least she had a clear conscience and the comfort of knowing she was doing what was best for her daughter, however much it hurt.

But Avery Falconer was tying her in knots.

They had shockingly frank conversations about desire and yet she could be open with him about nothing else. She wanted him with a directness that was unmistakable, but she did not know why. Was it because he looked so much like Piers, but mature and reliable? Or was it that he was a devastatingly attractive man who was open about his attraction to her? Perhaps it was simply that she could not forgive him for stealing Alice, however well meant his actions, and therefore everything about him, good and bad, was exaggerated.

Whatever she thought of him, and however much he loved Alice now, she could not forget that love and concern for an unknown baby could not have motivated him to buy the child. Pride, arrogance and the certainty that he knew best for anyone who might be connected with the lofty Earl of Wykeham was what had driven him then and it was pure chance that good had come of it.

Oh, but she ached for him.

'Cutting off your nose to spite your face, are you?' Mab demanded over the breakfast table the next morning.

'Probably.' Laura bit into a slice of toast,

chewed, thought, swallowed. 'Do sit down, Mab, you make my head ache stomping about. I have so few days left with Alice and I'm a fool to allow one mystifying man to stop me spending them with her.'

'Mystifying, is he?' Mab poured herself some tea and planted herself on the chair across the kitchen table. 'Not the word I'd use, myself. Downright—' She broke off and was lost in thought, searching for the word. 'Edible. I could think of other ways to describe him, but none of them decent.' She buttered a slice of toast and applied plum preserve with a lavish hand. 'Saw him riding past yesterday morning, first thing. Got a handsome pair of shoulders on him. And thighs,' she added. 'You'd know you'd got something in your bed with that one, right enough.'

'Mab!'

'Well, I'm female with eyes in my head and I've got a pulse, haven't I? Good-sized nose and feet…'

'Mab!' *Piers had big feet, too… Oh, stop it, you are as bad as she is.* 'All right, I am not dead either. Avery Falconer is very attractive. And intelligent. And he is good to Alice. And I like him. I just cannot forgive him.'

'Worse things to forgive a man for than giving a child a loving home.' Mab demolished the toast and picked up her tea. 'You and Mr Piers made a right hash of things between you, thinking with your…well, not thinking at all, if you ask me. You should have insisted he marry you before you got into bed with him and he ought to have cared enough about you not to have risked it. And don't look at me like that, you know it is true.'

It was like being slapped in the face. No, it was like having a bucket of cold water poured over a fragile sugar tower of illusion. Young love, passion, an undying, innocent romance— or two young people being thoughtless? She had built a castle in the air and inhabited it with her perfect knight, her gallant soldier, and hadn't the wit to think through the likely consequences of sleeping with a man off to a battlefield in the near future. And Piers had not fought hard enough to behave like a gentleman and not a randy young soldier.

More than time to let go of girlish fantasies. There was no such thing as undying love or she wouldn't feel so much as a twinge of desire for Avery Falconer. And Avery was guilty of nothing more than a strong sense of family duty and an honourable obligation to the child of a cousin he was probably very fond of. He had taken Alice for Piers's sake.

Mab eyed her warily, braced, no doubt, for a blistering retort about the impudence of maid-servants daring to speak their mind, or floods of tears. 'Thank you, Mab. You are quite right.' Not that it didn't hurt or was shaming to have the truth pointed out so bluntly, but it was probably like lancing a boil, she'd be glad later when the agony subsided.

'And you are quite right about today, too. I'll walk up to the Manor now. It is foolish to waste a minute with Alice.'

I will be pleasant and friendly and make it quite clear I want neither flirtation nor kisses, she resolved half an hour later as she negotiated the steps up the ha-ha and tackled the sloping lawn. Halfway she met Jackson, the footman, his hands full of a dew-wet hoop and ball.

'Miss Alice forgets her toys, ma'am,' he said with his friendly grin. 'Were you coming to see her? Only Miss Blackstock's taken her off to Hemel Hempstead in the gig to buy new shoes. You've just missed them.'

The disappointment was ridiculously sharp, not less for it being her own fault. If she hadn't been sulking over Avery she might have been in time to have joined the shopping expedition. 'I will just say good morning to Lord Wykeham, in that case,' she said, summoning a smile.

'He's in the Blue Sitting Room, ma'am. The window's open if you can manage the step.' He pointed. 'Or I can go in and announce you?'

'No, you continue your search for the contents of the toy box, Jackson. I can find my own way.'

Her footsteps were silent on the smooth flagstones. Laura stooped to look into the unfamiliar room and saw Avery. He was half-seated on the edge of a desk, his long legs out in front crossed at the ankles, his hands behind, bracing him. His head was down as though he was deep in thought. Laura hesitated, her hand on the window frame for balance, then caught her breath as he looked up, his face stark and naked as she had never seen it.

He must have heard her involuntary gasp, for he turned, his expression under control so fast she wondered if she had imagined the pain. 'Caroline. I was not expecting you today.'

'I know. I have missed Alice, haven't I?' She stepped down into the room. 'Avery, what is wrong?' The shadow of that inner agony was

still on his face, now she knew to look for it.
'My dear man...' She went towards him, her
hands held out and he stood, pushed away from
the table and she was in his arms.

He said nothing before he kissed her, his
mouth urgent and demanding, his tongue tan-
gling with hers as she responded, opened to him
as though they were old lovers who knew each
other's bodies with utter familiarity. She knew
how he would taste, how he would feel in her
arms. She knew, as she kissed him back, how
he would angle his head, how he would explore
her mouth, how she would melt into him. He
was everything her restless night-time imagin-
ings had promised he would be and more. *And
he is* this *man, not another, not Piers.*

He had turned as he kissed her and she felt
the hard edge of the table press into her buttocks, the hard ridge of his arousal press into
her belly. Desperate for air so that she could
kiss him again, Laura dragged her mouth free.
His eyes were dark and fierce and wild, the
eyes of a man whose control was always perfect—until now.

'Caroline.' It was a growl, a statement, not
a question.

Caroline? Who? Laura froze. Caroline was

not her. Caroline was a lie and she could not be like this with a man she was lying to. 'Avery.' She slid her hands down so they rested on his chest. Under her palms his heartbeat thudded. He stared down at her and slowly the darkness of passion faded out of his eyes.

'Avery,' she said again. 'I cannot—'

'Hell. No, of course you cannot.' She blinked, confused. How could he know what she was going to say? 'I apologise. That was outrageous. I had no right to touch you. I'll leave.'

'No.' Of course, he thought she was saying she could not make love to him. He was not a mind reader. But thank goodness he had stopped before things had gone any further. 'You do not need to do that. It takes two to be as imprudent as we have just been. I take responsibility for my actions. And reactions,' she added with a smile in the hope of easing the tension that showed in his jaw and clenched hands. *Yes, this time, I will take responsibility and I will think of the consequences.*

'Thank you.' Avery turned and ran one hand through his hair. 'I was feeling a trifle blue devilled, not that it is any excuse for attempting to ravish you on the desk.'

She was never sure afterwards what she had

intended to say to him. Laura looked up and saw the portrait on the wall behind him and the words simply dried in her mouth. *Piers*.

Chapter Seven

Avery turned to follow her gaze. 'That is my cousin Piers Falconer,' he said. 'I inherited this estate from him. I do not wonder that you look surprised. It is uncanny, is it not? People often take it for a picture of me and remark that they hadn't realised I had ever been in the army.' He did not appear to find it amusing.

Laura looked into the clear green eyes in the youthful, unlined face in the painting and her feet took her, with no conscious volition, to stand on the hearth where she could reach up and touch the hilt of the sword. *Go away,* she willed Avery, but he did not move. 'He was killed in battle?' She knew the answer, but she had to say something.

'A stupid, unnecessary skirmish with the enemy where they were not supposed to be because of a failure in communications. Ironic that a man who dreamed of glory and great epic battles should die defending a ford over a stream that shouldn't even have needed defending.'

'Ironic indeed.' *That was what you left me for, Piers,* she thought. *I was so angry with you.* 'He was a romantic about war?' Her fingers slid off the leather of the hilt, still too new to have lost its grooves or to have softened and moulded to the hand of its owner.

'Piers was army-mad. But he was an only child, the heir. His father died when he was seventeen and I became his trustee, although I was not that much older—four years. I pointed out that he could not join, that he had responsibilities, that his mother would be desperately anxious, but he only laughed. She would be proud, he said, and of course he would not be killed. He thought himself immortal, I suppose. He was very young in some ways.' Avery sounded bone-weary, perhaps with the memory of endless arguments.

'But he joined anyway.'

'Oh, yes. As soon as he was twenty and came into some money from his godfather he went to London and bought himself a commission.

There was nothing I could do and his mother, who had always indulged him, hid her fear. She died six months later. I suppose I cannot blame him for it, he never knew Aunt Alice's heart was weak.' Avery had wandered across to the window and stood leaning his shoulder against the frame, staring out over the parkland. 'He came back to England on sick leave. A combination of a minor wound and a fever. They gave him three months to recover and to settle affairs after his mother's death, although I'd handled that already.' He shrugged one shoulder as if to push away the memory. 'She was more like a mother to me than an aunt.'

'That is why Alice is named as she is.' Piers had never told her his mother's name or that she had died such a short time before they met. It seemed strange, she had thought they had shared everything. How little she had known him.

'Yes. Anyway, he recovered his health well and he was due to return on the next troop carrier, two days hence, when he told me he was going to make some excuse and delay.'

'Why?' Laura breathed, knowing full well why.

'He had become entangled with some airheaded chit and wanted to stay with her. I pointed out that by the terms of his father's will he could not marry without the consent of his trustees until he was twenty-one in six weeks' time and I was not giving my approval. He said in that case he would suffer a relapse and miss the ship.'

'She was so ineligible?' Laura asked. By some miracle she kept the shake out of her voice.

'No.' Again that shrug. 'Excellent family, no doubt a perfectly adequate dowry. But she was too young and he most certainly was, and they'd known each other a matter of weeks.'

Five weeks. Four weeks as lovers, long enough to create a child.

'Piers became very agitated, said he'd go sick for six years if it took that, let alone the six weeks until he could marry.'

'But he went back.' Laura held on to the back of the nearest chair. Piers had left, with only a brief note. *I have to go back to Spain. We cannot marry yet, but wait for me. I do not know how long it will be...* She had sat with it in her hand that morning, the morning when she had realised what the non-appearance of her monthly courses—usually as regular as clockwork—meant. She was pregnant and her lover had abandoned her.

'The boy was a romantic. A buffle-headed, muddle-brained romantic,' Avery said bitterly. 'He had broken his mother's heart by joining up, he had sworn an oath of allegiance, and the moment he fancied himself in love he would throw the whole thing over. He would lie to stay in England, pretend to be sick when his comrades went back to fight.

'I told him that to do what he was suggesting would be dishonourable, that his oath as an officer preceded any entanglement with some girl who could perfectly well wait for him—and if she could not, then she would be no wife for a soldier in any case. I asked him,' he said, his voice hard, 'if this was an excuse and he was too afraid to go back.'

Laura sat down, her legs boneless. 'You called him a coward?'

'By implication, yes.'

'And so he went back to Spain, abandoned the girl and was killed almost as soon as he returned?'

'Yes.' The stark word in the warm air of the room scented by the breeze from the garden was like the crack of a gunshot.

She had fallen from her horse once and the air had been knocked clean out of her. She had felt hollow then, but not as empty as she felt now. Laura stared at the dark head, still so firmly turned from her. What had that been? A confession? But he sounded angry, not remorseful, as though getting killed was Piers's fault.

Piers's sword rested almost within arm's reach. Laura saw herself pick it up and run it through that broad back as vividly as in a dream. She felt the jar as the steel hit bone and solid muscle, she felt the gush of hot blood on her hands. She blinked and it was still in its rack, she was still sitting down, her heart racing. When she spoke her voice came from a long way away and she wondered if she was going to faint. 'Do you regret it?'

'It was a matter of honour, it had to be said.'

'And you did not concern yourself with the girl he loved?'

'No.'

I had lain with a man I loved, because we loved. I was foolish and heedless, but does that make me worthless? It seemed that in Avery Falconer's eyes it did. *Hypocrite,* she thought. *I was... I thought I liked you.* Now she knew she had been right all along. He was arrogant, ruthless, judgemental and deeply unfair.

The clock struck, a thin, silvery note. 'My goodness, look at the time,' Laura said and stood up, half-expecting to find her legs would not support her. 'I must go and…and fetch something from the village. Something I promised Mab,' she added. She had the doorknob in her hand before he turned and she was out of the room before he spoke.

'Caroline—'

'Tomorrow,' she called back over her shoulder. 'I really must go now.'

He had shocked her. First by taking her instinctive concern as an excuse to kiss her and then by talking of battlefields and death. Avery watched the garden, but there was no sign of Caroline, so she must have taken the front path to the village lane. Tomorrow he would apologise. Now he had to shake off this mood before Alice came home.

Do you regret it? Caroline had asked. Regret was hardly the word, furious resentment was more like it. Damn it, he was not going to be plunged into this mental morass every time he came into this room to get a book. He could re-

move the portrait and the sword to the attic, but
that would be cowardly. This had been Piers's
home and his mother would have wanted them
there. Alice must grow up knowing what her…
her cousin looked like, hearing stories of his
courage.

He had failed Piers when he could not stop
him buying a commission and, somehow, he
had failed him if the younger man had been
capable of such muddle-headed thinking about
where his duty lay. Avery found the book he
had been looking for and deliberately sat down
at the desk to check the reference he was looking for instead of taking it to his study. If he
had caved in and let Piers stay and marry Lady
Laura Campion, he might have been killed in
the next skirmish after he landed in Spain. He
could have drowned on the transport ship. He
could have contracted a fever and died of that.

And he would have been leg-shackled to a
chit of a girl who had been loose enough to
throw her hat over the windmill for a handsome
face in a scarlet coat and who then hadn't the
backbone to cope with what being an officer's
wife would mean. He had read the few bloodstained tatters that were all that remained of the
letter that Piers had in his breast pocket when

he was killed: nothing but anger and petulance. And yet his cousin had kept it against his heart and it was probably the last thing he read. No soldier deserved to have those words ringing in his ears as he fought and died. *Coward... betrayal...I hate...I'm pregnant...fault...Laura.*

There were not many young ladies by that name and fewer still who vanished from the social scene because of a family crisis at a distant estate. He had gone to find Lady Laura, telling himself that Piers would have wanted him to, driven by grief and anger at the fates and at himself. When he tracked her down, the word locally was that Lady Laura was not well and consumption was feared. That was enough to keep visitors away.

Avery had had to return to his duties abroad, so he had bided his time, watched the calendar, paid a skilful agent to spy, to intercept the mails before they reached the receiving office. The girl had sent the baby away, far away, he learned. After that it was simple. Wait a short while, then a few weeks' leave and he was back in Vienna with Alice.

The agent was rewarded well for his discretion and for the reports he continued to send about Lady Laura Campion. She had returned to London society, but not heartbroken, not crushed by the shame or by giving away her child. Of course she'd had to do it, no lady in her position could have survived it becoming public knowledge that she had given birth out of wedlock. Her reputation would have been shredded if she had kept the baby.

But surely she could have kept the child close and found a respectable family where she could visit without suspicion to watch over her growing daughter? To have sent her to the other end of the country, to a remote dale and the hard life of a small farmer's child, that argued a complete lack of concern for anything but a swift removal of an embarrassment.

Scandal's Virgin they call her, Lambton had written. *She's the fastest of all the débutantes, she spends money like water and they say she leaves broken hearts behind her like so much smashed crockery. The chaperons shake their heads, the matrons are scandalised, the gossip sheets love her and the men pursue. The betting books in the clubs are full of her name— but no one can claim on the wagers because, it seems, she always stops just this side of ruin. An arrant flirt...*

Avery could think of other words to describe

Lady Laura Campion. Any guilt he might have felt at taking the baby vanished. If she had been heartbroken over Piers, if she had led a quiet, respectable life and married a decent man after an interval of mourning for Piers, then he would have experienced severe qualms about what he had done.

But Alice did not deserve a mother like that, a woman who showed no sign of mourning her dead lover or the loss of her child. He would move heaven and earth to make sure Alice never knew who she was. Sooner or later he was going to have to make up some fairy story for the child, create some perfect woman to be her mother and some satisfying, if romantically sad, reason why he could not marry her.

Not long now before he was in London and then he would see her, this witch who had so turned Piers's head that he forgot his honour and his duty, this lady with the heart of a harlot who had sent her own child far away so she could wallow in pleasure and break hearts as she had broken his cousin's heart.

'We are leaving. Now. Today.'

'What? Why?' Mab dropped the laundry basket onto the kitchen table with a thump.

'That man....' Her voice was shaking so much she had to stop, grip the edge of the table and breathe hard before she could steady it. 'That man forced Piers to go back to Spain before he could marry me. He called him a coward and he got him in such a muddle about his duty and his honour that he went—and he was killed.'

'Lovey, he might have been killed whenever he went back.'

'I know.' Laura sank onto the nearest chair. 'But he would have married me and Alice would be legitimate and Piers would not have died with that worry on his mind.'

'He knew?' Mab sat down, too.

'I wrote and it would have caught the next ship out. I think, from the timing, he could have received it. Perhaps I should not have done it, but I was so frightened and all I could think of was that I had to tell him.' *I feel such a coward. It seems like a betrayal of everything I told you I could be as a soldier's wife. I hate to worry you, but I am pregnant with our child. Please don't blame yourself, we were both at fault, but write, I beg you, tell me what to do...* There had never been a response, only the news of his death.

'I dare not risk being near Lord Wykeham or I will say something I regret, I know I will. I cannot believe I kept my tongue between my teeth just now as it is.' She covered her face with her hands as if the blackness could somehow bring a measure of calm. 'The boy from the Golden Lion can take the gig into Hemel Hempstead and give a message to Michael to bring the carriage right away.' She got to her feet and ran to the front parlour to scribble a note for her coachman, who was waiting at one of the big coaching inns and enjoying a quiet country holiday while he did so. 'If you go to the Golden Lion now with this, I will start packing.'

Mab, her bonnet jammed on her head and her mouth set in a grim line, marched in and took the note. 'Don't you be putting your back out pulling that trunk out of the cupboard,' was all she said before she banged out of the front door.

Laura pulled another sheet of paper towards her and wrote as swiftly as her shaking hand allowed.

Dearest Alice,
I am sorry I had to leave without saying
goodbye to you. I will always remember

*you and think of you. Please understand
that not everyone who has to leave you
wishes to do so.*

With all my love, your 'adopted aunt'.

They had not brought much with them, for
the cottage had been rented furnished and
Laura's pose as a widow in mourning meant
she could manage with a limited wardrobe. By
the time Michael arrived in the coach—the one
she had chosen specifically because it had no
crest on the doors—she and Mab had the trunk
filled and a neat row of portmanteaux lined up
in the hall.

It was not a good time of day to leave, for
they could not get back to London in daylight
and would have to put up at an inn overnight,
but Laura dared not risk staying another day.
As it was, there seemed little chance that Avery
could discover who she was, even if he wanted
to. The cottage had been rented through her
man of business in her false name, she had received no post and Michael had told no one who
his employer was.

The note for Alice was dropped off at the inn
for delivery the next morning. By then Laura
would be on the road again, heading for Lon-

don, the Curzon Street house, appointments
with *modistes* and milliners, the re-entry into
her world—the world of the Season and the
haut ton and oblivion in a whirl of pleasure.

Avery Falconer could advertise for a governess and then pack his bags and go back to
arranging the affairs of Europe wherever the
government chose to use his undoubted talents
for autocratically directing the lives and desti-
nies of others.

He had cared for his cousin Piers and yet,
when the young man had crossed Avery's line
of what constituted honour and duty, he had
bent him ruthlessly to his will. He loved Alice:
Laura told herself that she just had to believe
he would never break her daughter's heart because he thought he was doing the right thing.

For two weeks Avery kept the tightest rein
on his temper he ever had in his life. He inter-
viewed governesses and found none to his liking, he arranged for the Berkeley Square house
to be put in readiness and he dealt with a weeping child who could not understand why her
new Aunt Caroline had vanished. And that was
difficult to endure because he had the nagging
conviction on his conscience that she had fled

his kisses and Alice's distress was therefore all his fault.

After a few days of tears, followed by clinging, Alice seemed to settle down. After all, as she confided in Avery, poor Aunt Caroline had been sad, so perhaps it was best that she had gone home to her friends, the only excuse he had been able to come up with.

Now all he had to do was to find Alice a step-mama who would love her and she could forget a mother who had sent her away and a mysterious aunt who had vanished. He found he was quite looking forward to it. There would be no work, no worries, no sudden crises, simply a process of sociable, pleasurable wife-hunting and then marriage.

Must be getting old, he thought, studying himself in the pier glass and tightening the muscles of an already flat stomach. *No sign of grey hairs yet, but the prospect of a wife is surprisingly attractive.* There would be none of the expenses and tantrums associated with mistresses. *And none of the tension and guilt associated with respectable widows either,* his conscience added. But it was good that Caroline had gone, for an earl with diplomatic responsibilities could not offer marriage to the widow of some middling gentleman and the alternative would not have been honourable. Yes, it was fortunate that he would never see Mrs Caroline Jordan again. But he missed her.

Chapter Eight

'So who is chaperoning you? Hmm?' The Dowager Marchioness of Birtwell lifted her lorgnette to her eyes and fixed Laura with an unnervingly magnified gaze.

Laura paused in her wanderings through the crowds at Mrs Fairweather's May Day musical reception and dipped a curtsy. 'My cousin Florence, ma'am.' Laura reminded herself that one day she might be eighty with arthritis and managed a smile. She crossed her fingers behind her back—after all, Cousin Florence had promised to come and stay soon…she just wasn't here at this moment.

'Lady Carstairs? She always was an empty-headed peahen. If your poor dear mama couldn't keep you in line, what hope has Florence Carstairs?'

'I am resolved not to be a trial to her,' Laura said and was rewarded with a crack of laugher.

'Well, you are too pale to compete with this year's beauties—and you are getting to be too old for any nonsense into the bargain. Time to stop flitting about and find a husband.' The dowager flapped her hands at Laura as if she was a troublesome chicken. 'Go on, there are enough of them out there. In fact, I saw just the man a moment ago. Neither of you are in a position to be too fussy. Now where has he gone?'

There were limits to polite toleration of one's elders, Laura decided, murmuring an excuse and moving away into the thronged reception room before the old dragon spotted that Cousin Florence was nowhere to be seen or located the rather less-than-ideal candidate she had in mind for Laura's hand. She was too pale, too old and had too much of a reputation to be entirely eligible apparently, but what were the gentleman's faults, such that he could not afford to be fussy either? she wondered. Buck teeth, a spreading waistline and a gambling habit, perhaps?

'Lady Laura! You have returned to us and as lovely as ever.' Lord Gordon Johnston placed one elegant hand on his beautifully tailored chest, approximately where his heart would be if he possessed one, and sketched a bow.

'Nonsense, Lord Gordon. I have it on the best authority that I am too pale and too old and had best find myself a husband before I am at my last prayers.' She had known him for years and knew, too, that the only way to avoid becoming the victim of his barbed tongue was to show him no chink in one's armour.

Lady Birtwell was right: she *was* too pale, she had lost her bloom and it was going to take sunshine, excitement and entertainment to bring it back and drive away the memories of the past few months. Meanwhile she must take care to seem as carefree and as secure as ever if she wanted to hold her place amongst the *ton* and not slip into being *that poor Lady Laura, on the shelf and at her last prayers.*

'As white as the lily,' Lord Gordon agreed, running the tip of one finger down her cheek. 'Such a dutiful daughter to shut yourself away in your blacks for so long. And when will we be seeing the new Earl of Hartland in town?'

'Very soon, I hope. The house is all ready for him.' *Smile, don't let him see you care about another man in Papa's place.*

'And you are ready for a whirl of pleasure, my dear?'

'Of course. Now who is new on the scene and lots of fun?' *And why don't I care any more? Must pretend, must keep up the mask.*

'Let me think.' Lord Gordon surveyed the guests through narrowed eyes. 'How about Viscount Newlyn? Fresh in town, still a trifle gauche, pots of money and an itch to spend it. And such a pretty boy, if rather too aware of it. He's over there, I'll introduce you.'

Laura allowed him to guide her through the crowd to a group of old acquaintances clustered around a tall, blond young exquisite who looked as though he was all too conscious of every detail of his own appearance and who had spent a good hour before the mirror preening before he came out.

Irritating puppy, Laura decided, taking a mild dislike to him on sight. Still, if he threw good parties and was amusing she supposed she could tolerate him.

'Lady Laura!' He took her hand and pressed his lips to it. Laura extricated it with some difficulty and smiled at the various acquaintances who were greeting her. A year ago she would have called them her friends, now, she realised, she had not missed one of them while she had been out of society. '...delighted.' The viscount was still talking. 'I had no idea I would be so fortunate as to be introduced to Scandal's Virgin herself within a week of arriving in London.'

The circle around him fell silent. The nickname was whispered but never spoken in the presence of Lady Laura herself. Miss Willmott, always nervous, gasped and gave a frightened little giggle, Lady Pamela Tutt started an abrupt, desperate monologue about the problems she was having with her maid and Lord Gordon's rather thin lips curved in anticipation of an explosion.

Laura waited a heartbeat, just long enough for Lord Newlyn to realise he had made a major error, then smiled. 'Why, my lord, I had no idea we were already on such terms as to be using pet names. What is yours? The Blond Blunderer, perhaps?'

There was laughter all round the group at that and the gentlemen, several of whom had stiffened, ready to intervene on Laura's behalf, relaxed. The viscount coloured, his expression rigid, but there was real anger in his eyes, she recognised. He was obviously not used to setdowns. 'My apologies, ma'am,' he said before he turned out of the small circle and stalked away towards the card room.

'A clumsy youth,' Lord Petersfield drawled. 'A mother's boy, no doubt, used to being the centre of attention amongst his little circle in Essex.'

'Oh well, *Essex*...' Lady Pamela tittered 'that explains it. Now, my dear Lady Laura, how are you going to amuse yourself now you are back amongst us? Mrs Bridgeport is promising the most delightful picnic next week if the weather holds...'

Laura finally found herself alone after an hour, talked out and rather weary. She was, she realised, thoroughly out of practice for late nights, hot rooms and constant conversation. Either that or the social scene was no longer enough to hold her attention, which was alarming. If she did not have that, her drug to stop her thinking, then how was she going to cope with the cold, empty centre of her life?

She didn't even want to flirt and tease now, to punish any more men for her abandonment by one of them. Because now she knew it was not Piers who had thoughtlessly abandoned her,

but Lord Wykeham who had torn him from her
and made her baby illegitimate. *He is probably
to blame for Piers's death as well,* she thought,
staring up at a lurid battle scene in oils that
hung by the terrace doors. If Piers had not gone
back just in time for that skirmish…

'Lady Laura, allow me to offer you this glass
of champagne.' It was Lord Newlyn, a glass in
each hand and expression of contrition on his
handsome, boyishly smooth, face. 'Let me make
amends for my blunder just now.'

She could have snubbed him, turned on her
heel, or cut at him with some clever jibe, but,
Laura thought with a sigh, it was not his fault
she was in such a bad mood and perhaps she
should give him the benefit of the doubt.

'Thank you.' She took the glass and sipped.
'Please, do not regard it. I know you are but recently in London.'

'Indeed. Please, could we not step out onto
the terrace and talk? I am sure you could give
me valuable pointers about how to go on.'

*So that is to be my role in life, is it? Deliver-
ing wise words to young cubs.* But it was too hot
and too noisy and her head ached and her feet
in the new satin slippers throbbed. 'Very well.'

It was a mistake. She realised it as soon as

she set her glass down on the balustrade, as
soon as Lord Newlyn moved in and trapped
her in the angle of the stonework with far too
adroit a manoeuvre for the green young man
she had thought him. 'And who better to show
me all the tricks but someone such as yourself?'
he said as he put one hand on her waist and the
other firmly on her left breast.

Laura was taken off guard for a vital second and by the time she realised what she was
dealing with he had bent and was pressing hot
kisses all over her face. She twisted her head
away, jerked up her knee and freed one hand to
give him a stinging slap around the ear. 'You
lout!' she gasped as he crashed backwards, far
too far and violently for the blow she had struck
him.

'The very words,' a deep, hard voice agreed
and she realised a man had taken the viscount
by the collar and had sent him sprawling on the
flagstones. 'Pick yourself up, apologise to the
lady and remove yourself from this house before I find it necessary to deal with you further.'

They were all in shadow, but Laura pressed
herself back against the unyielding stonework in
one direction with as much desperation as Lord
Newlyn was scuttling backwards on the ground

in the other. With his back to her, obviously intent on shielding her, was a broad-shouldered figure she would have recognised anywhere.

'I…I'm sorry, ma'am,' the viscount managed. He got to his feet and hurried away, his tousled blond hair catching the light from the reception room as he stumbled past the doors.

'Are you all right?' The tall man turned, his face still shadowed. 'May I call your chaperon or a friend to you? It was perhaps not wise to have come out here alone with a young buck like that.'

'Thank you, no. I need no one.' It was impossible not to speak and impossible he would not recognise her voice, as she recognised his. 'Lord Wykeham.' What was he doing here, in London? In England, even?

'Caroline?' He went still.

'No.' Laura sidestepped and walked away towards the doors, stopped at the edge of the spill of light and turned to face him. 'No, my lord. That is not my name.' She could not make out his face beyond a pale oval against the blackness of the shrubs, let alone read his expression, but the shock and tension came off him like heat from a fire.

She lifted her chin and stood there, deliberately posed in the slender column of rose-pink silk overlaid with silver gauze. The neckline swooped low over her shoulders and bosom, the sleeves were mere puffs of ribbon and her hair was piled high in the latest style. She knew the rubies at her throat and in her ears would pulse in the light in time with her breathing because she had studied the effect in the mirror, and she knew she looked elegant, expensive and provocative, a hundred miles from the genteel respectability of the widow she had pretended to be. It was instinct to display herself and not to try to hide. Avery was here and there was no escape: she would stand and fight.

'Then who are you?' He took three long strides forward and confronted her. 'Step back into the shadow, we cannot be seen like this.'

Laura shrugged, a careless twitch of one shoulder that had his gaze dropping to the swell of her breasts as the silk shifted. 'No one will be surprised if I am seen on the terrace with a man.'

'Who are you?' Avery repeated. She could smell him, his familiar shaving soap, a discreet hint of cologne, the provocative warmth of a man who had been in a crowded room all evening. 'What are you hiding from?'

'I am not hiding from anything. Anyone.' She tipped up her chin. 'I am Lady Laura Campion.'

Avery went very still, the hiss of breath between his teeth the only sign of the shock she must have given him. 'How dared you insinuate yourself into my house under false pretences?' he said, the words low and even, at odds with the anger in the question.

'How dared you steal my child?' she flung back, unable to match his icy control. 'How could you accuse Piers of being a coward and send him to his death?'

'I sent him to do his duty. He made a choice when he took a commission and he knew the odds of being killed. If I failed him, it was by neglecting to teach him how to recognise a heartless wanton when he saw one. Just look at you now.'

'You hypocrite.' The stinging injustice of his words steadied her, gave her back some steadiness, even if it was only the rigidity of fury. 'You just like control, that is it, isn't it? You wanted to control Piers's life, you want to control his estate, you want to control his daughter's future.'

'I love that child.'

'I noticed. You love her so much that you let her think her mother left her.'

'Instead of telling her that you gave her away?'

'I—' Her parents had done it for the best of motives, she tried to believe that. 'It was the only thing to do.'

'Of course it was,' Avery said, his tone so reasonable that she gaped at him. He moved into the edge of the light and she saw his face, took a step back before she could control her reactions and stand her ground. 'The only thing if you wanted to forget about Piers, if you wanted to resume your gilded life, catch an eligible husband and had no care for your child.'

'What choice had I?' she flung at him and moved away, out of the light where he had her pinned like a moth against a lantern. 'You know perfectly well I would have ruined both my daughter and myself if I had kept her.'

'Of course I know that, but you could have gone to his family.'

'And what good would that have done?' Laura enquired. She groped her way to the balustrade and gripped the cool stonework, the dried lichen rough against the fine kid of her long gloves. 'His mother died shortly after he joined the army. There was no one to go to.'

'There was me. I came back.' Avery must have moved as she did, for he was very close now, the lepidopterist ready to skewer the captive moth with a long pin now she was fluttering, helpless.

'And what would you have done, pray?'

'Married you,' he said.

'*Married me?* Why? Why would you have helped me?'

'I would have not crossed the road for you,' Avery said dismissively. 'I would have done it for Piers and for his child.'

'Easy to say now,' Laura jibed. Inside she quaked. Where did the brave, defiant words come from? She was shaking so much she could hardly stand.

'You would not recognise a sense of honour if you fell over it.' The anger had finally surfaced and cracked his control. 'You sent the baby to the other end of the country to be brought up as a poor farmer's daughter. You had no intention of keeping watch over her, simply of getting rid of an embarrassing encumbrance. You might have found her a good home close at hand, but that is too late now. You will stay away from Alice, do you understand mc?'

'Or what?'

'Or your reputation will suffer for it. It is bad enough as it is, but I doubt even *Scandal's Virgin* could ride out that storm.' His lip curled. 'And that's the most inaccurate by-name I have ever heard.'

'If you betray my secret, then you ruin Alice,' Laura countered. 'No one would forget that story. All your scheming to make her eligible and respectable would go out of the window simply because of your spite against me. We are at check, my lord. If Alice is in London, then I will see her, even if you prevent me speaking to her.'

'I'll not let you near her. If you had loved her, you would have stayed in touch with the family you sent her to, not left her for six years and then arrived to play with her emotions on some whim.' All that hard-learned control had deserted him, she realised. Avery took a precipitate step closer, trapping her against the balustrade as Lord Newlyn had done.

'You cannot stop me—' Laura began. She had no idea what she was going to say, what she was going to do, for he took all her options away from her. His hands on her shoulders locked around the narrow bones as he pulled her towards him. Then his mouth took hers in a kiss that held nothing of sensuality or even simple arousal. This was punishment, anger, scorn and his own frustration at her defiance.

Laura stamped and kicked as Avery bent her back against the stonework. It took a few seconds to realise that there was cool air all around her, that his weight was gone, his hands had released her. 'There is no need to scream,' Avery said, his voice like a lash. 'I would not touch you again for any consideration I could imagine. Respectable widows are one thing, selfish pleasure-seeking chits are quite another. To think I was under the illusion I was rescuing you just now.' His laugh jarred, totally without humour. 'Just believe that I will do whatever it takes to protect what is mine—and Alice is mine in every sense that matters.'

It was on the tip of her tongue to tell him that she'd had no intention of trying to see Alice again, that she had resolved to leave her child in his care because she believed that was best for Alice. But now...now she would not admit that and let him think he had frightened her away, not if it killed her. Laura ran the back of her hand over her mouth and fixed him with a dagger glare that simply bounced off his disdain.

'We are all in London,' she said with a calm that belied her quaking knees. 'Unless you want to make a mystery of Alice and have people saying you are ashamed of her and want to hide her, then there is every chance I will see her again. I will not approach her because that would confuse her, but believe me, if I ever have the slightest suspicion that she is not happy, that you are not the loving father to her that you purport to be, then I will make such a scandal you would not believe and I will fight you in the courts for her.'

Laura gathered her long skirts in one hand and turned towards the house with all the poise of one of society's darlings. 'I will be watching you, Lord Wykeham. Never forget it.' She swept through the doors into the reception room again, into the heat and light and noise and almost stumbled with shock to find that this other world was continuing just feet from that encounter.

'There you are!' The dowager rapped on the floor with her cane as though she was rapping knuckles. 'Sent Newlyn to his rightabouts, I see. Good girl, he's a here-and-thereian, not

worth dallying on the terrace with that one.'
She looked around the room. 'Now where has
he gone?'

'Newlyn, ma'am?' The astringent old bat was
as effective as a splash of cold water in the face.

'No, you silly chit. Wykeham.'

'The Earl of Wykeham?' Had she gone white
or scarlet? Was her face a picture of guilt? She
felt as though the pressure of Avery's mouth
must have branded her. Surely anyone looking
at her would see her lips were swollen from
his kisses?

'There's only the one. He'd do for you. Rank,
money, good brain, although he's encumbered
with that by-blow he insists on acknowledging. He won't do for some innocent girl straight
out of the schoolroom, but you've enough town
bronze to carry off that little embarrassment
without any silliness. Eh? Men will be men.'

'Indeed they will, ma'am.' Laura agreed
grimly. 'Will you excuse me? I feel quite exhausted—I am not yet used to town hours
again.'

As she made her way to the exit she heard
the old lady cackle behind her. 'No stamina,
today's young misses. None at all.'

Chapter Nine

Damn it, I'm shaking. Avery summoned up every inch of control he possessed, thanked his hostess for a charming evening and strode out into the lobby. He looked down at his hands and willed them to stillness. He did not know what it was: fury at Laura Campion's deceit and defiance, the urge to shake the breath out of her or sheer frustrated lust. All three, he supposed.

Who the devil did he think he was punishing with that kiss? He was the one who was going to spend the night tossing and turning in frustration, not that deceitful, selfish woman.

'Your hat and cloak, my lord. Shall I call your carriage?' The footman waited impassively, too well trained to show that he found anything unusual about peers of the realm standing in the middle of the lobby eyeing their white-gloved hands and muttering.

I'll be a candidate for Bedlam if I carry on like this, Avery thought. 'Thank you. I'll walk. Find my driver and tell him to go home, would you?'

'My lord.' The coins hardly chinked as the footman palmed them. Of course, Avery could stand here threading the contents of the flower arrangement into his hair, provided he tipped well enough. The urge to do something totally mindless, utterly irresponsible, gripped him. Go to a hell off St James's Street and risk a few thou on the tables. Find a gin house down by the river and get stupid drunk and pick a fight. Or investigate a high-class brothel in Covent Garden and forget the taste of Laura Campion's mouth and the feel of her skin in a welter of costly, highly skilled flesh.

The gaming hells were closest, the thought of gin and a fight the most tempting and the brothel, he realised with a fastidious twist of his lips, the most distasteful. He began to walk, his stick casually in his hand, his senses, below the level that was furious and aroused, testing his surroundings for danger. Footpads abounded. Perhaps he could lose himself in violence that way.

* * *

It took him the ten minutes to Berkeley Square to cool down sufficiently to remember that he had a child to go home to. That would be behaviour to justify every one of Lady Laura's threats if he rolled in bloodied, drunk, stinking of gin and cheap perfume.

Avery turned around the square towards home and slowed his pace. Every night, whether she was awake or not, he went into Alice's bedroom and gave her a goodnight kiss. She was probably quite unaware of it—in fact, he suspected the only person gaining any reassurance from it was himself.

The fierce protective love he felt for the child still shook him to the core. He had taken her out of duty and a nagging sense of responsibility—it was only in the small hours of the morning that he admitted to himself that it might be guilt—for having sent Piers back to Spain. Miss Blackstock had cradled the baby in her arms as they bumped down the rough track away from the remote farm and then, when they turned onto the smoother turnpike road, she had handed him the swaddled bundle without a word.

Avery had never held a baby in his life. He

took her, looked down and was instantly riveted by the blue eyes staring into his. The baby looked at his face as though it was the only thing in the world, as though it was the entirety of her universe. Avery had looked back and discovered he had stopped breathing. *Is this love at first sight?* He could recall thinking that and then she freed one hand from the blanket, waved it, a tiny questing starfish, and found his finger. The grip was extraordinary. He looked at perfect miniature fingernails, at the smooth baby skin and knew, as his gaze blurred, that it was, indeed, love.

So much for setting Blackie up with a nursery and staff somewhere hidden away in England. Plans for bringing up the child at a distance in her own well-equipped, carefully staffed establishment went out of the carriage window. 'You will come with me to Vienna?' he asked Blackie and she had smiled and nodded, completely unsurprised by his instant infatuation. He supposed his smile must have been uncharacteristically sheepish, because hers had widened. 'You are sure?' he asked.

'Of course. A child should be with her father,' she had responded.

Her *father?* He had meant to be Cousin

Avery, a remote guardian. He'd had vague thoughts of visits on her birthday and at Christmas, of gifts, selected by Blackie. Eventually a governess, a pony—all taken care of while he dealt with the important matters of international statecraft that filled his days.

But they did not fill his heart, he realised during that long journey. His new-found adoration survived even the unpleasant realities of travel with a baby and the transformation of a sweet-smelling, endearing little creature into a squalling, irritable tyrant who wanted the wet nurse *now,* who needed her napkin changing *now*—regardless of whether his lordship thought it might wait until they reached the next inn. He could get out and stand in the rain while the women dealt with it or he could grit his teeth and put up with it. Human babies, it seemed, were just like any other small mammal: they had their needs and they were quite ruthless about getting them filled.

Slowly the months had passed, the baby-blue eyes became greener and greener as Avery observed, fascinated, all the stages of growth. Weaning, the first tooth, the first words and steps. And still that wide, intent gaze would find his face and the smile would curve Alice's lips and he knew he was never going to be Cousin Avery. He was *Papa,* to Alice and in the eyes of the world.

Now, when he climbed the stairs to her bedroom, he found her awake and was glad he had resisted the mad urge to bad behaviour. 'Why are you not asleep?' he asked, shaking his head in mock reproof.

Alice blinked up at him, then rubbed her eyes and yawned hugely. 'I'm excited, Papa.'

'By London? But you are used to big cities.'

'I know.' She burrowed down, eyes already closing. 'But something exciting is going to happen, I know it is.'

'I hope not, pet,' Avery said and smoothed her hair before he bent to drop a kiss on the top of her head.

It was not until he was in his own chamber, shedding his clothes into the hands of Darke, his valet, that the question struck him. How the blazes had Laura Campion discovered that Alice was her daughter? Had the Brownes decided to make even more money and had contacted Lady Laura to tell her that they had handed over the child? But why had she left it so late? Then he recalled that her father had died the previous year. It must have been, as he had accused, a selfish whim. Now she was alone in the world, she would take a very belated interest in the fate of her daughter.

Or, he decided cynically, she had ignored Alice all these years, but had finally resolved to take a husband and wanted to make sure her secret was safely buried in that remote dale. It must have been a nasty shock to discover that someone else knew and that the child was not growing up milking cows, baking bread and learning her letters in the village dame school, but was under the protection of someone of influence and power.

'Am I a cynic, Darke?' Avery enquired, shrugging into the proffered banyan. 'Am I distrustful?'

'Of course, my lord. And very proper, too, in your position, if I may say so. It doesn't do to think the best of people. You are a good judge of character, my lord. Very fair. But it is only right to assume the people you do not know well enough to trust will have only their own interests at heart.'

'Indeed. Just leave the hot water, will you? I'll sit up for a while.'

The valet effaced himself into the dressing room and eased the door shut. Avery lounged in the deep wing chair and followed his progress from tallboy to clothes press by the soft clicks and rustles until finally the outer door shut.

What exactly were Lady Laura's interests? He supposed that she had decided it would be wise to make certain that he would not betray her secret, but sneaking around disguised as someone else entirely would not achieve that— only a direct approach would have assured her of his silence.

Perhaps she had intended to find out more about him, see if he was the kind of man who would be a threat to her. He recalled her cool distance, the underlying *froideur* beneath her courtesy. And then she had met Alice and, he guessed, her plans had fallen apart. Unless she was a consummate actress she was deeply fond of the child...now. *Too late, madam,* he thought with a grim smile. *It is six years past the point where you should have discovered your maternal feelings.*

She knew now that he loved the child and would care for her and she had been correct to say that he would do nothing to cause a scandal. *Unless she strikes first and then she will be very, very sorry.* What he must do was to build the bulwarks up around Alice. He already knew he should marry and father an heir, but a woman who would treat Alice as a daughter, who would give her brothers and sisters and knit her into a normal family life, would benefit Alice as well as himself.

Avery got to his feet and tossed the banyan on the foot of the bed. Naked, he began to wash in the cooling water and pondered strategy as he worked the soap up into a lather. Picking out some chit from the flocks of them inhabiting every ballroom and park was too haphazard. He needed to study a prospective wife at closer range, assess her at nine in the morning as well as eleven at night, see how she interacted with servants and dealt with everyday setbacks and irritations. Watch her with Alice.

What he needed, in effect, was a house party. Avery scrubbed at his face with a towel and considered. He needed a hostess and he needed someone to suggest the guests. Which meant, he supposed with a sigh, he must ask his godmother. She was interfering and opinionated and she disapproved of Alice, but she was of impeccable *ton,* knew everyone and would not allow her disapproval to make her unkind to the child, only to lecture him on his supposed indiscretion. There was nothing for it, he was going to have to throw himself on the mercy of the Dowager Marchioness of Birtwell.

'And where are you going, my lady?' Mab demanded as Laura came down from her room after breakfast. 'You've got that look in your eye—you're up to mischief. And that outfit!'

'Really, Mab, any other employer would give you your notice. I am going out and I do not *get up to mischief.*'

'Then you'll want me along,' Mab said, refusing to be snubbed. 'You'll not be seen out without either maid or footman.'

Laura had no intention of being seen at all, hence the drab gown and pelisse that would not have been out of place on a governess, matched with a sensible veiled bonnet and sturdy half-boots. 'I am going for a stroll and dressed like this I am in no danger of being accosted by gentlemen on the strut.'

'You are going to find Miss Alice, that's what you're about.'

'I only want to see her,' Laura protested as she pulled on her gloves. 'I will not let her see me. You stay here, Mab.'

It was a sunny morning and no nurse worth her salt would keep a child indoors on a day like

this. Alice would be going out to take the air,
Laura would bet her new Norwich shawl on it.
The directory had given his lordship's address
and Berkeley Square, only a few minutes' walk
away, had a large central garden that would be
perfect to play in.

It was early, and quiet, without even a single
carriage drawn up outside Gunter's tea shop in
the south-east corner of the square. Servants
were putting the finishing touches to the brass-
work on doors and deliveries were in full swing.
A florist's boy staggered under the weight of
a vast bouquet, a dray dripped water outside
Gunter's as men in leather capes unloaded ice,
a milkman negotiated his hanging pails through
the area gate and down the service steps to the
kitchen entrance of politician George Canning's
elegant house and a giggling kitchen maid was
flirting with the greengrocer's delivery man.

Laura strolled into the garden and pretended
an interest in the flower beds as she made her
way towards the north-east corner and a secluded bench opposite Lord Wykeham's fine
double-fronted house. She did not have to wait
long before the door opened and Alice bounded
down the steps. A bag bounced at her side and
Miss Blackstock followed her out. Her voice

drifted across to Laura. 'Walk, if you please, Miss Alice!'

They walked down past Gunter's, and then past the high wall of the gardens of Lansdowne House into Bolton Row. Laura hung back, matching her pace to theirs, wondering where they were going. In a moment they would be in Curzon Street, walking past her own home. Then Alice scampered into Clarges Street and Laura realised they must be going to Green Park.

It was not the easiest of the parks to hide in, she reflected as she watched Alice, hand in hand with Blackie as they negotiated the traffic in Piccadilly. The nurse gave her a coin to hand the crossing sweeper herself, then they were through the gate leading to the narrow rectangle of the reservoir. Alice ran to the end nearest Queen's Walk where a group of ducks were clustered hopefully and dropped her bag on the ground, spilling what must be crusts of stale bread on the grass.

Laura walked in the opposite direction, to one of the benches at the far end where the ride towards Constitution Hill wound off around the gardens of the lodge-keeper's cottage. At this distance, veiled, she was safe from recognition, she was certain.

A few other nursemaids with their charges were walking towards the reservoir, all making for the end where Alice was surrounded by quacking and flapping ducks in the water and a flock of pigeons on land. Her laughter brought a smile to Laura's lips, even as her heart ached at the distance between them.

She glanced to the side as hoofbeats signalled the arrival of one of the park's rare riders, perhaps trotting back from an early morning gallop in Hyde Park. A raking black more suited to the hunting field than London hacking drew level with her and out of the corner of her eye she was aware of immaculate brown boots with tan tops, long legs in buckskin breeches and a gloved hand resting negligently on the left thigh as the rider guided the horse one-handed.

Her attention was still focused on Alice as she stood, intending to move her position to where a clump of bushed provided a little cover. The horse curvetted away, making her jump and she turned fully to face it as the rider swore. 'What in damnation are you doing here, Lady Laura?'

Avery Falconer brought the big animal under

control without taking his gaze from her veiled face. *How can he recognise me?* Her immediate instinct was to bluff, to turn a haughty shoulder and pretend he was just some importunate rake bothering a lone woman in the park, but she realised at once that was futile. Something about her had jolted his memory, now all she could do was brazen it out.

Laura tossed back her veil and raised one eyebrow in haughty distain. 'This is a public park, I believe, Lord Wykeham. I do not require your permission to take the air in it.'

'Dressed like a governess and without your maid?' He brought the gelding sidling forward, so close it took a conscious stiffening of her spine not to back away. 'You are spying on Alice, you devious jade, and I told you I would not stand for it.'

'Indeed?' Laura lifted the other brow and sneered at him, as best she could, considering their respective positions. 'And just what do you intend to do about it, considering that I am nowhere near her and in a public place?'

'Do?' Avery jammed his riding crop into his boot and smiled. 'Why, remove you, of course.'

Before she could realise what he intended he leant out of the saddle, took her by the

upper arms and hauled her bodily up in front
of him. Laura kicked, twisted and found herself dumped unceremoniously to sit sideways
across his thighs. 'Ouch!' The pommel jabbed
into her. 'Put me down!'

'In my own good time.' He turned the horse's
head away from the reservoir and shifted his
arms so they caged her and he could take the
reins in both hands. The gelding tossed its head
as if in protest at the additional load, but walked
on meekly enough.

'People will see,' she protested.

'Then resume your veil,' Avery said in a
voice of sweet reason.

Laura contemplated wriggling free and dropping to the ground, but the animal was a good
sixteen hands high and she risked a broken
ankle if she tried that. Besides, the strength
with which Avery had hoisted her up indicated
that he would have little trouble subduing any
attempt at escape. She was slender enough, but
she was a well-built adult woman and no feath-
erweight to be tossed about like a child. It was,
she realised, fuming, rather exciting.

Crude, animal instinct, she told herself severely. *He is big, strong and muscular, any*

woman would be in a flutter under the circum-stances. And he probably knows it, the wretch.

His chest was broad and steady and it was impossible to lean away from it—in fact, she was squashed so close she could sense his heart-beat, infuriatingly steady. Beneath her buttocks his thighs were hard and, she realised with ris-ing indignation as she worked out what was pommel, what was leg and what was...*some-thing else,* that he was finding this arousing.

A middle-aged couple exercising a pair of Italian greyhounds on long leashes stared, mouths open in comic synchronisation. Laura dragged down her veil with something like a snarl.

'That is a truly ghastly gown,' Avery re-marked.

'I did not wish to draw attention to myself.' *Oh, stop bandying words with him!*

'Which proves my point. You were spying.'

Laura firmed her lips over the retort she was about to make and assumed as dignified a si-lence as a woman being abducted by a peer of the realm in broad daylight within a stone's throw of two royal residences could.

Avery guided the horse across the Mall and into St James's Park. Laura stiffened. This park was full of trees, avenues and groves of them, and at this hour it was even quieter than Green Park had been.

'Where…what are you doing?' It was shaming that her voice shook.

'I thought I'd take you into that secluded little grove over there and see what effect wrapping my hands around that very lovely white neck of yours would have in persuading you to leave me and mine alone,' Avery said with a grim edge to his voice that had her twisting round in alarm. His face was set, harsh and every bit as grim as his voice had been.

Laura opened her mouth to scream and he shifted the reins and clapped one hand over her mouth.

'I do not like defiance,' he murmured in her ear. 'As you are about to find out.'

Chapter Ten

Laura bit the big, gloved hand over her mouth and heard Avery mutter what sounded like a curse under his breath, then they were within the grove. He reined in and removed his hand, leaving her with the taste of leather on her lips and rage in her heart.

'I really would not bother wasting my breath if I were you,' he remarked as she dragged air down into her lungs to scream. She ignored him and found herself slid unceremoniously over the horse's shoulder to land on her feet, with the breath jolted clean out of her.

Avery swung down out of the saddle and the horse stood there, reins on its neck, like a statue. Laura was the only creature who ever dared gainsay Lord Wykeham, it seemed. Running did not seem to be an option, not faced with those long legs: she wouldn't get three feet before he caught her. *After all, what can he do?*

She lifted her chin and glared at him. 'Go ahead, strangle me, although I have no idea what you can do with my body, not having a spade handy.'

The sun shone through the leaves, the birds sang. Distantly, on Horse Guards Parade, a shouted order spoiled the illusion of being deep in the countryside. Avery's eyes flickered over her, his mouth set in a grim line. He might be finding abducting a woman in the middle of London's parks arousing, but it certainly did not seem to be giving him any pleasure.

He walked towards her, drawing off his gloves. 'I can think of several things to do with your *body,* Lady Laura, but it's your stubborn brain that requires dealing with.' He pushed the gloves into a pocket as he stopped, toe to toe with her.

Laura made herself stand firm. 'Really, this is positively Gothic! I am not afraid of you, Avery Falconer. Whatever else you may be, you are a gentleman and not a raving lunatic. You are not going to strangle me and we both know it.'

'Of course I am not,' Avery agreed. This

close, without the slightest temptation to let her lids drop in erotic surrender, she could see how green his eyes were, a subtly different shade than Piers's had been. Gold flecks danced like fire. *Devil's fire.* 'I simply require your undivided attention for a moment.'

'Then you have it, my lord,' she drawled and gave him the look that worked very well with importunate gentlemen who became overamorous in conservatories. It always sent them off looking crushed. Avery merely appeared bored.

'I have said it once, but I do not think you have been paying attention. You will leave Alice alone. You will not watch her, you will not follow her, you will not contact her. Is that clear enough?'

'As crystal. And if I ignore your demands?'

'I will ruin you.' He smiled.

'Your threats are merely bluff. If you do expose me, then it will ruin Alice, too, you know that perfectly well.'

'Her name will not come into it, her parentage will not be an issue. You are not listening to my *threats,* as you describe them. Actually, they are promises. *I* will ruin *you*. Society will discover that *Scandal's Virgin* is actually *Scandal's Jade.*'

'That would be rape,' she flashed at him. 'I cannot believe it of you. Even of you.'

'It would, indeed, and *even I...*' his lip curled as he parroted her sneer '...even I would baulk at that. But fortunately for you, and for my scruples, all it needs is the appearance of the thing. Rumour, a whisper of scandal. A bet in the club books, a sighting of Lady Laura where she should not be, a few urgent and earnest denials on my part—and I will protest far too much, far too earnestly, just as a gentleman should—and the damage will be done.

'You have been very skilful, balancing on the edge, skating on thin ice. You dangle men on a string, leading them on. There's a nasty little phrase for women like you, Lady Laura Campion. Cock tease.'

On a gasp of outrage she stepped back and he lifted his hands from his sides, his palms open as though to demonstrate that he need not touch her, then he let them fall to his side, and smiled.

'Men have all the power,' she said as she found her voice at last. It trembled with anger, but she could not help that. 'You take what you want because the strength is on your side, the law, the double standards of behaviour. Men want my dowry, they want my bloodlines, they want my body and I do not choose to give those to *any* man because even the ones who protest undying love are unreliable. There is always something more important than a woman in their lives. I choose to entertain myself by playing the game with male rules and if that is uncomfortable for a *gentleman* I really do not care.'

She stopped because she was exposing herself and her pain all too plainly and his threats had the chilling ring of truth. He could ruin her with ease, just as he said, without laying a finger on her and without the slightest danger to Alice. 'You win, my lord.' She would not gratify him by squirming on his hook, she was too intelligent not to know defeat when she saw it. 'All I wanted was a few glimpses of my child. If you are threatened by that, so be it, I am not going to lose everything else in my life to your scheming.'

Laura turned on her heel and walked away before he saw the defeat in her eyes, while anger still gave her the strength to preserve the last shreds of her dignity.

'That could have gone better, Nero.' The gelding twitched an ear, but otherwise did not contribute anything to the one-sided conversation. 'She made me lose my temper. No…' Avery twitched his riding crop out of his boot and took a vicious swipe at some long grass '…she *did* nothing. I took one look, lost my temper and carried her off on my saddle bow like one of Scott's blasted heroes. And then what did I think I was going to do with her?' Nero cocked up one hind hoof and settled into the equine equivalent of a slouch. 'Kiss her senseless?'

Avery's body stirred, interested in this line of thought. The lack of control did nothing to improve his temper. 'How can I find her so damnably arousing when all I want to do is throttle the woman?' He gathered up the reins and remounted. As he moved, the scent of her rose from the front of his coat where Laura had been pressed against broadcloth and linen. Warm, angry woman blended with orange water.

Warm, frightened woman, he hoped. He had never threatened a woman in his life and it did not sit well with him now, but he'd carry out his threats without hesitation if he thought she was any danger to Alice's future. He would live with his conscience afterwards.

Laura Campion had courage, he'd say that for her. Avery dug his heels in and sent Nero back the way he'd come at the canter. Any other woman would have had hysterics, carried off like that. He recalled the look in her eyes as she'd faced him down. She had not flinched— yet how had she known he would not hurt her, one way or another?

But then she was a good actress with strong nerves—'Caroline Jordan' had been proof of that. It was a miracle he had not become even more wrapped up in the young widow than he had, attracted by her air of mystery, her sensual allure, her cool distance and haunting air of sadness.

It was humiliating for a man who prided himself on being a good judge of character that he had found himself intrigued by a woman whose morals were loose, who had written that scathing letter to a man who was risking his life for his country and who had given away her child and had forgotten her for six long years.

Avery reined in as the reservoir came in sight. He needed a few moments to restore a calm, cheerful face for Alice. Just why was Laura interested in her daughter now? The question kept nagging at him. Perhaps she was coming to realise that she had lost the chance of a decent marriage with her fast behaviour and her smirched reputation. Perhaps, with maturity, she was coming to yearn for a child.

Well, it was too late to claim this one, he thought, catching sight of Alice playing ball with three other small girls, their bright dresses like so many large butterflies as they ran and laughed over the grass. Laura Campion was never going to get close to Alice again.

Pritchett, her butler, was too well trained to remark on his mistress's flushed face, crumpled skirts or scowl. He took Laura's bonnet and pelisse and remarked, 'You have a visitor, my lady. The Dowager Lady Birtwell arrived fifteen minutes ago. I informed her you were out, but she said she was fatigued and would wait.' He lowered his voice to a confidential murmur. 'I believe she is resting her eyes. Naturally, I sent in a tea tray.'

'Lady Birtwell? I wonder what…?' Laura looked down at her drab gown and shuddered. 'Please send my woman to me, Pritchett, and have fresh tea prepared. I will be ten minutes.'

She hastened upstairs, untying her bonnet as she went. What on earth did the old dragon want with her? 'Mab, I need to change quickly. The Pomona-green afternoon dress.'

* * *

Laura came down within the time she had allowed herself, neatly gowned, her hair brushed into a simple style, a Norwich shawl draped negligently over her elbows. She could only hope that the dowager did not notice that her hands were still trembling and she was fighting for composure with iron determination.

'Lady Birtwell, I am so sorry to have kept you waiting. I do hope Pritchett has been looking after you. Fresh tea is on its way.'

'No need to be sorry, child. You weren't expecting me. Glad of the chance for a rest, if truth be told. I've been running about like a scalded cat all day.' She accepted a fresh cup of tea and a macaroon.

'Nothing is wrong, I hope, ma'am?' Laura sipped her own tea and wished for a large glass of Madeira instead.

'I have the whim to hold a house party next week. Short notice, I know, but the weather is sultry and is doing my breathing no good, the Season is slacking off and I thought a few days in the country would put me back in prime fettle. Just a select company, a dozen or so. Get some of those girls out of the hothouse at Almack's for some fresh air and invite some of my old friends for a comfortable few days, you know the sort of thing. Hmm? What do you think?'

'I am sure you will find it restores you in no time, Lady Birtwell.' The dowager was famous for her relaxed, cheerful house parties with a range of guests, excellent food and informal entertainments from shooting at the archery butts to impromptu dancing.

'Excellent. You'll come, of course.' The rings encrusting her plump fingers sparkled in the sunlight as the older woman put down her teacup.

'Me? I, er…I would be delighted, of course, but I don't…'

'There's nothing on in town of any importance, or I would know about it.' She narrowed her eyes and studied Laura, head cocked to one side. 'You look flushed, my girl. You courting on the sly?'

'What? I mean, certainly not, Lady Birtwell!'

'I'm pleased to hear it. Do your reputation no good to be carrying on some clandestine flirtation—what you get up to in public is bad enough.'

'Yes, ma'am.' *And what would you say if you'd seen me an hour ago?*

Her instinct was to refuse, upset as she was, but Laura bit back the polite words as she made herself reconsider. *She is offering me a week in the country, a week away from any risk of seeing Avery.* Was it cowardly to run away? Laura found she did not care whether it was or not. She was tired of being brave and bold. 'Thank you, I would very much like to come to Old Birtwell House.'

'Excellent. Do you need me to arrange transport?' The dowager reached for her reticule.

'Thank you, no. I will use my own carriage and bring my maid with me, if that is convenient.' Laura pulled the bell cord for Pritchett.

'Oh, yes, plenty of room in the staff wing and the stables. I will see you on Monday afternoon—bring the recipe for those macaroons with you.'

When the front door closed behind her guest Laura sank back on the sofa and closed her eyes. Lord Wykeham had defeated her, frightened her and humiliated her. He would keep her daughter from her and ensure she never got so much of a glimpse of Alice. Her only consolation was her conviction that he loved the child and would care for her.

Now all she had to do was to decide how

she was going to spend the rest of her existence, because now her former life, the pursuit of pleasure, the *frisson* of being Scandal's Virgin, held no attraction whatsoever. Dry-eyed, Laura gazed at the row of stiff, engraved and gilded invitation cards that lined the mantel shelf. Her old life was dust, her heart felt as though Avery Falconer had kicked it and she had no idea what she was going to do next.

Except escape to the country and ride and gossip and eat too much and try, somehow, to imagine a future.

She had been to Lady Birtwell's house parties before and the sight of the house, its warm red brick glowing in the afternoon sunlight, was pleasantly familiar. The journey from London into the Surrey countryside had been smooth and uneventful, despite Laura's wish for something to take her mind off her emotional bruises. A minor riot, an escaped bull, even a highwayman, would have been satisfying. Instead, she and Mab had progressed in respectable comfort, on good roads, distracted by nothing more than unsatisfactory coffee at one inn and a slow turnpike keeper.

Other guests were there already. She saw a

group of young ladies on the archery lawn attended by three gentlemen, one of them in scarlet regimentals. A carriage was being driven round to the stables as they drew up and Laura recognised Lady Frensham, one of the dowager's friends, being assisted up the steps to the front door by an attentive footman. It seemed that the party was an interesting mix of ages, if nothing else.

Her groom came to open the door and let down the step, the butler turned from delivering Lady Frensham into the housekeeper's hands to greet her and Laura took a deep breath, composed herself and entered the house, into a bustle of servants and luggage.

'Lady Laura, good afternoon, my lady. I am Rogers.'

'Of course, I remember you, Rogers. Good afternoon.'

The butler gestured to a footman. 'Lady Birtwell is receiving guests in the Chinese Room. Would you care to go to your chamber first—?'

The high-pitched screams of excited children drowned his words. The butler's carefully schooled expression slipped for a moment into something close to a wince. Laura realised she was wincing back. 'I beg your pardon, my lady.

I trust the children will not disturb you. Lady Birtwell enjoys the sound of young voices.'

'It is lovely to hear them enjoying themselves, Rogers.' Laura forced a smile on her lips. She had not realised there would be children here, that echoes of Alice's laughter would haunt every room. 'I will just go up to my…'

Her voice trailed away as the noise grew louder. Half-a-dozen children ran from the garden door at the back of the hall to tumble to a halt as they realised where they were. A sheepish silence fell, broken only by the shuffling of feet and the sound of a hoop being dropped with a clatter on the marble floor.

'Now then, young ladies and gentlemen, this is not the place to be playing, is it?' Rogers chided. 'Lady Laura has only just this moment arrived and she must think this a menagerie.'

The biggest boy piped up, 'Sorry, Lady Laura, we didn't mean to disturb you. We'll go out.' He turned and ran back, his companions eddying around him, leaving one small girl standing staring at Laura, her mouth open.

The solid marble floor seemed to shift under Laura's feet. Behind her she heard the sound of crunching gravel and voices and realised the archery party was coming back.

'Aunt C…' Alice Falconer whispered, her eyes wide and hurt on Laura's face.

Chapter Eleven

Laura froze, then instinct took over. She raised one finger to her lips and shook her head at Alice. The words died unsaid on the child's lips as Laura crossed the floor to her side. She bent and whispered, 'I am not really Caroline Jordan—that was just a disguise.'

'You were hiding?' Alice whispered back, eyes wide. The sparkle of tears had become one of excitement.

'Yes, a bad man was after me.' As soon as she spoke Laura worried that she had frightened the child, but Alice's eyes were alight with excitement.

'Like an adventure story? Is that why you had to go away from Westerwood?'

'Yes, I am very sorry.' Laura crouched down so she could murmur without Rogers overhearing. 'We must pretend we do not know each other. Can you do that?' It was wrong to ask the child to practise deception, but it was for her protection, too. 'You may tell your papa, of course.' Even if her father *was* Avery Falconer, she could not allow Alice to lie to him or to encourage her in deceit.

Alice nodded vigorously, then whirled round and ran after the others, ringlets bobbing. As she reached the door she turned, put her finger theatrically to her lips and waved. She seemed thrilled with her new secret.

'My goodness, do you not know who that child is?'

Laura straightened up and turned to find Lady Amelia Woodstock surrounded by a group of young ladies Laura knew, more or less, from that Season's events.

'Good afternoon, Lady Amelia. I have no idea,' Laura lied with a smile. 'A pretty girl, is she not?'

'*That* is Lord Wykeham's bastard.' The other girls gave shocked giggles at the word. 'I think it is disgraceful that he brings her to a respectable house party like this.'

'She is an innocent child.' Laura kept her voice reasonable and pleasant as she held on to her temper with an effort. 'You cannot visit her parents' sins on her head.'

'Perhaps *you* aren't as worried about appearances as the rest of us,' Lady Amelia said with a toss of blonde curls. 'But those of us who are not still on the shelf have to maintain higher standards.'

The effort to remain pleasant was so difficult that Laura scarcely registered the insult. 'Provided her father is not intending to create any more babies while he is here I really do not think we are in moral danger, any of us.'

'Ooh!' squeaked one of the young ladies. They were loving the *frisson* of scandal and her bold words, Laura could tell. Now they would giggle and whisper together and pretend a delicious alarm every time Avery hove into view.

Avery. In her shock at seeing Alice every other thought had fled. Now she realised that the only reason the child could be here was because Avery was, too. Why on earth hadn't Lady Birtwell told her? And why hadn't she had the sense to ask who the other guests were in the first place? *Because I was so agitated about Avery and that encounter in the park, that's why. I just wanted to run away and I have run right into the enemy's lair.*

'Lady Laura?'

Laura blinked at the woman standing in front of her, hands neatly crossed over her lace-edged apron. It did not take the large bunch of keys hanging from a chatelaine to tell her this was the housekeeper, new since her last visit. *Run away now while you still can. Turn and say it is a mistake, you aren't staying...*

'May I show you to your room, my lady?'

Reality swept over her, stark enough to steady her reeling thoughts. She could not leave now—too many people had seen her and this flock of silly, gossip-mad girls would make a scandal broth of speculation if she fled moments after walking in through the door. Somehow she would have to find Avery and tell him what had happened, make him understand she had meant no harm.

'Yes, of course. Thank you. Come along, Mab.' *Smile, walk, behave normally. See? No one has noticed anything is wrong.*

The door had hardly shut behind the housekeeper before Mab burst out, 'That was her! Miss Alice—so his lordship's here, too. What are we going to do, my lady?'

'It is all under control.' Mab's unexpected

panic calmed her, gave her focus as she reassured her. 'Alice will pretend she does not know me and I will seek a private interview with Lord Wykeham and explain.' She had said nothing to her maid about that last, disastrous encounter and Avery's threats. 'Now, help me tidy up because I must go down to see Lady Birtwell, it is only courteous not to delay.'

'What if he is down there?'

'Lord Wykeham will not make a scene in front of everyone, Mab.' At least, she hoped he would control his temper long enough for her to get him alone and explain.

Washed, tidied and outwardly composed, Laura made her way towards the head of the stairs. Someone moved in a cross corridor and she glanced along it to see a man close a door behind him and walk off towards the servants' back stairs, a coat draped over his arm. She recognised him from Westerwood Manor: it was Darke, Avery's valet.

Without giving herself time to lose her nerve, Laura turned into the passage. At the door she hesitated, hand on the knob, then the sound of voices from the direction of the stairs made up her mind for her. She could not be found standing alone on the corridor reserved for the bachelors outside a gentleman's bedchamber door.

With a twist of the wrist the door was open and Laura was inside, as breathless as if she had run. She closed the door and leaned against it while she caught her breath.

Avery, in his shirtsleeves, was standing with his back to her, head bent over the sheaf of papers in his hand. 'Yes, Darke?' he said without turning.

'It is not Darke,' Laura said.

He went very still. As the moment dragged on Laura saw the broad shoulders, the silk of his waistcoat drawn tight across his back, the point where the ties drew it in at his slim waist, the tight buttocks and the long line of his thighs, all exposed without the tails of his coat. He was a magnificent male animal and, much as she hated him, she knew she wanted him, too. And that made her even more vulnerable.

Avery laid the papers down on the dresser with care, knocked the edges together and then, only then, turned to face her. Laura realised with a flash of insight that he had needed the time to get control of himself, but whether he was controlling anger or lust, she was not sure. Both, perhaps.

'This *is* a surprise,' he drawled. 'Would you care to explain yourself or would you prefer to lock the door and undress first?'

'Is it necessary to be so crude?' she snapped. 'Or so arrogant? Your bed is the last place I want to be. I had no idea you would be at this house party, so I came to explain before you saw me and did something rash.'

'I do not do rash things, my dear.'

'Oh, yes, you do. You steal other people's children, you kiss women you hardly know, you abduct people in parks…'

'I'll give you the kisses,' he said, a smile curving his mouth. It was not a reassuring sight. 'Those were rash, I concede.'

'Stop pretending to flirt, or threaten or whatever it is you are doing.' With an effort Laura stopped twisting her hands together. 'Lady Birtwell invited me here and I accepted because I wanted to get away from London. And from you. I should have asked her who else she had invited, but I did not.'

'So how did you know I was here?' Avery pulled the emerald pin out of his neckcloth, put it down on top of the papers and began to untie the elaborate knot.

'I met Alice in the hallway just now.' She

seemed unable to stop herself watching the neckcloth slide through his fingers as he pulled it free.

'The devil you did!' He threw the crumpled muslin onto the bed. 'What happened?'

'I told her that Caroline Jordan was not my real name. I told her that I was hiding from a bad man.' His brows drew together in a frown and she added, 'She thought it was exciting, an adventure. She is going to pretend not to know me—you can make a game of it.'

'Can I, indeed? Or you can go right back to London. Now.' The waistcoat followed the neckcloth.

'Why should I? If I leave as soon as I arrive it will cause talk. I have already met several guests. In any case, I was only doing what you asked me to do, attempting to keep away from Alice. You go.'

'I am afraid I cannot do that, not without being extremely rude to Lady Birtwell.' He raised an eyebrow and began to unbutton his shirt cuffs. 'You did not know she was my god-mother? She has put this house party together to help me find a bride.'

Laura sat down on the edge of the bed, the nearest flat surface. 'A bride? For you? Oh my goodness, she was hinting the other night at Mrs Fairweather's reception, but I thought she was just teasing me.'

'Suggesting you would make me a good wife, was she? She has a strange sense of humour, although she does not know the truth about you, of course.' Avery pulled his shirt free of his breeches and gathered the hem in his hands.

What he was doing finally penetrated Laura's jangling thoughts. 'Will you kindly stop undressing while I am in the room!'

'I have a bath cooling in the dressing room and I have no intention of getting into it clothed. Do I need to remind you that you are here uninvited?' The last word was muffled as he drew the shirt over his head.

Laura was confronted by a naked, muscled torso and drew a sharp breath. Tailoring could make a man look a lot fitter and slimmer than he was, she assumed, but Avery Falconer needed no help from either his tailor or his valet. The intake of breath had been a mistake. He had been riding, obviously, and his skin exuded the tantalising musk of fresh sweat over the faint traces of Castile soap and a tang of spicy cologne.

She found herself staring at the silky trail of

hair that led down below the waistband of his breeches and, as if to indulge her curiosity, Avery's hands went to the fastenings of his falls.

'Stop it!' She closed her eyes, then slapped her hands over them for good measure. 'Go and check there is no one in the corridor so I can leave.'

He gave a faint snort of laughter and the bed beside her dipped as he sat down. 'In exchange for one kiss.'

'That is blackmail.' She opened her eyes and found he was removing his stockings. His breeches, thank heavens, were still fastened.

'Call it a forfeit.' He looked thoroughly amused now. No doubt this was highly gratifying, to see her embarrassed and at a complete disadvantage.

'If I let you take one kiss you will say nothing, you'll allow me to stay here?'

'I will speak to Alice. If she is not disturbed by having you here and I think she can treat your secret as a game, then, yes, you may stay. If she is upset or frightened by the thoughts of your *bad man,* that is another matter. I hardly feel you are going to enjoy this house party very much.'

'It will be amusing to watch you being pursued by a bevy of young ladies,' Laura said tartly. 'How will you decide—or will God-mama make that choice for you, as well?'

'I make my own choices.' The amusement had vanished, leaving his eyes hard, but not cold. There was heat there; he wanted her. 'And right now I choose to kiss you.'

Laura presented her right cheek, face tipped to the side. To her surprise he kissed it. Was she going to escape so easily? Then his lips moved, trailed to her ear and he caught the lobe lightly between his teeth. His breath was warm, fanning fires under her skin, teasing goosebumps along her arms. She gave a little gasp and he caught her in his arms, released her ear as he turned her and kissed her full on the mouth.

She wanted him to kiss her. She wanted *him,* despite everything that had passed between them, and she suspected he knew it perfectly well. Whatever else she could accuse Avery Falconer of, an assault on an unwilling woman was not one of them. But that did not mean she had to make it easy for him, or sacrifice her own self-esteem by simply melting into the kiss.

He growled as she put her hands on his bare shoulders and dug in her fingernails and paid her back by sliding his tongue between her lips so she was filled with his familiar taste. He shifted so that he fell back onto the bed, taking her with him to sprawl in wanton abandon over his half-naked body, her stomach pressed against his groin. She wriggled and he growled again and rolled over to pin her beneath him in a parody of mastery and surrender.

His weight and the slide of muscle under smooth skin beneath her palms was overwhelming. She wanted to yield and at the same time she knew she must not, did not dare. If she let him, he would burn her up, like tinder, leave her shattered. Leave her his.

Laura took hold of a double handful of hair and pulled. For a moment he resisted, his mouth still ravaging hers, then he let her pull his head up. 'Enough,' she gasped. *'Enough.'*

Avery braced his arms on the rumpled coverlet and then levered himself from her body. 'Enough,' he agreed. 'And now I have a cold bath waiting. How convenient.'

Laura got up, stalked past him to the mirror and began to push pins back into her hair. Her cheeks were flushed, her mouth looked as if… as if she had been ruthlessly kissed. Unable to meet her own eyes, she brushed at her skirts and retrieved her shawl from the floor.

'Kindly check the corridor.' If he so much as let his lips twitch, she would throw something at him, she swore, but Avery kept a perfectly straight face as he crossed the room and looked out.

'The coast is clear.'

'Thank you,' Laura said with awful sarcasm as she swept past him. And then, as she glanced back over her shoulder, he did smile.

A cool bath was certainly helpful. Avery dripped onto the bath mat afterwards and wondered whether he was bewitched or merely besotted. What was it about this infuriating, dangerous, flawed woman that attracted him so, against all prudence? It had attracted Piers, too, but his cousin had the excuse of being younger and a romantic. Now, on top of everything else, not only was she here, but she was expecting Alice to lie about her. He scrubbed his wet body dry, shrugged into his banyan and went to finish reading his correspondence while Darke set the dressing room to rights.

'Will you require me to shave you, my lord?'

'Hmm? Yes.' His concentration was all over the place, he'd probably end up cutting his own throat at this rate.

'Miss Blackstock said she would bring Miss Alice down to say goodnight early, my lord, at half past five. We understand that Lady Birtwell is holding a gathering before dinner to give the guests an opportunity to mingle.'

In other words, to enable her to parade her selection of young ladies before him, like fillies going down to the starting gate. 'You had better shave me now then and I'll get changed before Miss Alice arrives. She is capable of wrecking havoc with my attempts to tie a respectable neckcloth.'

'Quite, my lord,' Darke observed with some feeling. 'The hot water is ready.'

Avery sat back and closed his eyes as the razor scraped through the soap and the bristles of his evening beard. What the devil had his godmother been thinking of, to invite Lady Laura? She didn't know the truth, of course, but Laura's reputation was smudged enough as it was, even without the scandal of Alice's birth. Perhaps she had included her to throw the ladylike deportment of the other young women into relief by contrast.

It occurred to him that Blackie and Darke had both seen 'Mrs Jordan' at Westerwood. 'Darke, when Miss Blackwood brings Miss

Alice, I would like you to remain for a few moments. There is something I must tell you both.'

Alice arrived as he was sliding his arms into the swallowtail evening coat with the assistance of Darke. She bounced into the room. 'Poor Darke is going red in the face, Papa,' she informed him.

'So would you, if you had to stuff me into this coat.' Avery tugged down his cuffs, added his watch, chain and fobs, stuck in a cameo tie pin and decided he was as fancy as he was prepared to make himself for the purposes of wife-hunting. 'Miss Blackstock, Darke, a moment please.'

Alice pouted. 'I wanted to tell you a secret, Papa.'

'Is it anything to do with Mrs Jordan?'

She stared at him, open-mouthed. 'How did you know?' She glanced from side to side at the servants. 'She said I was to tell you, Papa, but perhaps I shouldn't tell Blackie or Darke.'

'She told you to tell me?'

Alice nodded. That was a surprise. He had not expected Laura to do that. He had misjudged her. 'Miss Blackwell, Mrs Jordan, who visited while we were in Hertfordshire, is actually Lady Laura Campion. She has had a personal problem that required her to conceal her identity.'

'She said she was running away from a bad man,' Alice explained, her face serious with the responsibility of the big secret. 'It is very exciting and we must not betray her.'

Avery grimaced at his two expressionless staff. 'A man she wished to avoid,' he explained. 'It would be best if you give no indication that you have ever encountered her under any other name.'

'Of course, my lord.' Darke gathered up the discarded banyan and removed himself to the dressing room.

Blackie shot a look at Alice, who was busy straightening the fob that hung from Avery's watch chain. 'If Lady Laura should approach Miss Alice...'

'Treat her the same as any of the other guests,' Avery said and stooped to pick Alice up, making her squeal with laughter. 'You are not to be naughty and disturb the grown-ups, puss. But if you behave nicely I expect the ladies will want to talk with you.'

And if they avoided her, or made any derogatory remark, then they would be crossed off his list at once. Whoever he married must accept Alice without reservation.

'Off with you to your supper now.' He set her on her feet, noticing that she had grown since the last time she had worn that dress. Before he knew it, she would be a young lady. How would he cope when she was the age the girls downstairs were now and men were courting her? He would be forever sharpening a rapier or cleaning his shotgun. But before then he would have a wife to look after her, one who loved the child as much as he did. He just had to go and choose her.

Chapter Twelve

This was nothing like he had expected it to be. Avery, his features schooled into the expression that worked for sensitive, yet boring, diplomatic parties, circulated the room, displaying an outer confidence while he fought an inner sensation that was something akin to panic.

Young women swirled around him like so many birds in an aviary, charming in their pastels and frills, smiling and flirting and chattering. Previously he would have been civil to the plain ones and the dull ones—not that Godmama had invited anyone who fitted those descriptions—and then admired the pretty ones with an appreciative male eye for their physical features.

Which was just what he would be guarding Alice against when she was their age—men like him. Shaken, Avery kept his eyes firmly raised above collarbone level and set himself to assess character, not curves. There were ten eligible misses assembled for him, the mix leavened— or perhaps the better word was *disguised*—by three married couples in their early thirties, eight bachelors of his age and younger, a couple of older widowers and a handful of widows of Lady Birtwell's age. And Lady Laura Campion who was, he decided, neither fish, fowl nor good red herring.

'Lord Wykeham?' Lady Amelia Woodstock looked up at him through wide blue eyes, delightfully fringed by darker lashes. 'Is something amiss?'

'Am I scowling?' he enquired. 'I do apologise.'

'No, not scowling, merely looking a trifle thoughtful and severe. No doubt matters of state are weighing on your mind.' Her lips quirked into a confiding smile which managed to convey that she was hugely impressed by his importance, but also recognised that he was a man who might be charmed. By the right woman.

'To be frank, they are not.' Avery lowered his voice and leaned towards her. With a twinkle Lady Amelia inclined her head for him to divulge the secret. 'I was wondering what a red herring was and why, precisely, it is always referred to as *good* red herring.'

'Or why it is the term for a deceptive clue.' Lady Amelia pursed her lips in thought. Full, kissable lips, Avery noted. 'Perhaps Dr Johnson's *Dictionary* would tell us.'

Us, not *you*. A clever little trick to increase the intimacy of the conversation. Not only a lovely young lady, but a bright one, as well. Not that he was ready to go off to the library and snuggle up on the sofa with only a massive tome as chaperon. Not quite yet, not with the first promising candidate.

He glanced up and saw Laura watching him. No, watching Lady Amelia and with an expression he could not read on her face. It was not approval. Jealousy? After that kiss in his bedchamber any other woman would be expecting either a declaration or a *carte blanche,* but Laura knew full well why he would never offer either of those. The only kind of relationship they might ever have was a flaming and very short-lived *affaire* characterised by lust on both sides and liking on neither. And, as he was a gentleman and had no intention of carrying out his threats to ruin her, that must remain in the realms of fantasy. It was a very stimulating thought though and his body reacted to it with a shocking lack of discipline.

With an inward snarl at his inner primitive male Avery wrenched his thoughts back to reality and the sensible thing, which was to avoid the blasted woman, get his rebellious body under control and stop reacting like a green youth whenever the scent of her was in his nostrils. But in the confines of one house, and with an innocent child in the middle of the thing, he was not certain how avoidance was going to be possible. He wondered whether it was still possible to purchase hair shirts.

He was certainly no fit company just at the moment for an innocent young lady, not without a moment or two to collect his thoughts. 'Will you excuse me, Lady Amelia? It is almost time for dinner and Lady Birtwell asked me to take in Lady Catherine Dunglass, so I had better find her and make myself known.'

'She is over there by the window in the yellow gown. So brave to wear that shade of primrose with red hair.'

Little cat, Avery thought, amused by the flash of claws. Lady Catherine had dark auburn hair and the primrose gown was a rather odd choice to complement it, but he doubted a mere man would have noticed without that little jibe. Was Lady Amelia aware of just why this house party had been assembled? Or perhaps she considered all single girls as rivals on principle and dealt with them with equal resolution. Perhaps they all did, he thought, startled by the notion that the ladies were hunting the single males with the same determination, although probably with rather different motives, as the gentlemen pursued them.

Parents were obviously searching for just the right husband for their daughters, but surely these girls, innocent, sheltered and privileged, were not ruthlessly seeking men? Weren't they supposed to wait passively to be chosen, exhibiting their accomplishments and beauty? He glanced across at Laura again. The fast young women like her were after excitement, obviously, but these other young women? He was obviously hopelessly naive in this matter of courtship and he did not like feeling at a disadvantage. It was not a sensation he experienced often.

Avery murmured a word to Lady Amelia and made his way across to the window and Lady Catherine, passing close by Laura as he did so.

She turned and looked at him, her gaze clear, limpid and implacable. Was it only obvious to him that she had been kissed to within an inch of ravishment only a short while before? Her lips were full and a deep rose-pink and a trace of rice powder glinted on her cheek where he must have roughened the tender skin with his evening beard. Marked her.

Mine, something primitive and feral growled inside him. *Madness,* his common sense hissed back. This woman was a threat to everything that was important to him. He had tried to put aside the knowledge that she was Alice's mother, his daughter's blood kin, and that by following his instinct, to keep the two apart, he was both punishing Laura and preventing Alice from ever knowing and loving her own flesh and blood.

Of all the awkward times and places to have an attack of doubt! Avery moved behind an ornate screen to try to collect himself for a moment. Alice would never stop wondering why her mother had left her. As she got older she would speculate on why her parents had not married—and would doubtless place the blame on Avery's head.

I could tell her the truth—but then she will

*know Laura sent her away, completely out of
her life. How could she face that rejection? She
will know I am not her father. And if she blames
me? I sent her father back to war and his death.
I am stopping her mother from being with her.
The shock would be terrible, her trust would
be destroyed, not just in me, but in the whole
basis of her life.*

Fear was an alien emotion, except when he
thought about Alice having an accident, being
ill, being frightened. Now he knew he was
afraid for himself. *If Alice discovers the truth,
I will have hurt her. And if I lose Alice, I have
lost the only person I love.*

Exerting all the control he had, Avery stepped
out of cover and found Laura's eyes still on him.
Hell, he wanted her. If he had not known all the
things he knew about her he would have liked
her as much as he had liked 'Mrs Jordan'. Her
dubious reputation as Scandal's Virgin meant
nothing to him now, he realised as he met her
gaze, filled with pain and fear and pride.

It took a physical effort to break that exchange of looks, to move. Then he was past
her and asking Mr Simonson, a club acquaintance from White's, to introduce him to Lady

Catherine. Avery forced a smile and turned all his attention on the young woman.

She was shyer than Lady Amelia, but with a sweeter expression. By the time dinner was announced, with Lady Catherine seated to Avery's left, she was chatting quite naturally, with no little tricks of flirtation. They agreed that they both preferred the theatre to opera, that the state of the king's health was very worrying and disagreed over the paintings of the artist Turner, which Lady Catherine found inexplicable.

'I prefer the work of Sir Thomas Lawrence. Papa had Mama painted by him and it is very fine. And I like paintings that tell a story.' She smiled nicely at the footman serving her soup, which earned her points with Avery. 'But then I like novels and I expect you think that very shocking.'

'Minerva Press?' he enquired. 'Gothic tales of horror and romance?'

'Of course!' She laughed, then hastily put her hand to her lips as though anxious her mama would chide her for expressing herself too freely. 'Do you despise novels, Lord Wykeham?'

'Certainly not.' He did not read them himself and the plots of most Gothic tales seemed improbable in the extreme, but he knew perfectly intelligent diplomatic wives who adored them, so he was not going to cross this young lady off his list just because of her tastes in reading.

Avery passed her the rolls and butter and found himself meeting the quizzical gaze of Lady Laura, diagonally across the table from him. Her glance slid from him to Lady Catherine and her mouth curved into a faint smile before she went back to her soup. Had he imagined that burning look with all its agonising emotions a short while ago? It appeared Laura approved of Lady Catherine. Perversely, he began to find the redhead a trifle vapid.

Laura was partnered by Lord Mellham, one of the slightly older bachelors. She looked exquisite, beautifully coiffed, dressed in an amber-silk gown that skimmed lower over her bosom and shoulders than the styles worn by any of the other unmarried girls. And she was wearing coloured gemstones, yellow diamonds, he rather thought. A slightly daring choice for a single lady, just as her rubies had been that night on the terrace, yet her behaviour was perfectly modest and not in the slightest flirtatious.

Avery studied her partner. Mellham kept glancing at the creamy curves displayed so enticingly close to him and seemed a trifle disappointed that he was not receiving more encouragement for his sallies. Soup finished, he put down his spoon and one hand vanished under the table. Avery felt himself stiffen. If Melham was touching her... Laura bit her lower lip, shifted slightly in her chair and whispered something. Mellham grinned and both hands appeared above the table again.

Avery caught Laura's eye again. She lifted one dark brow and murmured something to Mellham, who went red. Obviously the lady had no need of protection tonight. Avery felt a curious sense of disappointment. Something in him wanted action, would have welcomed violence.

The soup plates were removed, the entrées brought out and Avery turned to his other side to make conversation with Mrs de Witt, the wife of a politician and a notable society hostess. With her he had to make no effort. The conversation flowed with the ease, and at the level, he was familiar with from countless diplomatic receptions. As his inner composure returned he reflected that it was tactful of Godmama not to surround him with unmarried ladies and settled down to enjoy Mrs de Witt's opinions of the vagaries of various ambassadors.

Laura turned from Lord Mellham to chat to Mr Bishopstoke, the younger son of an earl and an old acquaintance. This gave her an excellent view of Lord Wykeham's averted profile as he talked to Mrs de Witt.

'Lady Birtwell has assembled a very creditable number of guests, considering the Season is still under way,' Mr Bishopstoke observed.

'I expect we all need a little rest and, besides, she always gives excellent parties.'

'I suspect she has another motive than simple entertainment on this occasion.'

Laura, who had just popped a slice of lobster cutlet in her mouth, could only look the question.

'Lord Wykeham is her godson,' Bishopstoke murmured. 'I think she is wife-hunting on his behalf.'

Laura disposed of the lobster in two irritable bites. 'You mean at his request?'

Bishopstoke nodded. 'He's too downy a bird to find himself the victim of a managing old lady's matrimonial schemes. No doubt he has decided it is time to settle down.'

'I imagine he is perfectly capable of finding himself a spouse without help. He is not a green youth in need of guidance.' *Was he ever?* It was difficult to imagine Avery was once as unsophisticatedly open as Piers had been.

'He has been out of the country a great deal and can hardly be familiar with the field, shall we say.'

'The *field,* as you put it, must be familiar with Lord Wykeham's standing and reputation, though. They can mark out an eligible bachelor when they see one: titled, wealthy, intelligent, powerful and acceptably good looking. He only has to stand around and the pack will hunt him down, if that is not mixing our metaphors somewhat.'

Mr Bishopstoke gave a snort of laughter. 'If you find him only *acceptable,* then the rest of us must surely give up the contest. I have it on the authority of all my sisters that the man is a positive Adonis.'

'Hmm. Are you not a trifle tactless in discussing Lady Birtwell's motives with someone who might be one of the field, Bishopstoke?'

'Would you have him? You will never give any of the rest of us a second's serious consideration, cruel one.'

'Oh, poor Bishopstoke! And I never realised you were dying of love for me.' She spared him a teasing pout and flutter of her lashes before she recalled her determination to be done with such nonsense. 'I am sure I am too scandalous for Lord Wykeham. Besides, there is a slight problem with his impeccable credentials, is there not?'

'The child, you mean? Would that matter to you?'

'No.' She made a show of considering it. 'Not if I liked the man.'

'And you do not even like him?' Bishopstoke raised an eyebrow. 'You amaze me, Lady Laura. Wykeham is being held up as a paragon of desirability.'

'I find him arrogant, manipulative—'

'Both useful characteristics in his profession, wouldn't you say? The hauteur to maintain his country's position and the ability to turn people and events to his will.'

'Admirable in a diplomat, but not comfortable characteristics in a husband, though.'

'Aha! Wicked girl, you want a man you can dominate.'

'Of course. And if I found one that I could,

then I would despise him for it. Do you wonder I have not married?'

'It will have to be a marriage of equals for you then, Lady Laura my dear.' He raised a glass. 'Here is to that impossible creature, a man who is your equal.'

Laura forced a smile and touched her glass to his. 'To a mythical beast, I fear.'

Lady Birtwell withdrew with the ladies after dessert, leaving the gentlemen in no doubt that they were not to linger over their port and nuts. Laura drifted over to the married ladies, unwilling to join the unmarried ones who, she was certain, would be chattering about the gentlemen and comparing their virtues. *Or lack of them.*

'Lady Laura, how pleasant to see you again. Such a sad business, the loss of your parents.' Lady Herrick patted the sofa next to her. 'Come and tell me how you get on these days. Who is chaperoning you?'

'My mother's cousin, Lady Carstairs.' She really must write and confirm the arrangements with Cousin Florence or word would get around that she was living scandalously alone with only the servants to maintain the proprieties and that

would just about finish her reputation. Lady
Herrick looked around and Laura added hastily,
'Lady Birtwell is chaperoning me here. I hardly
liked to impose another guest on the party when
I know I can rely on her.'

'She is a notable matchmaker, our hostess. I
have hopes that she will steer someone suitable
in the direction of my Emma.' Lady Herrick
nodded in the direction of her daughter, a very
shy brunette who was hovering on the fringes
of the group of girls.

'There are a number of eligible gentlemen
here, certainly.'

'And one for you perhaps, my dear.' Lady
Herrick lowered her voice. 'Lord Hillinger, perhaps?'

Lord Hillinger was forty, a widower with two
daughters and a passion for racing. His looks
were distinguished, his stomach flat, his hair all
his own and his fortune large. 'He is certainly
a most eligible gentleman, from what I hear,'
Laura agreed with caution.

'You have not met him? He is a connection
of my husband's family, I will introduce you.
See, the gentlemen have returned to us.' She
waved to the third man through the door and he
bowed slightly and came over. 'Max, my dear,

may I present you to Lady Laura Campion?
Lady Laura, Lord Hillinger.'

They exchanged greetings and the earl took
the chair opposite them and launched into perfectly unexceptionable small talk. Laura re-
ciprocated with half her attention. She could
discuss the Prince Regent's latest building proj-
ects in her sleep.

'I'm not certain Nash is the man for the job,
though,' Lord Hillinger remarked. 'What do
you think, Wykeham? Is Nash the man to create what Prinny wants down in Brighton?'

Laura was sure the hairs on the back of her
neck were standing up as Avery's deep voice
came from right behind her. 'Depends whether
Nash can pander to the Regent's shockingly bad
taste. If he can, then he'll do as dire a job as any
architect. If he tries for restraint or elegance,
he'll be out on his ear. He's got an eye to the
main chance though, so no doubt he will pros-
titute his talents to order.'

'Lord Wykeham!' Lady Herrick turned with
a shake of her head for his choice of words.
'How nice to see you again. It seems an age
since we met at the Congress, does it not? Come
and sit down, do.'

He could hardly refuse, Laura realised, not

without being unacceptably rude to the older woman. Avery came round the end of the sofa and took the other armchair in the little conversation-grouping.

'Do you know Lady Laura, Wykeham?' Lady Herrick was obviously more than happy to introduce Laura to men she would not consider suitable for her own, very young, daughter.

'We are acquainted, yes, ma'am.' There was nothing but polite acknowledgment in his slight bow to Laura and she flattered herself that no one could read a thing in her careful social smile in return. 'Do you have an opinion on the planned works to the Pavilion, Lady Laura?'

'They will certainly add to its entertainment value for those who spend the summer in Brighton. Whether it is an aesthetic experience or a circus show remains to be seen. Are you familiar with Brighton, Lord Wykeham?'

'Only on the most fleeting visits when it has been necessary to report to his royal highness. I may consider it for a summer break this year. I imagine my daughter would enjoy the seaside.'

Beside her Laura felt Lady Herrick stiffen so she kept her voice light. 'The beach is pebbles, unfortunately. But it is safe for swimming and her governess could take her out in a donkey cart. And there are delightful walks.'

The older woman relaxed, reassured, presumably, that Laura was not going to faint at the mention of the scandalous love child. 'Will you excuse me? I see my daughter wishes to speak to me.' The men rose and then sat again as she swept off.

'And boat trips,' Laura added, rather desperately. She really did not want to be talking to Avery at all, not in public and certainly not in front of anyone else. 'And the air is very healthy. Do you not agree, Lord Hillinger?'

He did not have a chance to respond as a pleasant baritone voice remarked, 'The air is always healthy and fragrant wherever you are, Lady Laura.' Mr Bishopstoke dropped into the newly vacated seat beside her. 'Never tell me you have identified *two* mythical beasts?'

'Sir!' Lord Hillinger was looking decidedly put out.

'I beg your pardon, my lord. A little joke Lady Laura and I were sharing, as old friends do. She seeks a husband who is her equal, one who she is neither dominated by, nor can dominate. I tell her that she seeks a mythical beast.'

'I do not find your humour amusing, sir.'

Lord Hillinger got to his feet, favoured Laura with a stiff bow and stalked off.

'Philip, you wretch,' Laura hissed, unable to look at Avery.

'He is a stuffed shirt, as well to get rid of him for he won't do for you, my girl. Now you have only got one mythical beast to deal with.' He flashed his charming, mocking smile at Avery.

Laura braced herself for Avery's crushing retort. There was silence. She risked a glance.

'What sort of mythical beast are you imagining?' Avery asked. He seemed faintly amused. Or perhaps that was simply the smile of a man about to knock another man's head off. 'I have wyverns on my coat of arms. Would that suit you, Lady Laura? Wings, scaly legs and a dragon's head? No doubt it would be a fair contest.'

'My goodness! That sounds like a proposal, Lady Laura.' Bishopstoke appeared to find his own dubious wit hysterical. 'Or a deadly insult. Shall I call Wykeham out for you?'

'Do go away, Philip,' Laura said with acid sweetness. 'Or you may find that both Lord Wykeham and I will upend our teacups over you.' He went, chuckling, leaving only Avery for her to be angry with. 'A fair contest? What kind of creature do you consider me to be, to equal a wyvern?'

'Perhaps they are like unicorns and will lie down at the command of a virgin.' He watched her from beneath heavy lids, like a big cat contemplating a dead antelope and wondering if it could be bothered to get up and eat it. 'Or no,' he added in a low voice that would not reach beyond their little space, 'that will not work, will it? A mermaid, do you think?'

Laura knew the symbolism as well as he did. 'The female embodiment of lust? The creature that lures men to their doom?' Why did he dislike her so? What was it about her relationship with Piers that seemed to anger him beyond reason? She found her hands were shaking and clenched them in her lap to still them. 'Sending you to your doom seems very tempting, Lord Wykeham.'

'I would like to see you try.' He looked completely relaxed, that faint, infuriating smile still curving his lips. *Those lips...* No one glancing in their direction would guess he was mortally insulting her.

'Then I would be delighted to oblige you, my lord.' Laura got to her feet, inclined her head and swept over to join the single ladies where she could retrieve the rags of her temper unobserved amongst their self-absorbed gossip.

Avery Falconer was going to pay for his insults. Just as soon as she worked out how to punish him.

Chapter Thirteen

The next day was sunny and Lady Birtwell swept her guests outdoors. 'The children need to run off their high spirits, the girls can renew the roses in their cheeks and the gentlemen may impress the ladies with their prowess at the archery butts and on the lake.'

There were canvas awnings set up in sheltered corners, with rugs, comfortable seats and footstools for the older guests and they were soon joined by the mothers who were glad to hand over their offspring to the small army of nursemaids on duty.

However, it seemed that the unmarried ladies had decided that a demonstration of their maternal suitability might be a good tactic, given that the bachelors were all assembled outside, as well. The babies were soon removed from the nurses to be cooed over and the little girls' dolls were admired. The small boys, far less appealing with their grubby knees and tendency to fight, received no female attention and were marshalled into an impromptu game of cricket by some of the fathers.

Laura felt a strong inclination to go and fire arrows into one of the straw targets, imagining the bull's eye painted on Avery's chest, but the opportunity to play with Alice was too tempting and, besides, she wanted to keep an eye on how the young ladies interacted with her.

Lady Amelia had apparently overcome her scruples at being seen with a love child. Laura put that down to her success with Avery the evening before when she had held his attention for at least ten minutes before dinner and had coaxed several smiles from him. Now Amelia was posed prettily on a rug, her pale pink skirts spread about her, a Villager straw hat perched on her curls to keep the sun from her face as she helped Alice dress her doll. She kept sending sideways glances towards the lower part of the lawn where Avery, coat and hat discarded, was fielding cricket balls.

Laura strolled across and sat down next to Amelia and Alice, her own forget-me-not-blue skirts overlapping the pink muslin. Amelia gave her own gown an irritable twitch to display it better.

'Good morning, Miss Alice.'

'Good morning, Au…Lady Laura. Lady Amelia thinks Clara needs a new sash.'

'I think so, too. That one is sadly frayed. You must ask your papa for a new ribbon.' Laura turned to watch the cricketers. 'He is working very hard.' Avery sprinted for a high ball, jumped, caught it in one outstretched hand and sent it back, fast and true, to hit the stumps.

'Oh, well caught, my lord!' Amelia applauded and Avery turned and sketched an ironic bow before walking back closer to the players.

'I wish I could play cricket.' Alice put down her doll and watched, her lower lip sticking out in a pout.

'Girls do not play cricket,' Amelia reproved. 'It is not ladylike.'

'We could play rounders if we can find enough players,' Laura suggested, knowing that Alice's natural energy would not last for many more minutes of sitting on the rug being good. 'I saw a bat and a soft ball with the cricket things.' She counted heads. 'Who would like to play rounders?' she called and found herself with five girls and four other ladies. Lady Amelia remained alone on the rug, looking decidedly put out.

They moved to the other end of the lawn from the cricketers, improvised four bases with branches from the shrubbery and began to play.

After ten minutes Laura had discarded her hat, rolled up her sleeves and was poised with the bat raised as Miss Gladman threw the ball to her. She had watched her bowling and was sure this ball would be as feebly delivered as all the previous ones. It was. Laura hit it perfectly, sending it flying away over Alice's head and towards the cricketers.

Alice ran for it, one stocking falling down, hair streaming behind her. Laura ran, too, straight for first base. Alice reached the ball and came running back, directly towards second base, which was closest to her.

'Don't run!' Lady Catherine at second base squeaked.

'Run!' Laura ordered, picked up her skirts to her knees and sprinted. It was a dead heat. Laura hurtled into the branch just as Alice did. They both went flying.

Alice landed on her bottom, ball still clutched

to her chest, hiccupping with giggles. 'You're out, you're out!'

Laura, twisted, threw herself to one side to avoid the child and landed in an awkward, jarring, heap. 'Alice, are you all right?'

She nodded enthusiastically and bounced to her feet. 'That was such fun!'

Bless her, she doesn't know enough other children to play games like this, Laura thought as she tugged her tumbled skirts down and began to get up. 'Ouch!' Her right ankle gave way under her and she sat back down with a thump.

'Lady Laura!' Alice dropped the ball and crouched down beside her. 'Have you hurt your poorly ankle?'

'Shh!' Laura warned. 'Yes, I must have twisted it.'

'I will get Papa and he can carry you again.' Before she could stop her, Alice ran off towards the cricketers. 'Papa! Papa!'

And this time it really is twisted, Laura thought grimly as the other players, realising at last that something was wrong, gathered round her. 'No, no, I will be all right, just a sprain, I think. Oh, thank you, Miss Gladman, I would be glad of a hand to rise.'

'Stay exactly where you are, Lady Laura.' Avery stood over her, coat and neckcloth discarded, sleeves rolled to his elbows. His shadow blocked out the sunlight as she looked up at him. 'I will carry you inside.'

Time seemed to slip back as he bent and slid one arm beneath her bent knees, the other behind her back, and lifted. The awareness of her body, of her femininity, was heightened by the thin barrier of his shirt, by the sensations of fine fabrics over the bare skin of his forearms. They were both hot from exercise and the scents of two warm bodies mingled in his nostrils. *It would be like this if we were making love.*

Lady Amelia hurried up. 'Your skirts, Lady Laura! Here, allow me.' She smoothed them about Laura's ankles with a show of concern that effectively drew the attention of anyone who hadn't noticed to the display of Laura's legs to the knee. Somehow the little tricks did not seem so amusing when they were directed at Laura. Perhaps Lady Amelia really did want him and was jealous. He could understand jealousy...

'Now, don't fret, Miss Alice,' Lady Amelia, said. 'You take my hand and we will go in with

Lady Laura and Papa. You are so active, Lady Laura, I do so admire your energy, but you have quite spoiled that pretty dress. How fortunate it seems to be an old one.'

She really was a little cat, Avery thought, unable to suppress a rumble of laughter, deep in his chest. Laura must have heard it, or perhaps felt it, for she moved in his arms and he caught her to him more securely with a murmur of reassurance before raising his voice. 'So kind of you to assist, Lady Amelia. Perhaps you and Alice would walk on ahead a little to alert the staff?'

'Of course, Lord Wykeham. Come along, Miss Alice.'

Laura held her head as upright as possible, stiff and unyielding. She was not going to allow herself to relax against his chest. Perversely Avery tightened his grip and slowed his pace. 'Let go, Laura. I have you.'

It was a mistake. She gave a little gasp that wrenched at something inside him, provoked a wave of helpless tenderness, just as he felt when Alice fell and hurt herself. And yet it was nothing like that feeling. He did not want to offer hugs and a sweetmeat and a bandage with bunny ears. He wanted to lay Laura down on a

bed and pour out his doubts and fears and confusion until he understood them himself. He
wanted to make it all right for all three of them.
He wanted Alice safe and happy. He wanted to
keep her and her innocent, unconditional love.
He wanted this woman who could destroy all
that with one word.

Laura was watching Lady Amelia as she
moved ahead of them, her pretty skirts swish-
ing on the grass, her parasol tilted elegantly and
one of Alice's hands was linked with hers. *The
perfect picture of modish motherhood,* Avery
thought.

'Cat,' Laura muttered, echoing his thoughts
of a minute before.

'Jealous?' Avery murmured in her ear, the
merest brush of her skin on his lips sending
goosebumps down his spine.

'Of her gown? Certainly not. I do not be-
grudge her all the help her dressmaker can give
her. I have plenty of new gowns, I just do not
choose to flaunt them all the time,' she said
tartly as he shifted his grip to negotiate the
steps to the lower terrace from the lawn.

'Of my attentions to her, then?' What the
blazes was he doing, putting his thoughts into
words?

'Certainly not. You are implying that you and I have a relationship that might be threatened by her.'

But we do have a relationship, of sorts. We have a child in common. We have those memories of Piers. We have our own different guilt and our own needs. We have desire. Surely I am not the only one that feels that even after what has happened between us? Don't be a fool, Avery told himself harshly. He was keeping what she wanted from her—the thing most precious to him was threatened by her very existence.

'I am sure Lady Amelia will make some lucky man an excellent wife,' Laura said. Her voice was tight with an emotion he could not read. He could not tell whether she was flustered by being in his arms, furious with Amelia or simply in pain. 'However, you should be aware that she disapproves strongly of Alice.'

'Nonsense. Look at them now,' Avery said. *Jealousy, that is all it is.*

'You did not hear her in the hallway when I arrived, telling the other ladies that it was shocking to bring a bastard to a respectable house party.'

'That is low, even for you, Laura, to make up such a thing.' Yes, he had been correct. She was jealous at the thought that Lady Amelia might be Alice's stepmother, that the child might grow to love her.

'How dare you! I am not a liar—'

'Of course not,' he said. *'Mrs Jordan.'*

Laura ignored the jibe. 'She is making up to Alice because she has set her sights on you.'

'On the contrary, I imagine she cannot be unaware of my interest and is very sensibly finding out how she gets on with my daughter.' It was time to stop this agonising and self-doubt. He was right to keep Laura from Alice. His plan to marry, to give the child a new mother, was the right one.

Avery strode across the upper terrace. At any moment they would be at the side door into the house and he could put Laura down, get her out of his arms.

'You have heard how she makes snide remarks—'

'I have heard no more than the sniping that seems commonplace between young ladies in the Marriage Mart. And amongst married ladies, come to that.'

'You have made up your mind that she is perfection, in other words!'

'By no means, if by that you mean I intend to fix my interest upon her. Frankly, my dear, your antagonism towards her makes me incline towards Lady Amelia. I doubt I would wish to marry someone who had your approval.'

'And why, exactly, is that?' she demanded, twisting in his arms in an attempt to face him.

'Because you are inconstant, flighty, deceitful—' They were at the door. Avery bit off the words, smiled. 'Ah, thank you, Lady Amelia. Lady Laura's maid is just the person we want. And two footmen with a chair. Excellent.'

'You sanctimonious libertine,' Laura hissed and pushed against his chest as he turned to place her in the chair. It was so unexpected, he was so off balance that his grip slipped and she slid free. Avery reached for her, his wrist cracking down on the carved wooden arm with a sickening thud.

Laura landed on her feet, clutching at him. She gave a gasp of pain as her injured foot took her weight and then she was slipping down. This time he caught her, held her tight despite the pain in his wrist.

'I never faint...' she whispered, and passed out.

'That's a new pair of half-boots ruined. And a good pair of stockings without a single darn in them covered in grass stains and as for this gown, I don't know I'll ever get it clean.'

That was Mab. Laura turned her head on the pillow and squinted against the light. She was lying on the bed with her foot propped up and something cold and wet draped over her ankle. She wriggled her toes experimentally. 'Ow!'

'You're awake then.' Mab came over and peered down at her. 'What a pickle. His lordship's none too pleased, believe me.'

'And what has it got to do with him, pray?' Laura reached behind her for more pillows so she could sit up.

'Miss Alice was frightened and was in floods, saying it was all her fault that you hurt yourself, so he had to cope with that until Miss Blackstock arrived. Then he banged his hand on the arm of the chair, trying to catch you, and it must have hurt like the devil, but being a man, he can't or won't admit it. And on top of that he's surrounded by silly chits all of a-fluster because he was striding about carrying you, like some fool in a poem, and they were ogling his arms and his chest and cooing about how strong and noble he is... Well, you can imagine, I'm sure.'

'Only too well.'

'Like I always said, he's a fine figure of a man. But with his coat off I can see what they were carrying on about. Buttocks you could bend a sewing needle on, I'll be bound.'

'Mab!' But a snort of laughter escaped her.

'That's better. No use you looking like a dying duck in a thunderstorm, that ankle's bad enough without you getting yourself in a pother about a man.' She scooped up the discarded clothing. 'We had to cut that half-boot off. I'll take these downstairs and have a word with the laundry maids, see what we can do with the grass stains. I'll have some tea sent up, shall I, my lady?'

Alone, Laura lay back with a sigh. Now she was doomed to be an immobile audience as Lady Amelia wormed her way into Avery's favour. She did not trust her one inch over Alice, for surely no one went from spluttering with disgust over the presence of a love child to finding themselves charmed out of their prejudice in a matter of hours.

A tap on the door heralded a maid with a tea tray and, hard on her heels before Laura could think of the words to deny her, Lady Amelia.

'I thought I would come and keep you company as your woman is struggling to salvage your wardrobe,' she said with a sweet smile. 'Put the tray there.' She nodded to a side table and sat beside it, regarding Laura across the chinaware with perfect composure.

'How kind.'

'Not at all? Milk and sugar?'

'Lemon, thank you.' At least it would give an excuse for a sour face.

Amelia stood to place the cup on the bedside table, inconveniently, and no doubt deliberately, at the exact angle that ensured Laura must twist inelegantly to pick it up. 'Miss Alice is quite unharmed by the incident,' she remarked as she resumed her seat, sweeping her pretty skirts around her with some emphasis.

'I had no reason to suspect otherwise. She seems a sensible child who would say something if she was hurt.' Laura managed to pick up her tea without slopping any in the saucer and took a sip. 'You seem very concerned about a child who you referred to as a bastard and whose presence you deplored only yesterday.'

'Naturally, a lady is concerned for the well-being of any creature.'

'Especially if she is intent on ensnaring the creature's father?' *There, at least we both know where we stand now.* 'Might I trouble you to pass me a biscuit?'

Amelia stood again, placed the entire plate on the bedspread next to Laura and returned to her place. 'Do have them all. Ensnare? I have no need to aggressively hunt after a gentleman. They come to me and seek my approval.' She gave her skirts another twitch. 'After all, in addition to breeding, connections and style, I have an impeccable reputation.'

'Which I do not. That is understood. But this is not about me, Lady Amelia.'

'I could not agree more. You may throw yourself at Lord Wykeham, but a gentleman of his nature would have only one use for a woman demonstrating that kind of behaviour.'

'Are you suggesting that Lord Wykeham would set up a mistress?' Laura ate a biscuit without tasting it.

'They all do,' Amelia said with a shrug. 'A lady ignores that kind of behaviour. And the women involved,' she added with a faint smile. 'The child is evidence of his proclivities.'

'And yet you would accept his offer if he makes one?'

'Certainly he will make one. And I may well

accept it. After all, I doubt the other gentlemen are any different.'

'And Alice?' The teacup rattled in the saucer. Laura set it down awkwardly on the bedside table. 'It is rather difficult to ignore a child.'

'Once I am in control of the household the child's place will be clearly established. As soon as I give Wykeham a legitimate heir then he will lose interest in her, I will make certain of that. A separate establishment would be necessary. Naturally, one would not want her mixing with one's own children.'

'Naturally.' A biscuit snapped between Laura's fingers. 'And yet you have sought out her company here.'

'But of course. Wykeham might hesitate to press his suit if he thought she would be an obstacle, which is why he has brought her here. I realised that after the first shock, as soon as I was able to give it some thought. And I would not be unkind to the poor little thing. She will soon learn her place—it is not her fault she is a bastard.'

'Love child,' Laura snapped.

'So sentimental. Everyone has to learn their station in life.' Amelia dabbed carefully at the corner of her mouth with one of the tiny linen napkins. 'I thought we ought to have this little chat because I would like to avoid unpleasantness as much as possible, as it seems I cannot rely upon you exercising restraint when it comes to the gentleman for whom I am easily the most suited partner.'

'Lord Wykeham is quite well aware that some call me *Scandal's Virgin*,' Laura said. 'I doubt he has any illusions about me, nor any intentions towards me.' *Not respectable ones, that is for certain. Should I warn her that I will tell him what she says about Alice? That would be the honourable thing for me to do. On the other hand it would allow her to prepare some lies.*

'And do not think to tittle-tattle to Wykeham about me.' Amelia took a final sip and set her teacup down with a firm click. She was apparently a mind-reader. 'I have already confided in him how jealous you are of me and I confessed I was a little taken aback and surprised when I first realised Miss Alice was here. He is assured of my complete understanding and support and I believe he is impressed by my frankness.' She got up and regarded Laura with a complacent smile. 'Do rest, Lady Laura. I'm sure it would be a great disappointment to you if you were unfit for any boisterous activities that might take place.'

'You witch,' Laura said to the unresponsive door panels as they closed behind her visitor. 'You scheming, clever witch.' Was Avery taken in by her? Very probably he was. A frank confession of prejudice, followed by a touching demonstration of motherly care for Alice, was just what might convince a man who was desperate to see his child accepted. It might have convinced Laura, if she hadn't heard the spite in Amelia's voice in the hallway and if she hadn't known her motive for befriending Alice.

'Over my dead body are you going to become my daughter's stepmother,' Laura swore. But how on earth was she going to prevent it?

Chapter Fourteen

Laura insisted on going down for dinner. She sent Mab in search of a cane and, by dint of leaning on her maidservant's arm, hobbled downstairs, muttering unladylike curses under her breath every time she had to put weight on her injured foot.

'Why you insisted on this gown, I'll never know,' Mab grumbled as they paused for breath on the first landing. 'Thought we were saving it for the big dinner before the musical performance in two days' time.'

'I am trying to counteract the impression that I am a hoyden without an outfit in the latest mode to my name.'

'Hmm. One doesn't follow from the other. That Lady Amelia been poking at you, has she?'

'Yes,' Laura admitted.

'Pads her bodice, she does,' Mab confided. 'Saw her woman adjusting one of her gowns in the sewing room.'

It shouldn't have made any difference to her mood, but, reprehensibly, it did. 'Thank you, Mab.' Now, every time the witch batted her eyelashes at Avery, Laura could imagine a handful of wadding escaping to peep above her neckline.

Everyone was very kind when she limped into the drawing room and several gentlemen offered her their arm to go in to dinner. Laura made light of the accident and forced a smile when Lady Amelia studied her gown and then smirked. She had risen to the bait and her opponent knew it. It would have been better not to have shown she cared and to have worn a less fashionable outfit.

Avery came over after dinner and enquired politely about her ankle, Laura replied with equal courtesy and he strolled away to discuss carriage horses with some of the other gentlemen.

'Oh, this will not do! We are all so quiet this evening after our energetic day in the fresh air.' Lady Amelia clapped her hands and laughed.

'We should play a game, do you not think, Lady Birtwell? Charades, perhaps or, no, I have it— Truth or Forfeit!'

Immediately her bosom friends joined in, urging that they play the game. Lady Birtwell beamed approval. 'An excellent idea. Now, all you young people bring your chairs into a circle, and, yes, I do mean you bachelors skulking in that corner.'

She organised them with jovial ruthlessness. The elderly and the married remained seated on the sofas, the unmarried were chivvied into the middle of the room. 'You begin, Miss Gladman. Chose your victim.'

Miss Gladman went pink, but turned readily enough to Mr Steading on her right. 'What is your worst nightmare, sir?'

'Playing round games where pretty young ladies put me to the blush,' he said without hesitation.

'That is a fib, sir,' Miss Gladman said severely. 'What forfeit shall I impose?'

The unfortunate Mr Steading was forced to stand in the middle of the circle and sing all the verses of *God Save the King* in his wavering tenor, but he was greeted with loud applause when he sat down.

'My turn again,' Miss Gladman announced, looking to her other side. 'Lord Hastings, what was your childhood nickname?'

'Podger,' the reed-thin viscount replied. 'Believe it or not, I was a fat child.' That was accepted as being so unflattering it had to be the truth and Lord Hastings chose the next person to question. 'Lady Amelia, what characteristic do you admire most in a man?'

She swept the room with her wide blue gaze, lingering for a moment on Avery's face. 'Why, integrity, of course.'

Laura would have liked to challenge that. Wealth and status would have been nearer to the mark, but there was no way of disputing the answer.

'Now, who shall I…? Lady Laura, what do you desire most in the world?'

Taken off guard, Laura realised she did not have a believable, safe answer. *What do I want, most of all? Why, Alice, of course.* And she would do anything to have her, she realised. Anything. A murmuring in the room jerked her attention back and she found that she was staring at Avery and that everyone was staring at her.

'Something that was stolen from me years ago,' she answered directly to Amelia.

'Whatever was it?' Amelia demanded. Laura realised she must have hoped the answer was a gentleman, and, probably, Avery, which would have produced blushing confusion and no answer.

'I will not say.'

'Forfeit, forfeit!' one of Amelia's friends called. 'What shall it be?'

'A poem,' Avery said. 'We cannot expect Lady Laura to exert herself, not with an injury to her ankle.'

Amelia pouted. *I expect she hoped for something embarrassing,* Laura thought. 'I will recite a verse a young friend of mine wrote,' she said. *'I wish I was a little star, Right up in the sky very far. I would twinkle with all my might, And make everybody's dreams come right.'* She finished off the piece of doggerel with a flourish, amidst general laughter and applause. From across the room Avery's mouth curved into a smile. Alice had written that out in her very best handwriting and drawn stars at the top and a sleeping figure of her papa at the bottom and Laura had helped her paint it.

'How charming,' Lady Amelia murmured.

I shall have to be careful, Laura thought. *She is so suspicious of Avery and me. The slightest indiscretion and she will make a scandal.*

Make a scandal... What do I desire most in all the world? Alice. And how can I have her without any scandal that would risk hurting her? By marrying Avery, of course.

The thought was so shocking she almost gasped aloud. The game continued, but she heard none of it, laughing and clapping when the others did, joining in the choruses of disbelief like an automaton. Avery desired her physically, but that was all. For some reason she could not fathom, he held her in implacable dislike. Yet he had liked her when she had been Mrs Jordan. If she was living with him, surely she could convince him that his prejudice against Laura Campion was misguided and that he could find again what he had enjoyed in the company of Caroline Jordan?

Could she simply ask him to marry her? No, he had made it clear that the only union he could imagine with her was an irregular connection, so she would have to entrap him. Laura shifted uncomfortably on her seat at the thought. It was an unpleasant word, *entrap.* It was an unscrupulous thing to do.

But she was not contemplating it for material gain, to secure a title or wealth. There were three people in this: herself, Alice and Avery. She would be happy if she had Alice. Alice would be happy with a stepmama she liked and Avery, surely, would be content when he saw Alice was well looked after and flourishing. And Laura would make him a good wife. She had social poise, languages, experience in running both a large household and a country estate. She had given birth once, so there was a good chance she would give him an heir.

He was not in love with anyone else, for his feelings for Lady Amelia were surely only the result of a practical assessment of her suitability. *But can I make him happy?* She wanted to, she realised. She wanted Avery to be happy. She wanted him to love her and to feel loved in return. *And I can do that. I can love him. I am more than halfway there already if I could only get beyond the fear for Alice and my anger at his mistrust of me.*

Yes, Laura concluded, trying to put aside that tantalising fantasy of love, marriage to her would be at least as satisfactory for Avery as marriage to any of the other women assembled here for his choosing. He would be angry with her, any red-blooded man would be, but he would simply have to get over it for Alice's sake, she told her conscience firmly. It was still making uneasy sounds, but she tried to ignore them. The discomforting thought intruded that the last time she had ignored her conscience she had ended up in bed with Piers and, ultimately, become pregnant.

She glanced across at Avery, her resolution shaken. She had liked him, admired him. He was, for all his faults, a good man and she was thinking about seducing him into matrimony. Then she saw Lady Amelia watching him and thought about her plans for Alice. *I want and need him,* she admitted to herself. *Alice needs a mother who will love her without condition, without reservation.*

'Are you cold, Lady Laura? Or in pain?' Lord Mellham was at her elbow. 'You shivered.'

'I am a trifle tired, that is all. Would you be very kind and ask a footman to fetch my maid-servant so she can help me to my room?'

'I could carry you,' he offered with a grin.

'I think I have been carried enough for one day, thank you, Lord Mellham.'

Even so, when Mab came in he helped Laura to her feet and supported her across the room to the door, watched with sympathetic interest by the company and by Avery, whose thoughts might have been a complete blank, judging by the absence of expression on his face.

Avery watched Laura limping from the room on Mellham's arm, smiling up at him, leaning so that when he looked down it was at her white shoulders and the lace that scarcely veiled the swell of her breasts. She had made the man blush over dinner last night, although he was showing no discomfort in her company now. After that she had been whispering with that fribble Bishopstoke, as thick as inkle-weavers, the pair of them. And later she'd been giving Hillinger the benefit of that other low-cut gown at close quarters, the hussy.

It seemed that Scandal's Virgin had decided to retire from the field on the arm of an eligible husband. The bachelors that Godmama had invited to give some cover for his search for a bride were providing Laura with an excellent choice of gentlemen, although she was going to have to find one who was so blinded by love or lust that he either did not notice, or did not care, that she had borne a child.

She'd tell some tale, he supposed, as the game broke up with the arrival of the tea tray.

A youthful betrayal that ended with the child dying. Or perhaps she would not trouble with arousing sympathy, perhaps her wealth and her name would be enough for someone like Bishopstoke.

Or I could marry her. The thought hit like a thunderbolt.

Avery drank a cup of tea that he did not taste, excused himself and went upstairs to the nursery wing. Alice had a small room off the main nursery where a nursemaid slept, one ear alert for the charges in her care in the rooms on either side and in the cots around her.

As he expected, Alice was fast asleep, one hand tucked under her cheek, her hair in its bedtime braids, her favourite doll on the pillow. He watched her in the dim light of the glass-covered nightlight, marvelling at the perfection of her skin, the curl of her lashes, the pout of her lips. Perfection, until one saw the scratch on her hand where she had been teasing the stable cat, the tiny smudge of mud under one ear that bath time had not dealt with, the stubborn tilt of her chin, even in sleep. She was a real person, not a doll, and he found her endlessly fascinating.

She was his world. He had taken her out of duty and out of guilt and she had rewarded him with unconditional love and trust and all she had asked in return was the love he felt for her. And all that was missing from her life was her mother and an end to the fear that he knew she had buried deep inside her, that somehow it was her fault that her mother had left.

Unable to resist, Avery stroked her hair, so soft under his hand. He could give her that mother, although how they could ever explain the circumstances of her birth and Laura's rejection of her, he did not know.

He tried to think it through logically, assess the facts as though they were terms in a treaty. Laura had behaved shockingly, thoughtlessly, with Piers and she had turned on him when he had returned to war and his duty. She had sent her daughter away, as she was bound to do or face ruin. But instead of finding her a home close by, one of ease and elegance, one where she could watch over her, she had sent her to a remote dale and a life far removed from her rightful place.

And she had simply forgotten her for six long years while she lived a life of pleasure and reckless enjoyment. *But,* he struggled to be fair, *she had been very young. She loves Alice now. Can I take the risk that she will be a faithful wife*

*and a good mother? Can I take the risk that
she will not steal Alice's love from me and then
hurt the child?*

Selfish, he castigated himself. *This is not
about you, this is about Alice. She will not stop
loving you. Will she...?*

He stood there, wrestling with his demons,
watching the child. The prickling sensation at
the nape of his neck came on gradually, then
the unease crystallised into the sound of another person breathing in the room. Someone
was behind him.

Avery turned, swift and silent on the balls
of his feet, and saw Laura sitting quite still on
a low chair in the shadowed corner. 'What are
you doing here?' he hissed.

'Watching her, as you watch her. Loving her
while I can.' The breathy whisper was quite
clear in the still room.

'You cannot stay here.'

'No,' she agreed softly, a ghost in pale ivory
and dark shadows. 'Will you help me to my
chamber?'

Avery bent to drop a kiss on Alice's cheek,
then turned and lifted Laura out of the chair
and into his arms. She gasped and clung and
he murmured, 'Quieter this way, there is less

chance of you stumbling.' That was true. So, too, was his need to have her in his arms again, soft and fragrant and dangerous. Desirable and vulnerable. Yes, he would ask her to marry him. And pray he was right to trust her.

She did not struggle, only curled her arms around his neck and was silent as he nudged the door closed with elbow and hip and strode to the top of the stairs. Her room, and his, were on the floor below. He had taken the precaution of discovering which was hers—why he was not certain, unless it was to help him sleep more easily at night, knowing she was not close.

The stairs were dimly lit and the froth of her skirts and petticoats were enough to stop him seeing where he was putting his feet. 'Keep still.'

'I am,' she murmured, and he realised that she had not moved. Only his body was reacting as if she writhed against him, his skin sensitive as though every nerve was exposed, the fret of linen against flesh almost intolerable. There was a tightness, a weight in his groin, and he set his teeth to ignore it and to ignore the whisper of her breath, warm against his shirt front, the tickle of her hair against his chin, the subtle assault of some expensive, elusive perfume in his nostrils.

It seemed to take an age to negotiate the stairs. He was two from the bottom when she murmured, 'I am sorry, Avery. I wish…'

He stopped. 'Sorry for what?'

'For this antagonism between us.' Her voice was husky with something that his body recognised at a visceral level. *Desire. For me, or simply for physical pleasure?* 'I wish…' She twisted in his arms and lifted her face. Her lips grazed his chin and then his throat, and fire shot through him. 'Please, Avery.' He felt the words more than heard them. Then she tipped back her head. 'You are right, I tease. But I am not teasing now.'

Avery did not speak. This was no time for words. Nor place, not here. He had decided to offer her marriage, now it was as though the Fates had been listening to his mind. He took the final steps to the floor, then turned left to his bedchamber, not right, to her door. In his arms Laura gave a little sigh and curled herself closer.

He held her one-handed as he turned the knob, then froze at a faint sound. It was as though something had fallen. But there was nothing to be seen and he shouldered open the door.

Darke had gone, as usual, leaving a lamp turned down low on the dresser. Avery disliked being attended at the end of the day. He preferred to undress himself and wash slowly in cool water, taking his time, thinking over what had passed and what the morrow would bring, shrugging on a banyan and taking a book to the fireside chair until his eyes were heavy with sleep.

Now he carried Laura to the bed and set her carefully on her feet beside it before returning to the door. His hand hovered over the key. 'I will lock the world out, not you in.'

'Leave it, I trust you.' She smiled faintly at his raised eyebrow. 'In this, at least.'

'Why, Laura? Why have you come to me?' *Propose to her now, or afterwards? Afterwards,* instinct told him. *Do not complicate this moment.* In passion, in the aftermath of passion, surely he would see the truth in her.

She half-turned from him and ran her fingers pensively over the old chintz bedcover, tracing the twining flowers and stems that some long-dead lady of the house had embroidered. The curve of her neck, the elegant line from bare shoulder to ear, was exposed to him, pearl-pale in the lamplight. Between her breasts was a shadowy, mysterious valley where a gold chain glinted.

'It has been a long time,' she said finally, without looking up. 'You think me loose, but there has not been anyone since…since before Alice was born. And there is this thing between us. This desire. I feel cold inside almost all the time. Flirting and laughing is no longer enough. And with you there is heat, even if there is nothing else but dislike and suspicion.'

Avery had not expected this frankness, this simple confession of need. His body stirred, eager, but he did not move. She spoke of nothing but desire, dislike, mistrust. Could he ever replace that with even the basic tolerance marriage would require? He probed a little, testing how open she would be. 'You know you are fertile. Why take such a risk again?'

Laura did look up then. The brown eyes that could look so cold seemed pansy-soft in the lamplight. 'We were young and foolish. We were to marry, so what did it matter? And Piers was inexperienced. You, I think, are both experienced and not inclined to be careless.'

Avery could argue that all the care in the

world was sometimes not enough, but somehow his prized self-control was slipping away,
sand through his fingers. Tomorrow he would
take that huge risk with his life and his heart
and with Alice's love. Tomorrow he would dis-
regard all the lessons of his own parents' disastrous marriage.

Tonight he would lie with this woman who
was ruining his sleep, haunting those dreams
he could snatch from a few hours of slumber.
He would not get her with child and he would
purge himself of this obsession, replace it with
clear-eyed logic. A small, cold voice of common
sense told him that neither could be guaranteed by force of will, but he was sick of common sense.

'You will be missed from your room.' The
handful of sand had almost trickled away.

'I told my woman to leave me. As you have
sent your valet away. It seems we value being
alone—that is one thing we have in common,
you and I.'

'Beside Alice there is little else,' he said as
he crossed to her side. 'Except this.'

She quivered as he trailed one finger down
her neck, over her breast to lift out the golden

chain, warm from her flesh, but she did not speak, only turned so her back was to him.

Avery lifted the weight of hair and kissed the nape of her neck as he began to unfasten the gown. He was slow because his fingers were not steady and slow because he wanted to prolong this moment, this silent surrender, this unexpected trustfulness. Under his lips the delicate skin over her spine was cool satin vanishing into fragile lawn and lace.

He unfastened the gown and pushed it from her shoulders to pool at her feet, brushing down his legs, covering his evening shoes. The wisp of a camisole was next and he followed it down with his hands, over the hardness of the corset, down to the feminine curve of her hips, then back up to free the laces.

Laura sighed as he loosened the garment, tossed it aside and bent to kiss the red marks it had left on her tender skin. Only then did he allow his hands to circle her waist and then drift up to cup the weight of her breasts, his thumbs sliding over the hardening tips. She murmured something too softly for him to hear and tilted her head back to rest against his shoulder and he closed his eyes while he struggled to find control and finesse and care.

She lifted her hands and pushed down the remaining petticoat, then turned slowly, within his embrace, to stand naked in front of him. There was colour on her cheeks and her eyes were lowered and it came to him that, for all her directness and bravado, Laura was shy. *It has been a long time,* she said. Six years for a sensual, beautiful woman who had known physical passion was indeed a long time. Time to ache—and time to grow reticent.

'Would you like me to put out the light?' he asked.

She looked up at that, eyes wide. 'Oh, no! I want… I want to see you.' A smile trembled on her lips. 'I want to be very bold and I fear to shock you.'

'Shock me?' Avery tugged his neckcloth free and stripped off coat and waistcoat. 'I would love you to shock me, Laura.' He finished undressing, arousal stoked by her unwavering gaze. When she ran her tongue along her lower lip he almost lost control like a callow youth. He dragged a deep, steadying breath down into his lungs. 'Show me. Let me show you.'

Chapter Fifteen

It had worked. She was naked with Avery in his bedchamber, all that remained was for them to be discovered and she had done what she could to ensure that. Now she had to deliver what she had promised and her courage was failing her for so many reasons.

He looked so like Piers and yet so different, so unsettlingly different. This was no idealistic, lovestruck youth, still growing into his body and his confidence. This was a man, self-assured, experienced and physically in his prime. And the overwhelming masculinity and sexuality he exuded shook her own poise. She desired him, he, very obviously, desired her, but it was six years since she had lain with a man. Could she entrance him sufficiently that he allowed her to stay the night, that he became careless of discovery?

She was acting out of calculation, acting against every instinct except the one that propelled her towards Alice. And yet she could not hate this man. She still could not find it in her to forgive him taking Alice, sending Piers back to war, but in everything else she desired and liked him. *I love him,* she realised, her breath taken by the realisation. *I love him and I am going to betray him.*

The only way she could go on was by drugging herself with lovemaking. Laura reached out and laid her palms on his chest, curled her fingers and raked down, lightly scoring. Avery closed his eyes and growled, deep in his throat, but he did not move as her hands moved downwards, winnowed through the coarse curls on his chest, circled his navel. She felt the skin tighten under her fingertips and she stayed still, deliberately tormenting him. Who would break first?

To her amazement he did. 'Touch me,' he ground out and opened his eyes, green and intense.

So she did, not tentative and not gentle, taking him in a bold grasp, stroking hard from tip to root and back. 'Like that?'

'Like that,' he agreed and lifted her, both

hands under her buttocks, and pushed her back onto the bed so her legs dangled over the side as her shoulders hit the mattress. It was outrageously arousing after the memory of Piers's tentative, gentle caresses. Heat flashed through her and when he stroked between her thighs with arrogant possession she knew she was already wet for him.

'Now,' she gasped and reached for his shoulders as he bent over her, his feet planted on the floor, the high bed presenting her wantonly to him. Her conscience stirred and she blanked her mind to it the only way she knew how. 'Now. *Avery.*'

He did not hesitate. One thrust and he entered her, filled her, shocked her into startled awareness of him, only him. Avery froze, poised over her, deep within her. 'Did I hurt you?'

'No.' He had not, only overpowered her with his size and his certainty. 'I am not sure I can move, though.'

'Curl your legs around my hips,' he prompted and, as she obeyed, ignoring the stab of pain from her ankle, the pressure eased. *'Ah.'*

Avery began to move slowly, his arms braced either side of her, his eyes never leaving her face as though he was reading her thoughts, her soul. It did not occur to Laura to close her eyes and escape that gaze as he remorselessly drove her higher and higher, tighter and tighter until she began to writhe and sob beneath him, begging for release. He shifted the angle and growled, 'Come for me', and she did, shockingly, suddenly.

When she surfaced out of the darkness and back to herself Avery was still moving within her, but he had shifted again, brought her up with him to lie on the bed. 'Again,' he ordered.

'I...I can't.'

In answer he bent his head to her breast, kissing, licking, nipping while she reached helplessly to caress the autumn-leaf hair, threading her fingers through the springing strength of it, holding him to her. The careful, sliding penetration had changed into a demanding rhythm that built the need back up in her, hot and swirling and tight almost to the point of pain.

'Avery.' And she was lost again. This time she heard him gasp, felt him go rigid and then withdraw before the swirling light and dark left her with nothing but the awareness of her own body, her own disintegration.

She came to herself to find him cleaning her with a cloth and cool water from the washstand. It was a curiously tender gesture from him. Laura realised she would not have been surprised if, having done with her, he had put her from the bed and left her to her own devices. *As I deserve. Finally I have earned my reputation.*

He had better manners than that, Laura concluded. She should be shy, ashamed even, to lie there naked amidst the tumbled sheets while a man showed her these intimate attentions, but she was too sated with satisfied desire to move. *I love him and he has made love to me as I never could have imagined. Oh, Avery, I love you so much.* Could she tell him, risk everything, admit what she had done and why? Would it convince him of her desperate need for Alice or would it simply disgust him? *He will never believe me if I admit how I feel.* She had done this all wrong, she realised. She should have told him she loved him, told him she trusted him with Alice. She should have loved both of them enough to risk letting them go.

And now she had to stay here, stay in this bed or this, this beautiful, stupid, wicked mistake, would have been in vain. She had chosen the wrong path, but now she had to follow it to its end.

'Thank you,' she murmured as Avery tossed aside cloth and towel. She reached out and touched his arm. 'Come back to bed.'

'You can hardly keep your eyes open,' he said, his own heavy-lidded gaze resting on her face.

'We can sleep a little and then later...' Laura let her voice trail off as she held out her hands to him. She did not have to act. Avery smiled and slid down beside her, pulled the covers over them both and settled her against his side, her head on his shoulder. It felt so good to be held by a man again, to be held by this man. His skin was salty and musky with their lovemaking, warm and soft over hard-strapped muscle. She wriggled closer and tried to turn a deaf ear to her conscience. *It is too late. Too late to go back, too late to say* I love you. *Too late for trust.*

Laura closed her eyes and finally slept.

They had woken twice during the night and reached for each other without words. Laura woke for the third time to the delicious drift of kisses across her stomach, then lower. Light was streaming through the open curtains, early morning light that showed her Avery's broad shoulders and the top of his head as he eased himself between her wantonly spread thighs.

'Avery?' She had heard of this, but Piers had never touched her in that way. Avery silenced her with a kiss so deep, so intimate that her whole body arched off the bed. His hands held her ruthlessly while his lips and tongue and teeth destroyed every last inhibition she had. Her hands were fisted in the sheets, her breath was sobbing from her lungs and her voice was hoarse with pleading, but he was implacable. Laura convulsed, shaking and ecstatic, her blood thundering in her ears.

Then Avery cursed savagely and she realised the noise was not her blood pounding, but knocking on the door and an agitated female voice. Avery threw a sheet over her and twisted one around his waist as the door she had persuaded him to leave unlocked flew open to reveal Lady Birtwell, Mab and the indistinct shapes of other figures in the corridor behind.

Lady Birtwell slammed the door behind her, leaving everyone else outside. 'Avery Falconer, how could you?' she demanded, brandishing something at the bed, the evening slipper Laura had managed to drop from her foot the night before as Avery opened the bedchamber door.

Her plan had worked and now she felt sick with
nerves and self-reproach. *Alice, think of Alice.*

'And Laura Campion, I am shocked and disappointed. Thank heavens your poor mother is
not alive to hear of this. Well?' She turned her
furious gaze on her godson. 'What have you to
say for yourself?'

'Who knows of this?' he asked coolly. Laura,
close to him, could see the tension in his jaw,
the clenched fist on his thigh, but his voice betrayed nothing but bored enquiry.

'*Who knows?* The entire dratted household, I
should imagine!' Lady Birtwell snapped. 'Lady
Amelia found the slipper when she was on her
way to Miss Gladman's room to borrow something and she brought it to me immediately,
which was very proper of her, for, as she said,
something must have happened to you if you
were wandering about with only one shoe.' She
glared at them both. 'Well, Falconer? What are
you going to do about it?'

'I can do little about the fact that Lady Amelia is a prurient little busybody,' Avery drawled.
'My immediate plans are to get dressed and
have breakfast.'

The infuriated dowager raised both hands
heavenwards as if in supplication for more

strength. 'What are you going to do about Lady Laura?'

Avery swivelled round to look at Laura, as unconcerned by his near-naked state as some pasha disturbed in his harem, she thought with unreasonable resentment. The irritation helped her meet his green eyes with some semblance of calm while she waited for the outburst. 'Why, marry her, of course,' Avery said calmly.

'Thank merciful Providence for that.' Lady Birtwell did not sound very thankful. She opened the door a crack, hissed an order and Mab sidled into the room. 'Take your mistress in there.' Lady Birtwell gestured towards the dressing room. 'Get her clothed while I make sure no one else is still wandering about.' She went out, closing the door behind her with a decided snap.

Laura swathed the sheet around herself, slid off the bed without looking at Avery and hobbled painfully after Mab, who had been gathering up scattered garments. The maid closed the dressing-room door and leaned against it. 'What were you thinking of?' she demanded.

'Getting Alice. It worked,' Laura said, pulling on her petticoat. If she sounded confident and pleased, then perhaps she could convince

everyone else that was how she felt. It was a
pity she could not convince herself. For one
night she had known how it felt to be loved by
the man she was in love with. Now, although
she would lie with him for the duration of their
marriage she had forfeited the right ever to tell
him how she felt, ever to expect his love in return. 'Stop lecturing and fasten my corset.'

'But the scandal!' Mab jerked the strings
tight and shook out the chemise.

'Lady Birtwell will squash it and he will
marry me. I will be Alice's mama-in-law.' She
turned on her maid who was unrolling stockings. 'What are you muttering about?' she demanded and sat down to take the weight off her
ankle. She must have twisted it again during the
night for it was throbbing like the devil.

'You are getting Alice, but you are also getting a husband who is going to hate you—and
he didn't care for you too much to start with!'
Mab knelt to roll on the stocking, tutting over
Laura's swollen ankle.

'Avery will not show his feelings for Alice's
sake,' Laura said, praying she was correct. 'And
I will make him a good wife.' *Somehow I must
make amends.*

'He'll not forgive you,' Mab warned. 'He's a

proud man used to having his own way, used to
being in control. You've trapped him in a net of
his own honour.' She stood and began to stick
pins into Laura's tangled hair with emphatic
force. 'You've got a tiger by the tail, my girl.
Let go and he'll eat you alive.'

Avery waited until Laura had been bundled
out of the room by her maid, waited until Darke
put his head round the door and retreated, wary
and silent, to fetch hot water, and then swore
viciously and inventively until he ran out of
words. When he looked down, the sheet between his hands was ripped across.

Thank heavens he had not asked her to marry
him before she had revealed her true nature, not
let her glimpse the feelings he had not been able
to acknowledge to himself until those moments
when he had held her in his arms and thought
he had read truth and pain and some stirring of
emotion for him as a man.

Now his questions had been answered. He
could not trust her, she was as manipulative
and deceitful as he had feared. She had told him
yesterday evening as clearly as it was possible
that the thing she wanted most in the word was
the thing that had been stolen from her. Alice.

Avery smiled, with a bitter kind of satisfaction. Laura thought she had trapped him, cockled him into matrimony. All that had happened was that she had betrayed herself, armed him thoroughly against her future wiles. There was nothing she could negotiate with now and he had what he wanted, a mother for Alice whose devotion to the child was assured.

Darke eased himself in from the dressing room and cleared his throat. 'Your shaving water is ready, my lord. Will you require me to shave you this morning or…?'

'I will shave myself.' Avery looked down at his clenched hands. 'No, you do it, Darke.'

Twenty minutes later he sat back in the chair, chin raised while Darke negotiated the tricky sweep around his Adam's apple, and resumed the outward calm that had seen him through one duel and numerous diplomatic crises. Laura Campion was just one more crisis to be dealt with.

'My lord!' Darke stepped back, the razor dangling from his hand. 'My lord, I almost… I am so sorry, I do not know what came over me.'

'My fault, I moved abruptly.' Avery dabbed gingerly at his throat and regarded the bloodstained towel with a rueful smile. 'I hope you can dress the cut or the guests are going to assume I would rather cut my own throat than wed.'

'Hah, hah,' Darke rejoined, clearly uncertain whether that was a jest or not. 'I am sure no one could think such a thing. A very delightful young lady, if I may be so bold as to offer my congratulations, my lord.'

'Yes, thank you, Darke.' Avery sat back in the chair and allowed the nervous valet to complete the shave. *Laura.* He had thought himself armoured against her—it seemed his nerves were not as steady as he had thought.

Avery went down for breakfast with a dressing on his throat under his neckcloth and an expression of complete blandness on his face. The breakfast parlour was almost full of house guests all eating very, very slowly in the hope of catching the scandalous lovers when they came down.

He smiled amiably, returned mumbled *Good mornings* with studied calm and sat down. 'Something of everything,' he said to the footman. 'And coffee.'

'You have a good appetite this morning, Falconer,' Simonson said and then blushed when two ladies giggled and several gentlemen cleared their throats noisily.

Avery regarded him steadily for a moment. 'Indeed I have. This excellent country air, I imagine.'

Lady Birtwell entered and the men got to their feet as she cast a repressive glance around the table and announced, 'The carriages will be at the front door at ten for morning service. For those who wish to walk, it takes twenty minutes and one of the footmen will direct you.'

From the expressions around the table it was obvious that the fact this was Sunday had escaped almost everyone, swept up in the delicious scandal bubbling in their midst. Avery accepted a plate of eggs, bacon, sausage and kidneys and made himself eat. He could not recall ever being so purely angry.

There had been fury mixed with grief and guilt over Piers's death, he had been more than annoyed when he discovered Laura Campion in London and realised what she was doing, but now he was conscious of little else but a desire to shake her until her sharp white teeth rattled in her head. It did not help that some of the anger was directed against himself.

He made himself converse with his neighbours on topics that were suitable for a Sunday which, eliminating horse racing, royal scandal, the latest crim. con. cases in the courts and most plays, none of which would have been approved by their hostess, rather restricted discussion.

There was a desultory exchange underway about the death of an ancient royal cousin and whether court mourning would be decreed when the door opened and Laura came in, leaning heavily on the arm of one of the footmen. The gentlemen rose to their feet and then sat again when she took her place, reminding Avery of a flock of lapwings, alarmed at a passing hawk, rising off a ploughed field and then settling back.

'Good morning,' she said generally, then, 'Tea and toast, please,' to the footman.

'You are very pale this morning, Lady Laura,' Lady Amelia said with sweet smile. Avery regarded her with dislike. How the blazes had he thought this sharp-tongued cat might have made a suitable wife? Laura's judgement had been quite correct.

'My ankle is very painful,' Laura said. 'How kind of you to be so concerned.'

Avery almost smiled before he recalled how

furious he was with her. The wretched woman looked, pallor aside, completely calm. *Actress,* he thought. *No shame, not an iota.*

The room had gone very quiet except for the scrape of knives on plates and the rattle of cups in saucers. The other guests did not appear to know where to look—at him, at Laura or at their plates. What did they expect—that he was going to fall to his knees at her side and ask for her hand? Well, he might as well give them something to twitter about.

'With your injury I imagine you would wish to drive to church, Lady Laura.'

All eyes moved to her. 'Certainly I will not be able to walk,' she agreed and took a sip of tea. Over the rim of the cup her eyes met his, brown, unreadable. Last night he could have sworn he could see into her soul. Last night he had believed he could love what he would find there.

'Then perhaps I may take you in my phaeton? It is not a high-perch one, so I imagine you will find it easy enough.'

'How very kind, Lord Wykeham. That would be delightful.'

Not a blush, not a moment's hesitation, the hussy. 'Excellent. It will be at the door for ten.'

He would drive her to church and make only
the most banal conversation. He would sit next
to her in the pew and find the hymns for her.
He would behave impeccably until her nerves
were as tight as a catgut violin string and then
he would drive her into the depths of the park
and…settle this matter.

Chapter Sixteen

They think I am brazen and immoral, Laura thought, watching the avid faces around the breakfast table. Only a few of the guests had the decency to make conversation. Lady Birtwell seemed frozen and Avery, damn him, looked like a cobra waiting to strike.

When was he going to say something? It was obvious he wanted to torture her with suspense, because he could hardly propose to her in the phaeton with Alice there. It was beginning to dawn on her that Avery Falconer had reserves of self-control that made her own seem like those of an hysteric.

Laura came down for church in a sombre deep-brown pelisse over an amber gown with a new French bonnet.

'Put your veil down,' Mab whispered as she helped Laura descend the stairs.

'I am not going to hide from them,' she murmured, then raised her voice. 'What a charming bonnet, Lady Amelia. So harmonious with your complexion.'

The bonnet was green silk. Miss Gladman tittered, Lady Amelia showed her teeth in what might have been taken for a smile. 'And yours is delightful, too. I always think fawn is so flattering with an older skin.'

'Very true,' Laura agreed warmly. She moved closer and added, low-voiced, 'And one of the benefits of passing years, as you will inevitably discover, Lady Amelia, is the awareness of the danger of making gestures which, however satisfying they may be for a moment, actually work against one in the end. All that effort to attach a certain gentleman, thrown away in one moment of spite. Oh dear.' She smiled. 'Look, Mab, Lord Wykeham has just arrived in his carriage. Help me to the door, if you please.'

And not a moment too soon, she thought as she heard the sharp hiss of indrawn breath and saw Lady Amelia's gloved fingers turn to claws on her prayer book.

The tiger was at the horses' heads and Avery

stood waiting for her with Alice perched up on the seat. There would be no room for Mab.

'Allow me, Lady Laura.' He put a hand either side of her waist and lifted her up to sit beside Alice, then walked to the other side, climbed up and took the reins. The tiger ran round and scrambled up behind.

'Good morning, Lady Laura.' Alice, band-box-neat and clutching her prayer book, peeped up at Laura from under her bonnet brim. 'Are you safe now?' she whispered. 'From the bad man?'

'I hope so,' Laura whispered back.

Alice slipped her hand into Laura's and gave it a squeeze. 'Papa will protect you,' she said confidently. 'Are you having a lovely time? I am.'

'Do you get on well with the other children?' Laura asked, conscious of Avery's silent figure looming on the other side.

'Oh, yes. Tommy Atterbury was horrid because I do not have a mama, but I said I would rather not, if mine dressed me up in such a silly way. His mother makes him wear a velvet suit with a floppy bow at the neck and he has ringlets, you know. Anyway, the others all laughed at him and Priscilla Herrick said I was a good sport and they've all been very nice.'

Laura could feel her lips twitching into a smile and bit her lips until she could answer with a straight face. 'That was very quick-witted of you, Alice. Well done.' Given Lady Atterbury's own appalling dress sense poor Tommy's outfit was no surprise at all.

She glanced sideways and found Avery looking at her. 'I can't be with her all the time,' he remarked mildly.

'Of course not. Self-defence is important. No doubt Alice has learned her quick wit from you.'

'And the sharp edge of her tongue is doubtless inherited.' His eyes were on the road again, fixed between the heads of the pair of handsome greys he was driving.

'Attack is often the best form of defence,' Laura remarked. 'Especially for a woman. We have fewer natural weapons.'

'I would beg leave to disagree,' Avery remarked, looping his reins as he guided the pair down the lane to the church. 'Men are constrained by honour from retaliating.'

'Given their natural superiority of strength and the unfair advantages law and society give

them over women there has to be a balance
somewhere.' With Alice listening Laura struggled to keep her tone light and free from the
anger she felt. *Honour! What a hypocrite he
was.*

'Papa, may I have the money for the collec-
tion plate?' Alice asked, cheerfully unaware of
the battle raging over her head.

'When we get down, sweetheart.' Avery
reined in and waited for the tiger to jump down
before he descended and swung Alice to the
ground. 'Allow me, Lady Laura. I trust the ride
did not jolt your ankle.'

'Not at all.' Laura took his arm and limped
into the church. Eyes followed their path down
the aisle towards a box pew whose door was
held open by one of Lady Birtwell's footmen.
'Not that one. I will sit there, with Lady Atterbury,' Laura said, recognising the towering
confection that her ladyship considered suitable
as a church bonnet.

'I imagine Lady Birtwell has given instructions on who is to sit where.' Avery continued
down the aisle, her hand trapped against his
side.

'But we look like a family group,' Laura
hissed.

'And?' Avery let Alice go in first, then ushered Laura through. 'That is your aim, is it not?'

'But not yet,' she hissed. Without creating a scene there was little she could do except sit down on the embroidered pew cushion. Laura leaned forward to place her prayer book on the shelf and said, 'I would prefer to be asked first.'

'You have already done the asking,' Avery remarked. He picked up a hymn book, consulted the numbers on the board and rifled through until he found the first before placing it before Laura. 'I am merely trying to exhibit some dignity by not screaming and thrashing about in the trap you believe you have sprung.'

To her horror her eyes began to sting. Laura dropped to her knees on the hassock and buried her face in her hands until she got the urge to cry under control.

The congregation came to their feet and Avery put a hand under her elbow to hoist her up. 'Or do you propose to remain there, praying for forgiveness?'

Laura ignored him, sat down and remained seated through the entire service. She helped Alice with her hymn book, moved her lips as though she was singing and fought her temper and her fear.

Finally the vicar and choir processed out and the congregation gathered their possessions and began to file down the aisle towards the south door. Laura had no idea what she said to the vicar as they left, although she must have said something reasonably coherent because he smiled and shook hands and no one seemed shocked.

Avery waited for his phaeton. 'Gregg, take Miss Alice to Miss Blackstone, please. If she has already left, then walk Miss Alice back to the house.'

With a sinking sense of helplessness Laura allowed herself to be helped into the seat and waved to Alice with the best imitation of cheerfulness she could manage. Avery got in, took the reins and sent the greys off at a brisk trot in the opposite direction to the house.

'Where are we going?'

'To hell in a hand basket, I imagine.' Avery turned into a lane and drove on until it widened into a little meadow beside a stream. The sun was shining, the birds were singing and the brook plashed cheerfully amongst its stones. An exquisite spot for a proposal, Laura thought, wondering if Avery's sense of irony had led him to select it for that reason.

He pulled off onto the grass, stuck the whip in its holder and tied the reins around the handle. 'I have to give you full marks for tactics, my sweet.' The endearment was like a slap in the face. 'The slipper on the floor outside my door was masterly.' She did not trouble to deny it had been deliberate, but concentrated on aligning the markers in her prayer book as though the fate of nations depended on their straightness. 'And as for your performance in bed, why, that was positively professional. Anyone would have thought you were actually enjoying yourself.'

The book fell to the floor of the carriage, the markers blew away in the breeze that did nothing to cool her burning cheeks. 'I was not pretending and neither were you. You know there is something between us. You said as much back in the village after we first met. Desire.'

'I am impressed by your ability to separate your emotions from your passions, then.' Avery looked down at his hand, opened his clenched fist and began to strip off his gloves. Laura saw one had split along the seam. 'The general wisdom is that it takes a kick in the groin or a bucket of cold water over the head to stop a man performing, but that ladies are far more sensitive. I doubt I could have lost myself in the moment quite as thoroughly if I was engaged in such a masterpiece of deceit at the same time.'

'You drove me to it.' She turned her shoulder to him. If she could just spring down from the carriage, confront him face-to-face instead of being forced to sit passively next to him. If only she had the courage to tell him she loved him. 'If you had not forbidden me any access to Alice, I would have been content, but you had to take her from me utterly. Utterly. How could you be so cruel?'

'Well, you have got what you wanted, for I doubt any respectable woman is going to accept an offer from me now, with this on top of the prejudice about Alice's birth.'

She had to be certain. Laura swivelled on the seat to look at him. Avery had leaned forward, rested his forearms on his long thighs and was staring at his clasped hands. 'You...you will marry me?'

He looked up at that and his lips curved into a smile that chilled her to the marrow. So must a master swordsman look when he was about to run through some hapless opponent. 'But of course.'

'And we will live together, with Alice? Be a family?'

'Of course,' he repeated. 'Your powers of acting are established and you will find mine are almost as good. Alice will not be affected by any household rift. As for when we are alone, my dear, we will keep separate suites. I will come to you when I wish to get you with child, for as long as it takes, and, how shall I put this... doing only what it takes. I think I will settle for the conventional heir and a spare. You need not fear my demands will be onerous.'

The ice congealed around her heart so she could almost hear it cracking. 'I imagine your mistress will be glad to have so much of your company, then,' Laura said. She could almost feel pleasure that she sounded so indifferent.

'I keep my vows,' Avery said, and now she could hear the anger beneath the even, slightly mocking tone. 'I have no mistress now, nor will I take one. You may be sure I will be faithful, my dear.'

'So you expect us both to suffer?'

'Suffer?' He shrugged. 'Sexual release is a mechanical matter, I do not expect to experience any pain of deprivation.'

'But we could have had so much more,' Laura

flung at him and took hold of his lapels, shook him, desperate to crack the mocking facade.

'We could have had,' Avery agreed. 'You have ensured we never will.'

When her hands dropped away from his coat he dug in his pocket and produced a small box. 'You see, I came prepared. Think of the pleasure of displaying this to Lady Amelia and her friends.' The square-cut diamond glittered in the sunlight. Beautiful, cold, expensive.

'Thank you,' Laura said steadily as she drew off her left glove and held out her hand. 'I must obviously take my pleasures where I may. You can be sure I will gloat in the most ladylike manner.'

He said nothing, but took her hand in his and slid the ring onto her finger. It was a perfect fit. Laura looked at the arrogant, masculine, beautiful face and did not flinch when he raised his eyes and met her gaze. *I love you,* she thought. *I would have shown you that love, heart and soul.*

Avery's eyes narrowed as if he saw something in her face, then he turned away with a slight shake of his head. He pulled on his ruined gloves, unwound the reins and clicked his tongue at the horses.

Laura kept her eyes on his profile and felt

the ice crack even further until the pain told her everything she needed to know. *It is too late. What have I done?*

She had her composure intact when they returned to the house. She smiled and thanked Avery prettily for the lovely drive, she laughed gaily at her own clumsiness as she hobbled up the front steps on his arm, she lowered her lashes demurely when she saw her hostess approaching and let her see the great diamond on her finger.

The reaction was most gratifying. Or it would have been if all she cared about was securing a husband and suppressing gossip. The sideways looks, the sharply indrawn breaths, the tutting disapproval, all vanished as if they had never been. Lady Laura Campion had secured the hand of a most eligible nobleman and all was as it should be.

Even the young ladies who had hoped to receive a proposal from Avery and who had sniggered with horrified delight over her disgrace that morning had the sense to hide their chagrin now. Lady Wykeham was going to be a power in society and they had no intention of earning her enmity now.

Laura could only feel relief at the change, although she gave no sign of her feelings about their hypocrisy. After all, she was the greatest hypocrite there. She showed off her ring, feigned modest delight, fluttered her eyelashes at Avery when he was not looking at her and did everything expected of her other than summon up a blush.

'Yes,' she agreed, dabbing at her dry eyes with a lace-edged handkerchief. 'It is so sad my parents are not here to share my happiness. No, I have no idea where we will be married. I will leave that decision to Lord Wykeham.'

'St George's, Hanover Square,' Avery said, strolling up to the tea table in time to hear her. 'I intend to stay at the town house for the remainder of the Season and I can see no reason to delay the ceremony, can you, my dear?' His look of polite enquiry dared anyone to so much as think an early date might be a necessity, not a matter of choice. 'Have you finished your tea, Laura? I think it time we shared our news with my daughter.'

'Of course.' She stood and took his arm and allowed herself to be guided from the room, but instead of walking through to the garden entrance and the terrace where the children were playing Avery opened the door to a small sitting room.

'In here. I need to make something very clear.'

'Well?' Laura shook off his hand and swung round to face him. 'What is your latest demand?'

'You will give me your word that you will never, under any circumstances, tell Alice the identity of her mother.'

Laura stared at him. The thought that she was now in a position to tell Alice the truth had never occurred to her, she was just so happy that she would be with her, despite Avery's loathing. Now she realised that it would be the most natural thing in the world to tell her daughter the truth.

'But I must tell her! Not yet, of course, but when she is of an age to understand. She has the right to know her mother loved her, always.'

'She has the right not to be hurt any more than she has been,' Avery said.

'Why, you are afraid I will tell her you are not her true father! That is it.' His expression became even stonier. 'You coward, you think she will cease to love you.'

Avery moved like a snake striking. His hand

fastened around her wrist like a manacle and her pulse jolted so he must have felt it like a hammer-strike. 'Tell her who either of her parents is and you will regret it. Alice has a hard enough path to follow in order to shake off the legacy you bequeathed her and establish herself as an accepted member of society with the hope of a decent marriage. Will you shake her understanding of who she is, destroy everything she accepts as the truth in order to satisfy your own need for forgiveness?'

'No! I need her to understand she is loved—'

'She knows that already.'

His fingers encircled her wrist, not tightly, just keeping her there. Laura tugged. 'Let me go, you are hurting me.'

'It hurts when you resist me, not when you do as I say.' He waited until she stopped pulling and established his point for him. 'In our marriage you will find the same thing. Obey and you will be happy enough. Run counter to me and suffer the consequences. Now swear.'

He did not spell out what those consequences were. To banish her from Alice, she supposed. He was intelligent enough to know an unspecified threat would work more uncertainty on her mind.

'I am surprised you would accept my word, but, yes, I swear not to tell Alice the truth about her parentage. Let me add another promise. I will never let her realise that the man she loves as her father is a blackmailing, unscrupulous tyrant.

'Now, let us go and tell her our joyous news.' She smiled at him, the glittering smile that had always masked her deepest hurt. *And I swear you will never discover my greatest weakness: my love for you.*

Chapter Seventeen

They sat together on a broad garden bench under a lilac bush, well away from the laughter and shrieks of the playing children. Alice stood in front of them and listened, wide-eyed, her hand clasped in his as Avery told her that he had found her a stepmama and that Lady Laura would be his wife. He had hoped she might be pleased, but he was unprepared for the emotional kick in the gut when she wriggled her hand free of his and threw herself into Laura's arms with a shriek of delight.

Alice's joy should not have been a shock, he knew she liked Laura, had seen their rapport when the child had grown to know her *Aunt Caroline.* Surely he could not be jealous, or worse, resentful that the child had found another adult to love? Avery shifted that uncomfortable, unworthy thought away and watched Laura. He was not prepared for the tears on her cheeks, nor the fierceness of her embrace in return for Alice's. She had protested all along that she loved her daughter and now he knew he had to accept that was the truth. No actress, however skilled, could feign the depth of her emotion and, in his heart, he had always known it.

And, despite her fierce independence, her dislike of him and her desperate need to be with Alice, she had yielded on every occasion when he had put pressure on her for the sake of the child.

Now, against his every prejudice, he had to accept she would do anything for Alice. Even, it seemed, marry a man she detested. But why leave it so late to try to claim her child? It could not even be that she had refrained from making contact while her parents were alive for their sake, because it was not until over a year from their deaths that she had sought Alice out. And the conventions of mourning would not have kept her from the child, he could see that. There had to be some good explanation, he wanted to believe that.

But could he trust her with anything else? She had turned on Piers, furious and full of spite, when he had simply been doing his duty. She had flaunted herself amongst the fastest set in society for years, earning a reputation that had been an inch from ruin. And she had lied to him, disguised herself, wormed her way into Alice's affections with a charade she could never have sustained. Even when she had come to him, acknowledging the dangerous sensual attraction between them, it had been a lie, a stratagem, a cold-blooded manoeuvre to trap him. It had not been her fault that she had delivered exactly what he had decided he wanted.

No, he could trust neither her word nor her virtue. She was a danger and he knew he did not understand her. Last night as she lay in his arms and had yielded with passion and fire to his lovemaking he had almost believed he was falling…

Avery gave himself a sharp mental shake. He could not afford weakness. He had gone to her room this morning when it was empty and he had taken that pair of evening slippers. Now one was locked in a dresser drawer, a physical reminder of a deliberate betrayal.

'May I call you *Mama?*' Alice asked.

Laura looked at him over the top of the child's head, her face tranquil, her eyes stark.

'Of course, darling. As soon as I am married to your papa, then I will be your mama.'

'Do you love Papa?' The innocent question startled him, and Laura, too, from her expression. Her gaze switched instantly to Alice's face and she smiled. It was not the smile she kept for him, edged with icicles, and not the genuine warm one that transformed her face whenever she looked at Alice. This, Avery realised, was a smile that hid something very deep.

'He will never know how much,' she said.

There was nothing he could return for that, not with Alice listening. For a moment he had thought it sarcasm, directed at him, and then he saw the glimmer of a tear as the dark lashes lowered to veil Laura's eyes. Her teeth caught her lower lip for a second and then she was calm again. She had not responded about her feelings for him, but for Piers, Alice's real father. But then she had written that letter to Piers. He shook his head in an attempt to clear it. Had he somehow misunderstood her? The woman tied him in knots.

'Is it a secret or may I tell everyone?' Alice was already off the seat, hopping from foot to foot in her eagerness.

'Yes, you may tell,' Laura said and sat, her

hands lax in her lap, watching Alice as she raced across the lawn to the other children.

'You loved him, then?'

She turned to stare at him, a frown of puzzlement between her arched brows. 'Him?'

'Alice's father.'

'Piers?' Her confusion puzzled him. 'Why, yes, of course I did. I would never have lain with a man I did not love.'

'Really? And last night?'

'What do you think?'

'That you overcame your revulsion very well.' He got to his feet and took a few angry paces away from her, furious that he was letting his guard down, that she might suspect he cared.

'I am not an innocent girl barely eighteen years old any longer.' She kept her eyes on the children, over by the house. 'And you are an attractive man and, as I expected, skilled in bed.'

Avery felt himself flush at the dispassionate description. 'I am glad I gave satisfaction.'

She looked at him then and this time there was more than a hint of tears in the brown eyes. 'You know you did. Stop trying to sound like a…a…as if I was paying you.'

'You do not have much good fortune with

your lovers, do you?' He had not meant to mention Piers, ever again, but that last accusation splintered his resolve. 'How did you feel about Piers when he left you? Went back to do his duty?'

'Bereft,' she said and stumbled as she got to her feet. Avery put out a hand to steady her and she hit it away with a swiftness that betrayed the depths of her turmoil. 'In the moment when I read his note I felt betrayed, alone and frightened. You would have been proud of what you had achieved, sending him back to his honourable death and making me hate him, if only for a second.'

Laura turned and walked away from him, away from the house, into one of the winding walks through the shrubbery.

His hand hurt like the devil. She had slashed out with the edge of hers and caught him on the side of the palm. He stood rubbing it while he watched the laurel branches sway and then settle in her wake. *Innocent girl, barely eighteen. Bereft, alone, frightened.* Pregnant. The wave of guilt swept through him, leaving the taste of bile in his mouth as it had so often in the months after Piers's death. *What had I done? Was I wrong? Should I have listened, helped?*

Too late now and, however hurt and frightened she had been, surely no woman who was truly in love could have written those cruel words to a lover facing battle?

Avery turned from the shrubbery and went towards the house. He needed a glass of brandy and straightforward male company with its certainties and its emotional directness.

'You may kiss the bride.'

The church swam into focus as Avery lifted the veil and folded it back over the wreath of myrtle and orange blossom that crowned her hair. Laura closed her eyes as he bent and touched his mouth to hers and a sigh went round the sophisticated, fashionable congregation. An excellent marriage of equal status and a great deal of land and money. How very satisfactory.

She clung to the cynical thought as Avery's lips moved over hers, warm and possessive. Her hands were on his lapels and she had no recollection of placing them there, but it was a good gesture, one that confirmed her affection and her submission to him in front of witnesses.

They went arm in arm to the vestry and she signed her new name carefully, as she had rehearsed. Laura Caroline Emilia Jordan Falconer, Countess of Wykeham. Beside her, Avery made a sound, quickly bitten back, presumably as he realised she had not lied about her name at least, those days in Hertfordshire.

Then they were in the chancel again, surrounded by faces in the pews and peering down from the wide, dark-panelled gallery. Her hand felt heavy with the broad gold band as she lifted her skirts to negotiate the steps to the nave and the great organ over the west door thundered into life, making her jump. All her senses seemed to be alert, raw. But not her feelings—those were numb.

On the steps she smiled and threw her flowers and waved as she sat in the open carriage and was driven away into New Bond Street and no one seemed to notice it was all an act.

'You look beautiful, Lady Wykeham.' Avery resumed his tall hat and sat back beside her.

'Thank you.' He looked exceedingly handsome, barbered and groomed to perfection, dressed with elegant formality, his patrician features suited to the grave solemnity he had projected all through the service. 'Alice behaved very well.'

'She was feeling so grown up in her miniature version of your gown that I think she was afraid to move.' Avery's face relaxed as he smiled. 'Do you mind not having a proper honeymoon?'

For a moment she could not follow his train of thought. 'Oh, you mean taking her with us tomorrow when we go to Westerwood? No, of course not.' Conscious of the groom clinging on behind she lowered her voice. 'After all, it is hardly as if we would wish to be alone together, is it?'

Avery was silent, occupied for several minutes with pulling off his gloves and smoothing them flat over his knee. 'We did not get off to a very good beginning with our relationship,' he said eventually, equally low-voiced.

Was this a flag of truce? Or a trick? 'No,' Laura agreed. 'We did not. However, I keep my word. You may be certain that I will do my utmost to be a good wife and you know I will do everything in my power for Alice.' He sighed, just on the edge of her hearing. 'What more do you want?' she demanded sharply, then caught herself before the groom could hear. Avery did not answer.

The wedding breakfast went exceptionally well. Laura knew everyone and, with the confidence of maturity, knew how to make a social event a success, even when her brain seemed numb and the house, her new London home, was unfamiliar. The guests retired to the vast drawing room after the meal, champagne continued to flow, the noise level soared. It was, people were saying on all sides, the wedding of the Season. And, of course, it was spiced by the speculation about how Avery Falconer would tame Scandal's Virgin.

At six o'clock Laura went searching for Alice and found her curled up asleep on a sofa.

'I'll carry her up,' Avery said behind her.

'But—'

'Blackie will put her to bed, you can look in later. We cannot both disappear together.' His expression became sardonic. 'Not this early, anyway.'

Laura watched him lift the child in his arms and remembered the three occasions when he had carried her in his arms, the feel of his body and the strength of his hold. She bent to kiss Alice's cheek and felt an answering pressure on the top of her head as if he had laid his cheek there for a moment, or pressed his lips to her hair in a kiss. Her heart fluttered, then she realised he must be acting for their guests.

The smile was perfect on her lips when she straightened and she did not look back as she swept back into the centre of the room. She could act, too, be the loving stepmama who was still less to the child than Alice's papa was. Someone made an observation and Laura nodded in agreement. 'Indeed, Mrs Nicholson. Such a delightful child, so pretty and affectionate. So easy to love.'

Three hours later Laura sat bolt upright in the big bed with its froth of lace and net hangings and tried to decide what to do. Avery would be coming in soon, she had no doubt. He would insist on his marital rights until she was with child, of that she was certain.

But she was equally certain he would not force her. She could say *no,* but that would be to break her word to be a good wife, and besides, she wanted him to make love to her.

A somewhat humiliating realisation, that. But she loved him and she desired him and she knew he made love with toe-curling skill: she would have to be perverse indeed to recoil from him because he did not love her.

She could do what ladies were supposed to do, or, at least, what some young ladies were told was proper: lie still and allow one's husband to do what he wanted. Laura suspected that Avery, if he did not laugh himself sick at the sight of her apeing a virtuous lady, would treat that response as the equivalent of a refusal.

A draught of air amidst the draperies was the only clue that the door leading from hers into Avery's bedchamber had opened. Laura stiffened, unprepared and with no plan at all for what would happen next.

Her husband appeared beside the bed clad in a vivid red-and-green banyan, a tight smile and, apparently, not a lot else. Laura swallowed.

'Shall I put out the candles?' He must have noticed the convulsive movement of her throat.

It was a tiny kindness, but it made up her mind. 'No, thank you. I want to see you.'

Avery lifted one eyebrow, untied the sash, dropped it to the floor, shrugged out of the heavy silk and stood regarding her quizzically. Laura stared back, then let her gaze slide slowly down over the sculpted muscles of his chest, the flat belly, the dark hair, to the inescapable evidence that whatever else her new husband was feeling it was not rampant sexual desire for his wife.

Laura closed her mouth and studied her interlaced fingers on top of the satin coverlet.

'I have discovered,' Avery said drily, 'that it is one thing making statements in the heat of anger and another altogether to carry them out.' He tugged on the banyan again and sat on the end of the bed, his back against one of the carved posts. 'It occurred to me that you would be lying there expecting me to march in and… Hell, I can't find a word that isn't downright crude or—'

'You certainly do not want to say, *make love,*' Laura agreed.

His mouth tightened at the sarcasm. '—*have you,* whether you want it or not. You wouldn't be aroused, I would hurt you.'

'Many, perhaps most, men would, without a second thought.'

'I am not most men.'

No, my love, you are not and that is why I love you, despite everything. 'I cannot think of an unexceptional euphemism either. Would it help if I said I would like to have sex with you?'

'You would?' The unfastened banyan fell open as he shifted to look directly at her. He was not so very far from arousal after all, or perhaps her frankness was stimulating.

'I think you would have noticed if you repelled me. Despite everything, I enjoyed lying with you before. You must have noticed *that*.' Laura pulled the ribbon tie of her negligée open. Catlike Avery watched the moving silk. 'Women do enjoy sex, you know. They don't have to fool themselves by imagining they are in love, or have to be wanton and abandoned.'

It was half the truth. She wanted him, badly, yet just as badly did not want the suspicion and hostility that lay between them like a hedge of thorns. She needed tenderness and affection and the slow slide of those long brown fingers across her flesh, the gentle torture of his mouth on her body.

'Then let us, as you say, *lie together* and whatever follows from that.' Avery flipped back the covers and shifted up the bed to prop himself on one elbow next to her. She could not imagine speaking so frankly with any other man under such circumstances. Somehow that very ease made her sadder. They could have so much, share so much if only they did not have this history between them.

Bold, because she knew what she wanted and needed him to want it, too, Laura pushed the heavy silk from his shoulders and ran her fingers into his hair, pulling him down to kiss her. Avery obliged, his fingers deft in the ties of her negligée, the urgency in contrast to the slow, almost lazy sweep of his tongue between her lips.

Avery disposed of her nightgown with an efficiency that made her smile against his mouth. One warm hand moved down her body, slid between her thighs. She was ready for him, embarrassingly so if she had a particle of shame left in her. Laura pressed against the questing fingers, arched into his palm to find it gone. He shifted his weight over her, nudged her thighs apart with his knee and entered her in one hard stroke.

Surprised, yet excited, Laura curled her legs around his hips and looked up into his face. Avery's eyes were closed, his face stark, the tendons of his throat taut. He thrust steadily without kissing her, his hands still on the pillow beside her head. Laura struggled to meet his rhythm, to pace her own pleasure. Then he stilled, groaned deep in his throat and thrust hard, hanging over her, his face contorted into a mask of effort. She felt the heat of his release deep inside her, braced herself for his body as he relaxed onto her and held him to her when he subsided, crushing her breasts against his chest.

Her body was throbbing and tingling with unsatisfied desire, but part of her was flattered and titillated by his urgency. She rubbed her cheek against his hair as he lay, his face buried in her shoulder.

Then, taking her by surprise, he rolled off her body, rose from the bed and pulled on his robe. 'Thank you,' Avery said politely, as though she had poured a cup of tea or hemmed a handkerchief for him. 'Goodnight, Laura.'

Chapter Eighteen

The pattern continued for four days and four nights. Avery was unfailingly polite, mildly affectionate to her in front of Alice and the servants and consulted amicably about what changes she might wish to make to the house. In the evening he listened intently to Alice's news, courteously to Laura's description of how she had spent her day and made unexceptional small talk over the dinner table.

At night he came to her bed, ensured she was adequately prepared for him, which, to her humiliation, was easy enough, and removed himself to his own chamber as soon as he had obtained his own release. Laura was furious and frustrated and had no idea what, short of chaining him to the bed, she could do about it. Easy though she had found it to speak frankly to Avery about desire, she found her tongue stuck to the roof of her mouth when she tried to ask him to stay and actually make love to her.

'You're as cross as crabs,' Mab observed on the fifth morning when Laura managed to upset her trinket bowl on the dressing table, sending ear bobs and silver chains flying. She knelt on the floor, muttering curses under her breath, and tried to gather them up while her maid-servant nagged. 'What's the matter with you? You've got little Alice, you've got a lovely home and a fine husband who isn't lacking in his attentions to you...'

Laura sat up abruptly and banged her head on the underside of the table. 'Ow!' She crawled out and glared at Mab. 'I will thank you not to refer to private matters of that sort. Nothing is wrong.'

'Then sit down and let me do your hair.' Mab was, as usual, unsquashable. She swept the brush through Laura's hair, provoking a gasp of pain as the bristles found a tangle. 'There, of course! I know what's wrong, its that time of the month. I lost count, what with the excitement over the wedding and all. That's why you're so down in the mouth, just like normal.'

'So it is.' Laura rubbed her back, which now

she thought about it, was aching. She did some rapid calculations. 'Tomorrow.' Now she had the knowledge that she was not pregnant to add to her usual monthly misery. She would be fine by the day after, once she had got through a day of being clumsy, achy and prone to tears and another day of cramps. Tonight, she thought, with the feeling of someone glimpsing a small patch of silver lining in a very dark cloud, she could tell Avery to keep to his own bedchamber for a few nights. He'd be hoping he had got her with child, she was sure, gloomily pleased to be spreading the misery.

By the time she went downstairs she had talked herself into a more positive frame of mind, although she was grateful that Alice was going to be spending the day with her friends, the granddaughters of Mrs Gordon. Avery had ridden out early to inspect some distant woodland with a view to selling some of the timber, Pritchett informed her.

She had been reluctant to turn off any of her old staff so Avery had agreed to Pritchett taking over at Westerwood while his own butler remained in control of the town house and the Westerwood butler, who had been feeling his rheumatics, moved to the easier duties at the Leicestershire hunting lodge.

Pritchett refilled her coffee cup. 'Which room do you wish to look at today, my lady?'

The rooms at Westerwood Manor were all in excellent condition, but some seemed dated, others were not very comfortable. Laura had been working round them, making notes and listing necessary work. It made a neutral topic of conversation with Avery and it was helping her learn his tastes before they moved to his main country house, Wykeham Hall. It was best for Alice, they had agreed, for her to become used to the changes to her family in a house she was familiar with.

'This room, I think… No, the Blue Sitting Room.' Avery was away, that was the safest time to investigate the room where Piers's portrait hung.

'Very well, my lady. I will send Jackson and one of the maids along to assist you.'

'No need for that, thank you, Pritchett. I do not expect to have to change anything around. I just want to familiarise myself with that room.'

It took an hour of procrastination before Laura finally shut the door behind her and went to sit at the writing table that faced the fireplace and Piers's portrait. This was the table where Avery had kissed her with such passion, the place where she had learned the truth about Piers's return to Spain and his death.

Laura folded her hands on the blotter and made herself look steadily at the picture until she felt her calm return. He looked so young, so unformed in that flamboyant red jacket. Had he really loved her or was it simply a boy's first calf love? If she had refused to make love with him, would they have drifted apart naturally?

Yes, she thought, sadly. *Yes, what we had was sweet and strangely innocent. Or perhaps naive is the better word. If he had lived, we would have married because of the baby and by now we would have outgrown each other and yet be tied together for life.*

She got up and went to lift down the heavy cavalry sabre from its stand on the mantelshelf. It was not even scratched, Piers had owned it for such a short time. A bullet in the chest had killed him before he was able to raise his sword in anger at the enemy. Laura touched the tassel that hung from the finger guard, then set the weapon back in place.

It felt as though she had said goodbye, finally. Laura went back to her seat at the table and straightened the blotter, the paper knife and the inkwell automatically, unable somehow to leave the room yet. Presumably there should be writing paper and sealing wax in the drawers, she had better check that was all in order.

She opened the shallow right-hand drawer and found expensive paper, a knife for trimming pens, a taper and a coil of wax. All as it should be. She pulled at the left-hand drawer and it stuck. When she bent down to check she realised it was locked, although the wood of the drawer had shrunk so that the tongue of the lock was visible. Impulsively she picked up the paper knife and pushed it into the gap. The flimsy lock popped open and the drawer slid out.

It was empty except for a tattered, much folded, piece of paper. Curious, Laura picked it up and flattened it out on the blotter. It was not even a full sheet of writing paper, just a torn quarter of a page, ragged at the edges, covered in a brown stain with only a few words visible.

Then she realised she was looking at her own handwriting and that this must be part of that desperate letter she had written to Piers when he had left for Spain and she had realised she was carrying Alice.

These brown stains must be blood, Piers's blood. She snatched her hand back, then, ashamed at her squeamishness, traced the few faintly legible words with her fingertip, seeing again the full message she had tried to send. Her fear, but her trust in him despite his apparent desertion. Her anxiety and her desperate need for reassurance.

She had no idea how long she sat there or when the realisation came to her that he must have kept her letter beneath his uniform against his heart, and that was why it was rent and bloody, just as his body had been. He had died knowing she loved him, knowing he was to be a father. She hoped he had been happy at the news, even if, like her, he would have been apprehensive.

Something dripped onto her hand and she realised she was weeping, the tears sliding silently down her cheeks. Laura found her handkerchief and mopped her eyes.

'How very touching.'

She started and the paper fluttered to the desk, as brown and tattered as a dead leaf. Avery ducked under the raised window and stepped down into the room, just as she had all those weeks ago when she had found him here.

'This is the last letter I wrote to Piers.' Why was Avery's face so set and hard? Because she had opened the locked drawer? She answered the unspoken accusation. 'I know the drawer was locked. I did not intend to pry, it must have been instinct.'

Avery shrugged. 'I wonder you care to touch it.'

'Because of the bloodstains? If he was wounded and in my arms I would not care about the blood.' She looked down at the scrap again, away from her husband's hard, inexplicably accusing, eyes. 'Piers must have carried it against his heart.'

'A strange thing to do, considering what you wrote.'

'I do not understand.'

Why did she sound so confused—surely she recalled what she had written in that last letter? Avery reached across and picked up the fragment and stared at it again. 'It was how I found you, and Alice,' he said absently as his mind grappled with the puzzle. 'Your name is not common.' It was like trying to read the occasional coded message that had come his way when abroad, the sort where individual words and the spaces between them had to be shuffled and...

The spaces between. God, had he been so blinded by his own guilt and grief, the need to blame someone? 'Read me what you wrote.' He thrust the paper at Laura.

She stared at him as if he was drunk, but she was prepared to humour him, so took it and laid it in front of her. One rounded nail traced the first line as she read, hesitating out of forgetfulness or emotion, he was not sure which.

'I feel such a coward. It seems...like a betrayal of everything I told you I could be as a soldier's wife. I hate to...worry you, but I am pregnant with our child. Please don't blame yourself, we were both at fault, but write, I beg you, tell me what to do... Please look after yourself, with all my love, Laura. There was only the one page. The beginning of the letter was me thanking him for his note and hoping he was safe.' Her voice trailed away.

'You really did love him, didn't you?' He was trying so hard to stop his voice shaking that it came out harder and more abrupt than he meant. What had he done? Instinct should have told him to look deeper. To have trusted this woman. Prejudice, guilt and fear. What a toxic mix.

'Yes, of course. I told you how I felt about him, I would never have made love with him if I had not.' Laura's hands clenched into fists. 'I am sorry, but the fact that I loved Piers does not mean I cannot be a faithful wife to you.'

'That is not why I asked.' *Hell, this was difficult.* 'I have a confession to make.' He made himself meet her startled gaze. 'When I found that letter all I could read were isolated words, negative, angry words. Together they sounded like a diatribe from a woman who felt bitter and betrayed, who was writing to accuse Piers of abandoning her. I thought those were the last words he received from England, that he had gone to his death not with a message of love over his heart, but one of furious rejection.'

Laura gasped and stared down at the letter. '*Coward, hate, blame.* But…you condemned me on those isolated words alone? How could you!'

He almost said it aloud, spoke of the grief and the guilt, the awful guilt, but how could he excuse himself when he had done Laura such an injustice? It would sound as though he was trying to justify the unjustifiable. 'I am sorry. I was wrong and I was prejudiced.' *I love you.*

How am I ever going to be able to say those words to you now? How will you ever accept them from me?

'I should have been open with you from the start. Told you what I thought, asked you to explain.' He was unused to being in the wrong so completely. *The great diplomat, the man who can read faces, delve into minds. Look at you now.* 'I should have been totally open and honest.'

'Open and honest,' Laura echoed, almost to herself. When she stood she seemed paler than normal, frailer somehow, as though she was in pain. 'I cannot speak of this any more now. It is too… Excuse me.'

Avery was still standing on the same spot when little Annie, the downstairs maid, came in, her hands full of feather dusters and polishing cloths.

'Oh! I'm sorry, my lord. I thought the room was empty when I saw her ladyship come out. I'll come back later.' She bobbed a curtsy.

'No, I am just leaving.' Avery folded the bloodstained letter into a piece of fresh paper and took it with him. He would lock it in the desk in his bedchamber where there was no risk of Laura finding it and being upset all over again.

Who am I trying to deceive? I was the one who upset her, not the letter. She was weeping, yes, but that was simply normal grief. The pain came later when she realised what I had thought, how little I valued her. I thought all I was risking with this marriage was my place in Alice's heart. He had glimpsed something more than he had ever hoped for. A wife he loved and who might love him, a family built on truth and trust and not lies and secrets. And he had thrown it away.

Laura did not appear at luncheon, although it was not unusual for them to miss each other for that informal meal. Perhaps she had gone to collect Alice early so she could enjoy the company of someone who trusted her, he thought, spearing a slice of ham with unnecessary force. But how could he tell what she thought or what she wanted? He was coming to realise he did not understand her at all and that she might never trust him enough to let him try.

Laura had been still pale and quiet during dinner. She had left him to his port and was sitting with a book open on her lap when Avery joined her in the drawing room. After ten minutes of stilted conversation she announced she was going to her room, said goodnight and left him standing on the hearthrug with no idea of how to reach her.

After half an hour spent brooding Avery came to the conclusion that they had only two things in common. Alice could not be involved in this, but perhaps they could talk honestly in bed. He felt a glimmering of optimism as he shed his clothes and donned his banyan.

Laura was sitting up in bed, pale against the white pillows. When she heard him she opened her eyes and said, quite simply, 'No.' Then she closed them again and lay back.

Avery found himself out on the landing with no very clear memory of how he had got there, only the knowledge that he had never been with an unwilling woman in his life and he was not going to start now with his wife. Even persuasion was unacceptable.

He thought about the library and its decanters, only to be jolted out of his inertia by a snort right behind him. When he turned Laura's woman Mab stood there regarding him with disapproval over an armful of clean linens.

'Yes?' he enquired in the tone that normally had staff scuttling for cover.

'Have you been bothering my lady?' Before he could tear her off a strip for impertinence she added, 'You men! And now of all times.'

'What do you mean?' Was Laura sick? 'Come in here.' He steered her into his bedchamber where Laura would not be able to hear them.

'I mean, she'll be feeling poorly for a couple of days, bless her. Always has taken her badly. And it's no good you glowering at me. You might be upset she's not going to give you your dratted heir this time, but I expect she's not too pleased either.'

'Poorly? Heir?' Light dawned. 'You mean it is that time of the month?' No wonder the poor woman had looked so drained. He could not have found a worse time to distress her if he had tried for a year.

'Yes,' Mab said baldly. Her face softened a trifle. 'I'm sorry if I spoke out of order, my lord, but I worry about her. She might seem as if she's hard sometimes, but she's not. Not as sophisticated as her reputation makes out and not as strong either.'

'I cannot fault you for caring for your mistress.' He should not be gossiping with servants, let alone taking one into his confidence, but he had to ask. 'You've known her for years. She loved my cousin, didn't she?'

'Aye,' Mab agreed. She shifted the laundry onto her hip and scratched her ear as if deep in thought. 'Doubt it would have lasted though. Calf love.' She eyed him up and down, a purely feminine appraisal that brought the colour to his cheeks. 'He wasn't the man you are, if that's what's worrying you.'

'It is not. Thank you, Mab.' He opened the door for her. 'Is there anything I can do for her?'

'Stay in your own bed for a few nights.' He heard the wretched woman laugh softly as she padded off down the corridor.

Avery abandoned thoughts of the brandy, went to bed and lay awake, brooding on the enigma that was his wife. He had misjudged her badly over Piers, but why had she rejected the baby? Perhaps her grief for Piers was the cause. Or she simply could not face the scandal and then, if she feared she was never going to marry and have children, a belated maternal instinct had driven her to seek out her daughter. But if scandal worried her, why had she returned to society and behaved in a manner that was certain to brand her as fast, to put it mildly?

But he could hardly demand an explanation now, not when he had so obviously destroyed whatever shreds of trust she had in him. He shifted uncomfortably, going back in his head over her shock and hurt that he had so misread her letter. It seemed that she was right not to trust him and yet he dare not risk trusting her utterly either, not when he loved her like this. It felt like baring his throat to a sword.

Alice had been his only vulnerability, his only weak spot. In everything else his life was his to command and he could rely on his determination, his intellect, his ambition, to achieve what he wanted. He was not used to failure. Somehow he had to turn this around for all their futures.

Chapter Nineteen

Laura took breakfast in bed the next morning. It was easier to yield to Mab's bullying than face Avery over bacon and eggs that would simply make her queasy. She was uncomfortably aware that he was probably very angry with her. No man would take a monosyllabic refusal with equanimity, she was certain. She should have explained, however embarrassing it was and however hurt she was by his interpretation of her letter to Piers.

And that did hurt, deeply. No wonder Avery had thought so little of her if he could believe she was fickle enough to send a letter full of accusations and recrimination to a man facing danger and death. He was a hypocrite, too, she told herself, stoking her anger. He had virtually forced Piers to go back to Spain when, who knows, if he had sold out to marry her and be a father to their child, he would be alive now.

What if, what if... No, it was a futile game to play. Piers might have walked out of his house and been run over by a cart, or have been struck down by typhoid. Every second of every day everyone made choices that could result in life or death. If Avery felt guilty, then that was his burden to carry and she had to learn to forgive him.

It was curiously difficult to do, even when she loved him. Perhaps that was the penalty of becoming older, one saw the shades of grey in everything, in everyone.

'Mama?' Alice peeped around the door. 'Blackie and Mab say you are poorly and I mustn't come and bounce on the bed.'

'But you may come in and sit beside me.' Laura patted the bed. 'I will be better soon, it is just a tummy ache.'

'Papa has written you a letter. He said I could bring it.' Beaming with importance, she handed over the note, folded but unsealed.

Laura opened it and read: *I have accepted an offer on the timber in the far woods and I must go to St Albans to my lawyers to finalise the sale and for other business. I may also need to go to Buckingham, but I will be back in four, or at the most seven, days.* There was no salutation, no signature beyond his initials.

'Papa has gone away for a few days on business,' Laura said and managed a big smile. 'So the ladies of the house are in charge. What mischief shall we get up to while Papa is away?'

That did make Alice bounce, until Mab wagged a finger at her. They would have a picnic with nothing but cake, go riding all day, buy a puppy...

Laura let her rattle on and told herself that it was only her present condition that made her feel so miserable. But she knew she wanted Avery back, needed to talk to him, needed to find a way through this suspicion between them.

Alice followed Mab into the dressing room to 'help' her sort out Laura's shoes and Laura smiled at Miss Blackmore, standing quietly in the corner, waiting with her usual patience. 'Do you think we should find Miss Alice a governess, Miss Blackmore? My husband was speaking of it a while ago.'

'That was when he did not know who he would be marrying so soon, if I might be so bold as to put it that way. He hasn't said any more about it to me, my lady.'

'She is still a little young. I could undertake her lessons for a year.'

'That would please Miss Alice, my lady. But might it not be a problem when his lordship wishes to travel with you and not always take Miss Alice? You haven't had your bride trip yet, for one thing.'

That was true. Somehow Laura could not imagine Avery wanting to whisk her away alone on a romantic journey, but he might want her to act as hostess if he was sent on a diplomatic mission and Alice was becoming rather old to take around the capitals of Europe with parents who were distracted by matter of state.

'A governess would give her continuity,' Laura agreed. She stretched and rubbed her back. The cramps were easing, by tomorrow she would feel her usual energetic self. 'Which carriage has Lord Wykeham taken?'

'The small one, my lady.'

'Well, in that case, I think I will take the travelling carriage and we can go up to London tomorrow and set about finding someone. Mab, Alice!' They looked around the door, one head above the other, and made her smile. 'I think we will have a ladies' trip to London, just the four of us, and we will see if we cannot find

Alice a nice governess. What do you think of that, Alice?'

The child came in, her face scrunched up in thought as she considered this hard question. 'Will she be fun?'

'Of course. She will be young and cheerful and she will teach you all kinds of exciting things.'

'And you won't go away, just because I've got her?'

'I will have to go away if Papa is travelling and needs me, but I will always come back, Alice. If we choose a governess now, then you will have plenty of time to get to know her before I go anywhere with Papa. And Blackie will be here, as well.' Alice nodded approval. 'In that case, ladies, this afternoon we will pack for London!'

Avery had intended to stay away a week, time for Laura to recover from her temporary indisposition and from her distress over the letter. Time for him to decide how to deal with a wife he desired, whom he had, undoubtedly, wronged and yet, somehow could not quite bring himself to trust. *She has wronged me,* a mutinous voice reminded him. She had never explained how she could shut Alice out of her life for six years. She had acted a part as Mrs Jordan. She had tried to entrap him into marriage. *And yet I love her.*

Avery gritted his teeth and looked out of the window at the sight of the park rolling past the carriage windows. The sun was just setting and the stands of beech trees cast long, lovely shadows across the grass.

He was in no mood to appreciate natural beauty. Four days he had managed to stay away, not long enough to get his own guilt and resentment under control and not long enough, he was sure, for Laura to be feeling very kindly towards him.

His mood was not helped by Pritchett's expression of surprise as he walked through his own front door. 'My lord!'

'Yes?' Avery raised an eyebrow. 'Why the surprise? I believe I live here.'

'Yes, of course, my lord. It is just that her ladyship—'

Something cold ran a finger down Avery's spine. 'What is wrong with her?' *Was she sick after all? He would forgive her anything. Anything at all—*

Pritchett took a step back. 'Nothing, my lord,

I assure you. It is only that her ladyship and Miss Alice left for London the day before yesterday. I assumed you knew, my lord, and would be joining them.'

'Of course.' *Whatever else was happening, preserve appearances in front of the staff.* One of his mother's favourite rules. Appearances are all, never mind the hell beneath. 'I will be joining them in London. Tomorrow.' *If they are there. Stop it. Trust her. Of course they will be there.*

'I feel confident we can find someone suitable from these five, don't you?' Laura conned the list of young women she had asked for interview the next day.

'I think so, my lady. I particularly liked that one and that one.' Miss Blackmore touched two of the names on the list that Laura held out to her. 'They all have the qualifications you are looking for, and are under thirty and seem to be of a kind and cheerful disposition, but those two gave me the impression of a natural firmness.'

'Which is what they will need to handle Alice,' Laura agreed with a chuckle. 'Miss Blackmore, I hope you do not feel that I am attempting to detach you from Alice. You have been such a major influence on her and she loves you very much. But I am hoping that perhaps there may soon be someone else for you to look after...'

'That is wonderful, my lady. His lordship—'

'No, not yet, Miss Blackmore, but I hope it will not be too long. And I do not want Alice feeling that not only has her little nose been put out of joint by a new baby, but her Blackie has also been taken away from her.'

'Of course, my lady. That seems very sensible and farsighted.'

'Thank you.' The carriage lurched as they rounded the corner into the square. 'Almost home. I wish now I had not told Alice we were seeking a governess for her. When they call tomorrow and meet her I have no idea how she will react to them.'

'Ah, well,' Blackie said with a smile, 'if the worse comes to the worst and she is difficult it will scare away the faint-hearted ones.'

Laura met Blackie's gaze over the top of Alice's head and raised an eyebrow. The nurse nodded the merest fraction. On the other side of the room Miss Pemberton, candidate number five, was deep in discussion with Alice over whether, as Miss Mirabelle was a French doll, Alice ought to learn some French words so she could talk to her. The young woman's references were excellent and all from ladies Laura knew. She was quiet yet cheerful, bright-eyed, intelligent and decisive, and Alice took to her from the start.

'Miss Pemberton.'

The woman looked up. 'Excuse me, Alice.' She came and took the chair next to Laura. 'Lady Wykeham?'

'I would like to offer you the position. Do you need time to consider the offer?'

'No, I would be delighted to accept. Thank you very much, I greatly appreciate your confidence, Lady Wykeham.'

'Excellent. So when would you be able to start?'

The door opened. 'Lady Wykeham, what the blazes are you—?' Avery stopped on the threshold apparently silenced by the sight of his usually elegant drawing room. The table was littered with dolls and their clothes, the Chinese carpet was obscured by a drift of drawing paper, the side table bore evidence to a hearty tea and Alice was bouncing with excitement.

'Papa!' She threw herself into his arms as Blackie and Miss Pemberton got to their feet.

'Good afternoon, my lord,' Laura said with a calm she was far from feeling. 'Alice, please stop squealing, I wish to introduce Miss Pemberton to Papa. My dear, this is Miss Pemberton, who is to be Alice's new governess. Miss Pemberton, my husband, the Earl of Wykeham.'

'Delighted, Miss Pemberton.' He offered his hand, she took it with a calm, well-bred manner that made Laura want to cheer. Apparently cursing earls disturbed Miss Pemberton's composure no more than noisy six-year-olds did.

Avery was wearing his best diplomatic blank face, but she could not worry about that now, nor the butterflies fluttering in her stomach, nor the sharp pang of desire at the sight of him, windblown despite his immaculate riding gear, eyes sparking with tightly controlled temper.

'Do allow me to show you out, Miss Pemberton.' Laura stood and ushered the governess towards the door. 'If you would like to come with your trunks in two days' time?'

'Thank you, Lady Wykeham. My lord.' She dropped the slightest of curtsies. 'Goodbye for now, Alice. Miss Blackmore.'

Laura said goodbye in the hall and left Miss Pemberton to the butler to show out. When she went back into the drawing room Avery was hunkered down, talking to Alice. 'No, I have not brought you a puppy. Are you not glad just to have Papa home?'

'Of course.' She looked up winsomely from under her lashes. 'But I'd have been even gladderer if you'd brought a puppy with you.'

'You are a minx, young Alice. Don't try those tricks on me, I've had older ladies than you flutter their eyelashes at me and none of them has received a puppy as a result, let me tell you. Now off you go with Blackie, I must talk to Mama.'

He waited, smiling and apparently relaxed until the door had closed and the sound of Alice's excited chatter had faded. When he turned the smile had vanished. 'What the devil is going on, Laura? What are you doing gadding off to London without so much as a by your leave?'

'I have come to our house with my maid, our daughter and her nurse, using our carriage and leaving our staff fully informed of our whereabouts. I have engaged a suitable governess for our daughter as we have discussed in the past. I am not certain which part of that programme counts as *gadding,* but I am certain you will enlighten me.' Her knees were knocking and the ginger snaps she had eaten with her tea were lying heavy in her stomach, but at least she managed to sound both composed and polite.

'You did not consult me.'

'Neither did you, when you took off for a week with only the courtesy of a scribbled note.'

'Damn it, Laura, I was taking myself off while you were…indisposed. Mab told me.'

She raised her eyebrows at his language, but did not protest at it. 'I see. So having discovered that you were unlikely to get any sex for a few days you could think of nothing else to keep you at home.'

'There is no need to be so crude about it,' Avery snapped.

'Forgive me.' Laura got to her feet in a swirl of sea-green muslin. 'I was pleased to note that Miss Pemberton is able to withstand your violent language without flinching. She will obviously need to.'

'And to the devil with Miss Pemberton!'

'Miss Pemberton is not going to the devil, she is coming here. Alice, Miss Blackmore and I all agree she will be an excellent governess.' She pulled the bell cord. 'I would like some more tea. Will you join me and tell me about your business and I will tell you about Miss Pemberton and how Miss Blackmore and I decided upon her?'

'And Alice?' He sat, crossed one booted leg over the other and regarded her steadily. All the anger was under control. She wondered if she would ever penetrate that composure more than a fraction.

'Alice was very helpful in sorting out the final five candidates, you may be sure.' The door opened to reveal the footman. 'More tea, please, and another cup for Lord Wykeham.' *How very wifely I sound. How very hollow I feel.*

Miss Pemberton and her trunks arrived two days later. With Blackie's help she turned part of the nursery into a schoolroom and then Blackie went on a long-overdue holiday to her family in Somerset. She and Laura had discussed it at some length and concluded that not only did the nurse need the rest, but it would be best for Alice who would not be able to play Miss Pemberton off against Blackie, who warned Laura that she was quite bright enough to do so.

Laura saw no reason to inform Avery of Blackie's holiday. It was, she concluded, well within her remit as mistress of the household and he did not seem to notice her absence which was far less noticeable in town than in the country house.

The household settled down to a few more weeks in London as Alice adjusted to a new routine. It was best to remain there, Laura was certain. Alice was less familiar with the town house, the opportunities for distraction were fewer and it gave Miss Pemberton time to exert her gentle but firm authority.

Whatever else she was doing Laura made certain she was at home for nursery tea and games and Avery, even if he could not be at home then, made a point of being there for a bedtime story.

He was perfectly amiable, drove Laura about, took her to the theatre, walked in the parks, hosted a small informal dinner party. He took an intelligent interest in Alice's lesson plan and approved the light touch with much play amidst the learning.

What her husband was not, Laura thought resentfully on the fifth evening after he came to London, was in her bed. She dragged the brush through her hair, counting under her breath, but it was not enough to distract her from the fact that he had not come to her room once. It was, she supposed, retaliation for her blunt accusation about why he had left Westerwood so abruptly.

She dropped the brush onto the dressing table, tossed her hair back over her shoulders and snuffed all but the bedside candles. A new novel sat on the pillow where her husband's head should be lying. She frowned at it and then felt a sudden resolve that however sensational it might prove to be, it was not how she was going to spend another night.

The connecting door was firmly closed, but not locked. She had tried it an hour ago, eased the handle down while she laid her ear to the panel and listened. Avery had been speaking to Darke, a desultory conversation. Then she heard the valet say *Goodnight*. It was not even as though Avery had an evening engagement.

Laura looked from the pristine white bed to the door and back again. No, she was not going to climb between the covers and lie there patiently waiting on his lordship's pleasure. She smiled ruefully. That was what she had been waiting for all the nights of their marriage. His pleasure, not hers.

As she walked to the door and pressed down the handle she asked herself what was the worst he could do. Order her back to her bed? Without knocking, she opened the door and went in.

Chapter Twenty

A very was not in bed. He lounged in the chair reading, his bare feet propped up on the fender, a leather-bound book in his hands.

'Laura?' He dropped the book to the floor and stood up. 'Is something wrong?'

'It occurred to me that I had spent rather too much of my marriage lying in my bed waiting on my husband's pleasure. Literally, *his* pleasure. Certainly not mine.'

'Laura!' He sounded so shocked she almost smiled.

'I do not think I need to mince my words with a man who uses his wife for his carnal needs without any consideration for hers,' she retorted.

'The devil you say!' Avery strode across the room and confronted her. Laura took a step back and found her shoulders were against the door. 'Are you saying that I take you without your consent?'

'No, you pig-headed man,' Laura snapped. 'I am saying you leave me unsatisfied in order to punish me for trapping you into marriage. When you condescend to come to my bed at all, that is. There, is that plain enough for you?'

'You are saying that you want me even after I said those things about coming to you only to get an heir? Even after the way I leapt to assumptions over that letter to Piers?'

Suddenly she saw a vulnerability that she had never glimpsed before. Perhaps because she had never looked, perhaps because all she had been filled with had been her own needs—her need for Alice, her need to somehow survive loving this man who thought so little of her.

'Yes, I am saying that. We have always known it, you and I, haven't we? That there was an attraction, despite everything.' She reached up and touched his face, trying to convey a tenderness that she dared not put into words. 'I am a grown woman, Avery. A married one.' Laura looked deep into the troubled green eyes. There it was again. Avery needed something and perhaps, just perhaps, she might be it. 'You want me, too.' She did not dare risk saying *need*.

He did not answer and for a despairing moment she thought he would turn from her. Then his mouth came down over hers in a kiss that was hard and unapologetic and demanding. She fisted her hands into his hair and kissed back with equal force. There was the metallic taste of blood in her mouth, his, hers, she did not know, or care. She would probably have felt no pain if a bullet had hit her.

Avery put his hands on her waist and lifted her up, heedless of her hold on his hair, his mouth still fastened on hers. Pushed back against the door, all she could do was wrap her legs around his waist as her nightgown rode up and she felt silk, skin, coarse hair and blessedly hot, hard, fierce heat against the soft skin of her inner thighs.

He lifted her higher, freed her mouth, then with relentless control, let her slide down, down until their foreheads rested together and he filled her. They clung to each other, joined tighter and deeper than they had ever been before, the only sound their shuddering breaths.

Then he began to move. They were so locked, the position so strained, that he could make only the shortest withdrawals and thrusts, but the very constriction and restraint inflamed her beyond bearing. Laura found Avery's mouth and pressed her own to it open, her tongue searching and twisting against his, her breasts crushed against his chest, each movement fretting the hard, aching tips of her nipples against the lawn of her nightgown.

He growled deep in his chest and lifted her, holding her higher so he could thrust harder, making the door rattle at her back, merciless until everything knotted, broke, shattered and she screamed against his mouth, convulsing around him, until she felt him shudder and collapse against her, the spasms of his release sending her over into a second crashing climax.

He must still be supporting her, she realised hazily, otherwise she would have poured down the wall, boneless and limp. Avery was so still she might have thought him unconscious, the thud of his heart against her breast and the heat of his breath on her bared shoulder the only indications that he lived.

After a long moment he lifted her, shifted her in his arms and carried her to the bed. He laid her down and then simply collapsed on the covers beside her, limbs sprawled, eyes closed. Laura found strength from somewhere to roll over and push back the sides of his robe. The belt had been lost somewhere. She folded her arms on his chest and studied his face. His hair was dishevelled and there was a smear of blood on his lip. She wondered if he was asleep or simply as shattered by the experience as she felt.

Cautiously she sat up and dragged her nightgown over her head. It was torn and crumpled and she tossed it to the floor and went back to contemplating her husband. The dark lashes lifted and he regarded her steadily. 'Did I hurt you?'

'I don't think so. I did not notice if you did. Did I hurt you?'

'I have no idea.' His lips twitched into a fleeting smile. 'I had other sensations to deal with.'

'Mmm.' She curled up against his chest, a satisfyingly broad and strong pillow.

Avery tugged until he could flip covers over both of them. 'I regret that I may need to lie here awhile before I can repeat any part of that performance.'

'I will contain my impatience,' Laura murmured and heard his chuckle. 'Part of me wants to know where you learned to make love so skilfully, part of me does not want to hear the answer.'

'What happened just now was not skilful.'

'It was thrilling beyond words.' She wriggled so she could trace kisses across the flat pectoral muscles and feel his skin quiver at the touch. 'And the first time...'

'You mean that the way you responded to me that first night together, that was genuine? At the time I believed it was, hoped it was, but then when I knew why you were there, I did not know.'

Laura sat up abruptly. 'How good an actress do you think me, Avery?' *And how cynical? But he said* hoped. *Does he care?*

'I do not know.' He sat up against the pillows, turned so he could look her in the face. 'Your—'

'My reputation?' Her heart sank. So that was it, not the uncertainty of a man who cared, but the doubts of a man who thought he was dealing with an experienced lover. 'I was a virgin when I first lay with Piers. Thinking back, I expect he was, too. We made love six times. I told you I have been with no one else, Avery, whatever the gossip says. They called me *Scandal's Virgin,* did they not? That was the truth. I flirted, I kissed, I permitted liberties that I should not have, but that was all.' Part of her rebelled against justifying herself, part of her desperately needed him to understand.

'Why?' he asked. 'Why risk your reputation like that?'

'Frankly?' She shrugged, embarrassed by telling someone she cared about what had motivated her. 'I was angry. Angry with men, angry with society. Angry with myself. Piers had taught me to love, but then he left me. I know it was not his fault, that my anger was not rational, I understand that.

'I wanted a lover, but there was no one I could bear to be with and besides, I dared not risk falling pregnant again. Society expected me to return to the Marriage Mart after my *illness,* but how could I counterfeit an innocent little virgin? Besides, if I married, the man would have to be very naive indeed not to notice I had carried a child.'

'If he wished to marry you, you could have told him first.' Avery's thumb stroked the sensitive skin of her inner wrist. She doubted he realised he was doing it, he seemed so absorbed in her story.

'And have him break it off? Risk the truth getting out? No man would marry me knowing that.'

'I did.'

'I trapped you,' she flung back.

'Perhaps,' he said, puzzling her with the small, almost secret smile that touched his lips. 'You certainly secured the two things you wanted: your daughter and a man in your bed.'

'A man in my bed is a matter of no importance beside my daughter. I would have become a nun if I thought that would make Alice happy and secure,' she protested.

'That would be a waste,' Avery said. Had she wounded him, asserting that a man—he—was of no importance? 'It took you a long time to seek her out.'

There was a question in the statement, one she could not bring herself to answer. How could she tell him her parents, whom she had loved and trusted, had plotted and lied, had planned to take her child and break her heart, all in the name of respectability? She loved them still, but she could not forgive them, or bring herself to speak of that betrayal, the way they must have put respectability and appearances beyond care for their own grandchild and before her own wishes.

'The time was right,' she said abruptly. 'Avery, make love to me again.'

It seemed he was rested enough. There was no opportunity then, nor until they fell asleep finally and deeply at dawn, for questions, truths or lies.

Avery could not remember ever feeling so physically satisfied before. His muscles felt as though they had been massaged, his whole body was relaxed and yet sensitive, tingling with remembered orgasmic pleasure, the anticipation of more to come a constant awareness.

And yet, as another week passed in apparent harmony and the nights in mutual pleasure, he could not settle, could not be easy in his mind. He knew what was wrong, or, at least he could see the shape of the problem, looming like a nightmare beast in the corner of his vision. Lack of trust. Laura had lied to him and, he was certain, lied to him still. There was something she was hiding, something she was not telling him. He no longer believed that she feigned delight at his lovemaking, but he had been deceived by her too often to yield to the emotions that he feared would make him blind to more lies, more deceptions.

He loved Laura and if she ever discovered that weakness she had the intelligence and the ruthlessness to exploit it unmercifully. His own mother had been quite conscienceless in manipulating his father, who could never bring himself to believe the woman he loved was the wanton his friends tried to warn him about. She had smiled and charmed and, occasionally, confessed to a fault with tears and ingenious excuses. The poor devil had believed her until he was confronted by undeniable proof.

Avery had never believed the story of how the shotgun had gone off accidentally when his father was climbing a stile. He had gone to his Aunt Alice and she had simply accepted him into the family, treated him as an elder brother to Piers. His mother had shrugged, no doubt, and gone her own self-obsessed way. The accident that left her with a broken neck at the foot of her latest lover's grand staircase had been hushed up. Avery, aged just seventeen, had wept for the last time in his life and faced the fact that his mother had killed any scrap of love he had ever had for her.

Now, over breakfast, he watched his own wife and tried to force the lid closed on the feelings that left him vulnerable to hurt and disillusion, just as his father had been.

Why had she left it so long to come for Alice

and why, when she did, had she disguised herself and lied about her identity? Why had she
not simply come to him, told him who she
was, confessed her wish to become part of her
daughter's life? Why, when she knew he was
seeking a wife, had she not suggested to him
that they wed in order to provide Alice with a
loving home?

Her first deception had risked confusing and
hurting the child. It had certainly confused him.
He could accept that now and knew why he had
been so angry when he had discovered who she
really was. Her second piece of scheming could
have wrecked his reputation.

Was that it? Startled by the sudden thought,
Avery lifted his newspaper to hide his face. The
sheets rattled against his cup and he threw it
down. Did she hate him so much that she would
risk upsetting Alice, hazard her own, fragile
reputation in order to punish him?

He had taken her daughter, then she discovered he was instrumental in sending her lover
to his death. Once he knew her identity he had
forbidden her any contact with the child until
the house party had thrown them all together.
Had she manipulated her invitation to the house
party, relying on his godmother's cheerful love
of entertaining to ensure her welcome?

The enormity of it made him dizzy. Avery made himself breathe deeply until the charming, happy face of his wife came back into focus. She was coaxing Alice into eating some egg before the child attacked the jam and toast. The picture of perfect motherhood. The ideal wife who had every reason to hate him.

He had never found the words to convince her of his deep regret for the misunderstanding over the letter to Piers. And Laura had never mentioned it again. Was that because she did not *want* to forgive him? Yet there was no way she could wound him, not now they were wed.

'Papa?' Alice's clear voice cut through his churning thoughts.

'Yes, sweetheart?'

'Do you like my new hair ribbon?'

'Yes, sweetheart.' She could hurt him through Alice. If she took the child away…

'I don't seem to have seen Blackie for an age,' he said.

'No.' Laura smiled at him. Clear-eyed, innocent. 'I gave her a long holiday with her family. Now Miss Pemberton is with us I thought it was time she had a rest.'

Miss Pemberton, his wife's choice made without reference to him. His wife's employee, loyal to her. Avery schooled his expression into bland approval. 'Of course, my dear. She deserves her holiday.'

He waited until the next morning. It was Miss Pemberton's half-day and Laura went out shopping, taking Alice with her. Avery waited for the front door to close behind them, then he climbed to the nursery floor and tapped on the door of the governess's sitting room.

She was sitting at the table, darning stockings, but she got to her feet when she saw who it was. 'My lord. Please come in.'

Avery left the door ajar in case she felt uneasy about being alone with a male employer. 'Miss Pemberton, I hope you will excuse me interrupting you in your free time, I will not take much of it, I hope. Shall we sit?'

She took the chair opposite his and folded her hands neatly on the table. A self-contained, intelligent young woman.

'I do not interfere with my wife's running of the household, you understand. And, naturally, your appointment is within her sphere of influence.' She looked a trifle puzzled, but she nodded. 'However, Alice is my daughter. She is my wife's *step*daughter.' The governess nodded again and sat a little straighter in the chair. 'Naturally she is very fond of Alice, but she is not her guardian, not her mother.' His tongue almost tripped him on the lie.

'Yes, Lord Wykeham. I am aware of that.' Miss Pemberton was cool.

'I am sure you are. I wanted to make it clear that my daughter does not leave the house without my knowledge and consent. She most certainly does not go on carriage journeys without it. Do you understand?'

'Your instructions are very clear, my lord, although I confess I do not understand.'

'Lady Wykeham is prone to occasional flights of fancy that usually manifest themselves as erratic journeys. It would be unsettling for Alice.'

'I see.' She looked very perturbed. 'I can assure you, my lord, that if there is any suggestion of such a thing I will inform you at once.'

'Thank you.' Avery stood up. 'I can rely on you not to mention this to my wife? She becomes very distressed when we argue about these…whims.'

'Of course, my lord. I greatly respect Lady Wykeham, I would not wish to upset her in any way.'

* * *

Laura barely made it downstairs in time before the sound of footsteps on the upper landing sent her headlong through the first bedchamber door she came to. She closed it gently and leaned back, one hand pressed to her lips to stifle the sound of her panting breath.

She had come back into the house because Alice had forgotten her gloves and, leaving the child in the carriage, had run lightly upstairs in her thin kid shoes to fetch them herself. It was much easier than trying to explain to a footman where they might be.

The sound of Avery's deep voice coming from Miss Pemberton's room had caught her attention. What on earth was he doing there? Not interfering in the carefully constructed lesson plan, she hoped! She tiptoed along the landing and found the door ajar, so she stood and listened, indignation at interference swept away by horror at the tale Avery was telling about her.

She was within an inch of sweeping in and demanding to know what he meant by it when she realised what was happening, what he feared. Despite the lovemaking, the appearance of friendliness, the pleasant partnership that she was so hoping would blossom into something else, he trusted her not one inch.

He believed she would betray him. He thought she wanted to steal Alice from him.

Chapter Twenty-One

Laura listened to the sound of Avery's foot-steps dying away, then she heard the door to their bedchamber open and close and she ran down the stairs, jerking to a walk when she reached the hallway.

'I couldn't find them,' she said to the foot-man. 'Never mind.' She had to get out of there before Avery realised she had been in the house. 'I couldn't find them,' she repeated to Alice and sank back against the squabs as the carriage moved off.

Was Avery insane? He knew she had no hope of setting up a separate household with Alice. He could simply walk in and claim them both, order them back home. She had no legal power and, now she was married, virtually no money either.

Then she realised. He was perfectly sane, perfectly logical. He genuinely thought she would snatch Alice away from him to hurt him. To punish him for Piers, for the things he had said about that letter and for taking her daughter in the first place. He thought she would do something so rash simply to wound him, make him suffer. After all, she had jewels, pin money, so she could, she supposed, vanish and manage for weeks, if not months, before he found her. If she told the child the truth about her parentage she might be able to do it in such a way that Alice would come to regard Avery as some kind of monster, so that when he eventually caught up with them Alice would hate him...

'Mama, are you all right?' Alice bounced across to sit beside her. 'You look frightened.'

'Do I?' Laura conjured a smile from somewhere. 'Not at all. I was just...thinking.'

Pretending to be Caroline Jordan had been a dreadful mistake. But there was no going back from it, even if it proved fatal to her marriage. Avery condemned her for entrapping him, lying to him and she could not find it in her to blame him. Somehow she had to convince him that he could trust her and hope he might come to understand why she had done what she had.

Would he ever forgive her? She had no idea, but she had to try, she loved him too much not to.

Laura swallowed panic as Alice prattled happily about the shops as they passed and she contemplated the desert in front of her, the arid marriage of her own making. She had fallen in love with Piers with all the impetuosity of a girl, heedless of consequences, unknowing of what love truly meant. Now she loved Avery with a woman's understanding and a woman's heart. The heart that would be broken when he cast her off, for surely that would be what would happen unless somehow she found a way to reach him.

The realisation of what to do came to her as she helped Alice choose ribbons. 'The blue to match your new dress and the green for the new bonnet,' she agreed, her mind half a mile away where one tall, brown-haired gentleman dealt with his correspondence and perhaps contemplated ways of ridding himself of his untrustworthy wife.

The answer came with a jolt as she gave Alice the coins to pay for her purchases. *Tell him the truth. Tell him everything, however painful it is, however it reflects on Mama and*

*Papa. Be utterly and completely open without
trying to work out whether it will make things
better or worse. If he forgives me, I will tell him
I love him, tell him the new secret that is still
just a hope. If I tell him first he will think I am
trying to wheedle him into forgiveness.*

*And I will forgive him, however hard it is. I
will learn to understand and forgive, for Alice
and because I love Avery.*

'Avery?'

Avery turned from the bookshelves he had
been staring at for the past ten minutes. 'Laura.'
She was the last person he wanted to see, not
while he was wrestling with his conscience
over what he had said to Miss Pemberton. It
was probably a sensible precaution, a rational
part of him said. *You love her,* his heart urged.
Trust her.

'You want to talk to me?' He pulled a chair
round so she could sit, but she stood in the middle of the floor, her hands clasped in front of
her like a defendant in the dock.

'Yes, I want to talk.' She was very pale, but
her voice was steady. 'I overheard you speaking to Miss Pemberton.'

'Hell.' He did not try to justify himself or to

touch her. There was a core of inner steel there, he realised as he met her steady gaze. It was not hostile or tearful, just…strong.

'I had thought that we were…that things would be all right. It wouldn't ever be perfect, but we could be a family even if you did not love me, even with everything that had happened in the past. But I did not realise until I overheard you how little you trusted me, how little you understood why I had lied to you, why I had trapped you into marriage.'

'There are things you have not told me. There are still secrets,' he said and Laura nodded, slowly, accepting the accusation. 'But I should not have spoken to Miss Pemberton.' Her eyes widened at the admission, but he pressed on. 'I should have talked to you instead.'

'I did not trust you with everything I need to tell you. And you do not trust me and I cannot blame you for that.'

Avery turned away sharply, one hand fisted in the silk window curtain, his back turned, unable to meet the honest pain in her face. If he touched her now he would kiss her, lose this chance of honesty in the flare of passion that overcame him whenever he felt the softness of her under his hands, caught the scent of her in his nostrils.

'I would happily die if that would make Alice happier or safer,' Laura said. 'I do not know how to make you understand what I did and allow me to be a proper mother to her. I want us to be a family, a happy one,' she added, her voice a whisper he had to strain to hear.

Avery unclenched his hand from the curtain, leaving it criss-crossed with creases like scars. 'Tell me what happened when you knew Piers was dead.'

Behind him there was the rustle of silk as Laura crossed to the chair and sat down. 'I told my parents I was with child. They were… aghast. Will you forgive me not repeating what they said? It is very painful.'

'Of course.' His voice sounded rusty.

'We agreed that I would pretend to be ill and go to one of our country estates to recover. Luckily there were all sorts of fevers going around that year. I coughed and moped for two weeks, then apparently succumbed to the infection.

'It was a healthy pregnancy.' Her voice trailed away, then she said, almost angrily, 'You want to know why I waited six years to find her, don't you? That is what you cannot understand or forgive.'

'I can forgive if I understand,' he offered and turned. This was the sticking point, the thing that Laura found most difficult to tell, he realised. He took the chair opposite her and sat down, leaning forward, his forearms on his knees, just out of touching distance.

'My parents told me she was dead,' Laura said abruptly. 'When my baby was born my mother took her, wrapped her. I heard her cry, once. I thought Mama would give her back to me to hold, but she gave her to the nurse and they went out of the room. Then Mama came back and said she was dead.' She stopped and drew a deep, shuddering breath.

'I watched her from the park the day before you found me there. That was the first time I had heard her voice from that day. They told Mab her name in the village. A shopkeeper knew my daughter's name and I did not.'

Avery found he was on one knee in front of her chair, both her cold hands clasped in his. 'How did you find her?'

'I was going through papers, months after they died, because I was moving into the Dower House and I needed to make sure I was taking the personal documents and leaving all the estate papers for Cousin James. There were letters from the Brownes in a locked box. I thought she was alive and I could find her. And then they wrote to say she was dead.'

'Oh, God. I told them to do that.'

'I went there anyway. I wanted to see the grave. They told me everything, gave me your card.'

'How could your parents do that?' Avery demanded.

'I suppose they thought it was best for me. I tell myself that. Why, after all this time, the hurt should be so sharp, I do not know. They did it for the best,' Laura repeated on a sob, then caught herself, her hands over her mouth.

'Oh, my darling.' Avery reached for her. 'My poor darling.' By all that was merciful she stayed in his arms and her own went around him, her forehead resting on his shoulder.

'When I found you had taken Alice it was bad,' she said, her voice muffled. 'Then when you told me about Piers I thought I hated you. I will never know how I managed to say nothing to you that day under his portrait. I saw myself in my mind's eye with Piers's sword in my hand, running you through.'

The vision was so vivid he almost felt the blade of the sword, the sickening pain. 'I understand.'

'You do?' Laura released him and sat back, her eyes enormous and dark as she stared at him. 'You might understand now why I let Alice go in the first place, but still, I deceived you and then entrapped you.' Laura forced a smile that caught at his heart. 'You are only human, after all.'

'I am only human,' Avery agreed. 'I understand why you had to pretend to be Mrs Jordan, why you mistrusted the man who had taken your daughter. I understand why you could not bring yourself to suggest marriage directly.' But now she had told him the truth and he could be honest with her in his turn, he realised. Tell her things he had never told another soul.

'My father adored my mother,' Avery said, his tone conversational, as he sat back on his heels. 'We were such a happy family, I thought.'

'You thought?' Laura was still shaken from her own confidences. He could see her struggle to comprehend what he was telling her.

'She'd had lovers for years. She'd lied and deceived, she had wound my father around her little finger. I thought she was perfect, too. And then he found a letter and it all came out. I saw her change—it was like something from a medieval myth. One moment there was Mama, beautiful, loving, sweet. The next there was a bitter, mocking creature hurling contempt with her back against the wall, confronted with evidence she couldn't twist or hide. She had been acting for years.

'She left without saying a word to me—I was eight. She went to her lover and my father died in an accident with his gun a few weeks later.'

'An accident?' she ventured, her voice appalled.

'Everyone agreed it was best if it was. I found him,' Avery said. *He looked so small huddled there in the bracken and the blood.*

'Avery!'

'She died a few years later. It seems it has left me finding it difficult to trust,' he said with a wry twist of the lips. 'I suppose somehow I see myself in Alice, fear for her if her love is betrayed, just as I fear for my own heart.'

'Oh, my love. Oh, Avery.' Laura found herself on her knees, reaching for him without conscious volition, before her words or his came together in her mind. 'You fear for your own heart?'

'You called me your love?' Avery's voice clashed with hers. 'You love me?'

She could lie, but then she had lied to him so often. She could pretend, but she had done that, too, and it was hollow. Summoning all her courage, Laura held his gaze and said, 'I love you, Avery. Whatever happens, whatever you feel for me, I will always love you.'

'Thank God. I lost my heart to you, my love,' Avery said. The tautness had gone from his face and there was nothing in his smile but genuine, wondering, happiness. He gathered her in to him, his cheek against her hair. 'I had a glimmering of it. That night we first made love I was going to ask you to marry me. I was going to wait until the morning and do it properly with the ring. And then, what happened, happened, and I closed off all those new feelings for you, sank back into suspicion. How could I let old history teach me so wrongly about trust and truth?'

He felt so good, so strong and solid and male. Her man. *My husband.* 'When I met you again unexpectedly in London, I thought I hated you,' Laura murmured into his shirt front. 'But there was always something there between us though, right from the start. I thought it was simply desire.'

'I do not think there is anything simple about desire, my love.'

Laura twisted so she could drop a kiss on his wrist, feel the pulse beat against her lips. He loved her. Miracles happened. 'Perhaps that connection between us made the mistrust more extreme.'

'It would take a better philosopher than I am to understand the mysteries of the heart,' Avery said. 'Who would have thought that I could fall in love with Alice's real mother?'

'Who would think I could learn to love the man who stole her from me, the man who told the world he was her father?' Laura laughed at the sheer wonderful inevitability of it.

'Papa?'

The small voice from the doorway had them twisting round, clasped in each other's arms like guilty lovers in a melodrama. Alice stood there gazing at them, her face pale, her eyes wide, hair ribbons trailing from her fingers like some misplaced carnival decorations. 'You are not my father? I don't understand.'

Chapter Twenty-Two

'Alice!' Avery got to his feet and held out one hand to the child as he helped steady Laura with the other. 'Come in. We need to talk.'

Laura's heart bled for him as she saw the look in the child's eyes: doubt, anxiety, trust wavering on the edge of betrayal, but this was no time for displays of uncontrolled emotion. They had to reassure their daughter, nothing else mattered. She moved briskly across the room, closed the door and took Alice by the hand. 'Come and sit down, Alice,' she said with as much calm firmness as she could muster. 'This is going to be a very big surprise and it is a good thing you are such a big girl now and can listen carefully and try to understand.'

'We'll sit on the floor,' Avery said, folding down to sit cross-legged on the carpet. 'Then we can all hold hands and look at each other.'

'I am your mother,' Laura said without pre-amble when they were settled, Alice's cold little hand in her right hand, Avery's big warm hand in the left. 'Your real mother.'

'You left me.' Alice bit her trembling lower lip.

'I lost you,' Laura corrected gently. 'You know that people have been unkind to you sometimes because Papa was not married?' A nod. 'People get very cross if a man and a woman make a baby before they are married and I'm afraid that is what your father and I did. We loved each other and he had to go to war. And then, darling, I'm so sorry, he was killed. He was very brave and he was doing his duty.' Avery's hand squeezed tight around hers.

'Like Cousin Piers?' Alice was looking steadier now.

'Cousin Piers was your father, sweetheart,' Avery said. 'So I thought I must look after you. Only when I found you I knew at once that I loved you and that I wanted to be your papa. So I let you believe that I was.'

'But...' Alice turned to Laura, her forehead crinkled with the effort of working it all out. 'If *you* are my really mama, why didn't you marry Papa?'

'Because I didn't know where you were,' Laura told her. 'You see, my mother and father thought it was best if they sent you away so no one knew I had been in love with your father and that we had had a baby.'

'Because silly people get cross because of you not being married.' Alice nodded, obviously having sorted that out to her satisfaction.

'It took me six years to find you,' Laura explained. 'And I pretended to be Mrs Jordan because I didn't know what your papa would think of me.'

'So why didn't you tell me? And who was the bad man you were running away from?'

'Er...'

'Mama did not tell you because I was cross with her, too, which was exceptionally silly of me,' said Avery firmly. 'And the bad man frightened Mama in the park, but he has gone now and will never come back.'

'So it is all right now?' Alice asked, the anxious quaver back in her voice. 'Even though Papa isn't my really father and Mama is... Mama?'

'It is perfectly all right,' Avery said. 'Grown-ups make a lot of muddles about things sometimes and we can't tell everyone about who really is who because otherwise some people will be horrid to Mama. But now we are a family and nothing is going to spoil that.'

'Would Cousin…Cousin Piers be pleased? Can you tell me more about him?' Alice jumped up and put her arms around Avery's neck and kissed him. 'I don't love him like you, Papa, but I'd like to know about him.'

Laura found she was looking at her husband and daughter through a mist of tears. Avery appeared to have lost the ability to speak. 'We will talk about him lots,' she promised. 'And he would have been very, very proud of you, Alice.'

And then Avery opened his arms and pulled them both close and they clung together, murmuring disjointed reassurances to each other. There were tears, but when Laura finally stood up and took her daughter's hand and went upstairs so they could wash their faces and brush their hair it seemed as though none of them could help the smiles and the laughter of sheer happy relief.

'Are you tired?' Avery asked when finally Alice, who had been allowed to stay up for dinner, had fallen asleep with her head on the table-cloth and had been carried up to bed.

'Exhausted,' Laura admitted as she walked unsteadily into Avery's bedchamber and collapsed on the bed. 'I can't face going downstairs for tea. But I do not think I will ever sleep either.'

'Happy?' Avery asked. He kicked off his shoes, then leaned against the bedpost and began to untie his neckcloth. The dressing-room door opened and he called, 'That will be all for tonight, thank you, Darke.' It closed again and he joined her on the bed.

'Happy? I do not think I know the name for it. It is as though someone has swept away all the doubts and worries and pain and loss and I'm like a newly whitewashed house. Empty. And yet full. Confused,' she added when he laughed. 'Happy, content, terrified I will wake up and this is all a dream.'

Laura turned on her side and propped herself up on her elbow. Avery was lying on his back, eyes closed, mouth curved into a smile of pure content. 'How do you feel?'

He opened his eyes and studied her for so long that Laura felt herself grow rosy with the intensity of the look. Then Avery sat up. 'There are not the words. Let me show you how I feel.'

Time stood still as he kissed her, caressed the clothes from her body, then lay and allowed her to strip him and caress in her turn. All the urgency, the heat, that had driven their lovemaking before had gone, replaced with a tenderness that went far beyond the erotic. Avery made love to every inch of her body with lips and teeth and tongue and gentle, relentless fingers.

Laura was swept from one peak to another, her body saturated with sensation. When he finally took pity on her and fell back beside her she summoned what remained of her energy and moved on top of him, straddling the narrow hips. He closed his eyes as she rose up and took him into her body, sinking down until they were joined, perfectly, and she felt a tide of feminine power sweep through her, meet and meld with his maleness.

He let her set the pace, lay and watched her through heavy-lidded eyes, his lips parted, his breathing ragged as she slowly, slowly built the tension, twisting the rope of passion between them until he reached out, gripped her wrists and thrust up, taking them both over the edge, into the storm.

* * *

They lay there, blissfully relaxed, drifting in and out of sleep, for hours. Eventually a clock, somewhere deep in the house, struck three.

'I am awake,' Avery said. 'And hungry.'

'So am I. Shall we raid the pantry? There is plum cake and cheese.'

'A recipe for indigestion,' Avery teased, but he belted his banyan and followed her downstairs, through the sleeping house. They filled plates and made tea and then tiptoed out again.

'Goodness knows what we are going to have to tell Miss Pemberton,' Laura said as they curled up against the pillows and tried not to get cake crumbs in the bed.

'I will tell her that I was a foolishly suspicious husband. Miss Pemberton will consider me a brute and will probably order *A Vindication of the Rights of Women* from the library for you.'

'Poor Avery,' she teased and then, suddenly anxious, added, 'Are you truly comfortable with Alice realising you are not her blood father?'

'I am very happy. It has done my conscience no end of good, confessing. She'll have lots of questions, but we will deal with them honestly as they come up.' He put an arm around her shoulders and pulled her close.

'Thank you for agreeing to let Alice have a puppy,' Laura said.

'I had forgotten I had a bone to pick with you, my lady,' Avery said sternly. 'Whatever possessed you to promise Alice a puppy at dinner time? I foresee months of puddles on carpets, shredded upholstery and missing slippers.'

'Um...' Laura wriggled free and caught Avery's left hand in hers, fiddling with his wedding ring, keeping her eyes fixed on it. 'I thought it might be a good idea, because her nose is going to be very out of joint in a little while, I suspect, bless her.'

There was a moment when she thought he did not understand, then Avery pulled her round to face him, his fingers tipping up her chin so he could look into her face, his own intent and flushed. 'You are with child?'

'I think so. So does Mab. But it is very early, just weeks, and I have not seen a physician yet.'

'Oh, my love.' His arms around her were strong, possessive yet strangely tentative. 'You should be resting... You shouldn't have had all the strain and anxiety. You—'

'Avery.' She gave him a little shake. 'I am pregnant, not sick! Are you pleased?'

'Pleased?' He sat back and regarded her as if she had asked whether he had a head. '*Pleased?* I am delighted. Why did you not tell me before?'

'Because I thought I would never find out your true feelings for me once you knew,' Laura admitted.

'I see.' Avery rolled off the bed and got to his feet in one fluid motion and turned away. Her heart sank. 'Trust. It keeps getting in the way, doesn't it?'

'Lack of it does,' Laura admitted.

'You thought I would lie to you, pretend an affection I did not feel, if you gave me a child?'

She swallowed the lump in her throat. 'I wondered.' Surely, after all that had passed between them, she had not had lost him again? Trust was so important to him and so fragile and she had shown she doubted him. Her hand went instinctively to her belly. She shouldn't have said anything yet. It was to soon, she could be wrong and then he would think—

Avery paced back to stand in front of her. He looking down, his face shadowed. 'I wonder if perhaps we are being too hard on ourselves,' he said. 'We are going to make mistakes, hurt each other, I am certain. But that is part of it, part of growing together. Love cannot be a magic potion, can it? One moment we are just two fallible human beings full of faults and fears, the next we are in perfect harmony? No, this isn't a fairy tale, this is real life and real love.'

He reached out and pulled her gently to her feet. 'I love you. You love me. We will work it out, Laura. We will learn how to trust and how to tell each other of our fears. We will learn to argue and make up and not see that as a sign of failure.'

Her hand was still pressed over where she hoped his child lay. 'I may not be...'

Avery caressed her cheek. When he spoke his voice was husky. 'I think you are.' He laid his hand over hers. 'But if not, then we have time and love and what will be, will be.' He bent closer to look into her face. It was shadowy under the bed canopy, but the candlelight threw his face into relief, showed her both the strong man she loved and the tender lover she was coming to know. 'Are you crying? Oh, Laura, my love.'

She found her voice from somewhere. 'Only because I am happy. Ever since Alice was born there has been an empty, hollow place inside me. When I found her again it was filled and yet, somehow, something was still missing. I was not complete. Avery, I am complete now, with you.'

When he pulled her into his arms and kissed her there was no need for words. Impossibly, when she had given up all hope of happiness she had it all. A husband she loved, who loved her. Her daughter and the hope of all the years ahead would bring.

'Tomorrow, shall we pack and go to Wykeham Hall?'

'Start afresh?' Avery asked. 'Yes, my love. That house has been long neglected. It is waiting so we can make it ours. Let's go and build a home together. Raise a family.'

As he embraced her she saw their shadows, strong against the subtle silk of the wall hangings. *Two figures entwined, two hearts as one,* Laura thought as Avery began to kiss her and her eyelids fluttered closed. *Finally at peace.*

* * * * *

A sneaky peek at next month...

HISTORICAL

AWAKEN THE ROMANCE OF THE PAST...

My wish list for next month's titles...

In stores from 4th July 2014:

- ❏ A Lady of Notoriety – Diane Gaston
- ❏ The Scarlet Gown – Sarah Mallory
- ❏ Safe in the Earl's Arms – Liz Tyner
- ❏ Betrayed, Betrothed and Bedded – Juliet Landon
- ❏ Castle of the Wolf – Margaret Moore
- ❏ Rebel Outlaw – Carol Arens

Available at WHSmith, Tesco, Asda, Eason, Amazon and Apple

Just can't wait?

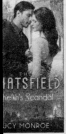

L5/21

MILLS & BOON
Book Club

Join the Mills & Boon Book Clu

Want to read more **Historical** books?
We're offering you **2 more** absolutely **FRE**

We'll also treat you to these fabulous extras:

- Exclusive offers and much more!

- FREE home delivery

- FREE books and gifts with our special rewards scheme

Get your free books now!

visit www.millsandboon.co.uk/bookclub
or call Customer Relations on 020 8288 28